Please return/renew this item by the last date shown
on this label, or on your self-service receipt.

To renew this item, visit **www.librarieswest.org.uk**
or contact your library

Your borrower number and PIN are required.

4 6 0215142 1

THE FICTION COLLECTION

VOLUME ONE

THE FICTION COLLECTION
VOLUME ONE

From Legends to the current lore...

This volume features a diverse collection of short stories which chronicle the exploits of intriguing assorted side characters along with some of the more familar names in the saga, including Lando Calrissian, Han Solo, and Darth Vader.

The tales include Legends stories—from the continuity pre-2014—such as a moving tale of Darth Vader reuniting with an old acquaintance, a dark story with the mysterious Darth Plagueis, and an edge-of-your-seat adventure with Han Solo and Chewbacca in action aboard the *Millennium Falcon*.

From the current lore—2015 to present—there are tales of Blade Squadron, the pilots of the Rebel Alliance's B-wing starfighters, as they strike out against the Empire; the story of Darth Vader and the Emperor making a surprise inspection of an Imperial facility; and a gripping tale of survivors of Alderaan evading the Empire's stormtroopers.

TITAN EDITORIAL
Editor Jonathan Wilkins
Managing Editor Martin Eden
Art Director Oz Browne
Senior Designer Andrew Leung
Assistant Editor Phoebe Hedges
Senior Production Controller Jackie Flook
Sales and Circulation Manager Steve Tothill
Direct Marketing Assistant George Wickenden
Marketing and Advertisement Assistant Lauren Noding
Publicist Imogen Harris
Editorial Director Duncan Baizley
Operations Director Leigh Baulch
Publishers Vivian Cheung & Nick Landau

DISTRIBUTION
U.S. Newsstand: Total Publisher Services, Inc.
John Dziewiatkowski, 630-851-7683
U.S. Distribution: Ingrams Periodicals,
Curtis Circulation Company
U.K. Newsstand: Marketforce, 0203 787 9199
U.S./U.K. Direct Sales Market: Diamond Comic Distributors
For more info on advertising contact adinfo@titanmail.com

Contents © 2021 Lucasfilm Ltd. All Rights Reserved

First edition: March 2021

Star Wars Insider: The Official Fiction Collection Volume One is published by Titan Magazines, a division of Titan Publishing Group Limited, 144 Southwark Street, London, SE1 0UP

Printed in China.

For sale in the U.S., Canada, U.K., and Eire

ISBN: 9781787736375
Titan Authorized User: TMN 3872

LUCASFILM EDITORIAL
Senior Editor Brett Rector
Art Director Troy Alders
Creative Director Michael Siglain
Story Group Leland Chee, Pablo Hidlago
Asset Management Chris Argyropoulos,
Nicole LaCoursiere, Sarah Williams
Creative Art Manager Phil Szostak

Special Thanks: Erich Schoeneweiss, Christopher Troise, Eugene Paraszczuk

CONTENTS

LEGENDS

The following stories are from Legends continuity,
originally published from 2011 to 2013.

VADER ADRIFT

WRITTEN BY **RYDER WINDHAM**
ART BY **JOE CORRONEY**

"Did you hear about Darth Vader, sir?"

The veteran stormtrooper turned his white-helmeted head to see his younger counterpart approaching across the spaceport's shuttle launch pad. In a gravelly voice, the veteran trooper said, "What's that, TK-813?"

The younger trooper came to a stop. "Darth Vader, sir. He's here."

The veteran glanced at the large box-shaped shuttle that had just touched down and was now resting on its thrusters beside a nearby gantry. "Lord Vader's at the garrison?"

"No." TK-813 pointed up to the sky. "On the *Tarkin*."

The two Stormtroopers were among those stationed at the spaceport on the planet Hockaleg in the Patriim system, where the *Tarkin*, an Imperial battle station, was under construction in Hockaleg's orbit. Named in honor of the late Grand Moff Tarkin, the battle station consisted of a massive, planet-shattering ionic cannon that was bracketed by hyperdrive engines and defensive shield generators. Shaped like a concave dish, the ionic cannon resembled the Death Star's main offensive battery, but was without the Death Star's flaws—or so its designers claimed. Although the *Tarkin* was considerably smaller than the Death Star, it was still so large that it was visible in Hockaleg's blue sky as a rectangular satellite.

The Empire had conscripted a number of humans for the ground operations at Hockaleg's spaceport—a tight sprawl of mostly ramshackle structures—and the veteran looked around to make sure none of the locals were listening. Satisfied, the veteran tilted his head back to look skyward and said, "Who told you Lord Vader was on the *Tarkin*?"

TK-813 thought for a moment, then said, "Grimes overheard someone at headquarters mention it."

"Grimes?" The veteran looked back at TK-813. "Who's Grimes?"

"You know, sir. He's TK-592. No, I mean, he's... uh, TK-529."

The veteran sighed impatiently through

his helmet's respirator. "When did he tell you?"

"Not long ago, sir. Just after you cleared the last flight to the *Tarkin*."

The veteran glanced at the landed shuttle, looked back at TK-813, and said, "At our next rotation, you, 'Grimes,' and I are going to walk over to headquarters so we can have a chat about the importance of maintaining military protocol and distributing information on a need-to-know basis. I suspect a number of laborers on Hockaleg have no fondness for the Empire. For all we know, some could be Rebel spies."

"Yes, sir."

But the veteran wasn't listening. He was focused on the bright, yellowish glint that appeared to be growing across the top of TK-813's helmet. The veteran twisted his neck sharply to look skyward again. The rectangular point of light he had seen earlier had transformed into an expanding blossom of fire.

TK-813 followed the veteran's gaze and said, "Oh, no. Is that the *Tarkin*?"

"It *was*."

"Sir, what should we—?"

But the elder trooper was already running for the shuttle, taking his blaster rifle with him.

Darth Vader was seated in the cockpit of his crippled TIE fighter. The fighter's transparisteel window was shattered and lits starboard wing was a mangled mess. If not for his armored pressure suit and the fighter's reinforced hull, the Dark Lord of the Sith might not have survived the collision with the large chunks of ice that had materialized in his path less than a minute before the *Tarkin* exploded. Because the explosion had released billions of pieces of debris, as well as electromagnetic radiation that prevented starship-to-starship transmissions— including distress signals—all Vader could do for the moment was sit in his fighter; listen to the rasping noise of his labored, mechanized breathing; and reflect on how he had once again missed an opportunity to capture his son, Luke Skywalker.

Only a few weeks had passed since his duel with Luke on Cloud City. He had traveled to Hockaleg in his personal flagship, the Super Star Destroyer *Executor*, to inspect the *Tarkin*. He had never had much regard for so-called superweapons, and had been morbidly amused that the new battle station was named after the commanding officer who had lost the Death Star. His interest in the *Tarkin* had changed, however, the moment he had sensed Luke's presence on-board.

Vader had previously failed to apprehend Luke at the shipyards of Fondor. And on the planet Aridus. And on Monastery. And

Mimban and Verdanth, and, most recently, in Cloud City. With those experiences behind him, Vader had no intention of letting Luke slip away on the *Tarkin*.

Suspecting the young Rebel would try to sabotage the battle station's main power reactor, Vader had instructed Imperial officer Colonel Nord to remove all security personnel from the reactor areas and to increase sentries along possible escape routes. And then Vader had stood outside a generator room and waited for Luke to walk right into his trap.

Vader had not anticipated that Colonel Nord would try to kill him.

The assassination attempt had distracted Vader long enough for Luke to escape on an Imperial transport. Vader had not had time to deal with the traitorous officer before going to his TIE fighter to pursue Luke. Nor could he stop Luke from transferring to the increasingly irksome *Millennium Falcon*, which had appeared from out of nowhere. And when someone had dumped the *Falcon*'s water supply, Vader had been unable to evade the wall of ice that had rapidly formed in the *Falcon*'s wake.

From his damaged fighter, Vader had watched the *Tarkin* rotate to direct its ionic cannon at the *Falcon*, and he realized the impending blast would destroy his fighter, too. He had no doubt that Colonel Nord was directing the weapon's aim, or that his chances of escaping the blast were less than nil.

But then the *Tarkin* had exploded over Hockaleg, launching wide tendrils]of burning fuel in all directions. Two nearby Star Destroyers and dozens of smaller vessels were consumed instantly. The explosion's shockwave struck Vader's TIE fighter, knocking it away from the ice and sending it tumbling across space. Debris from the *Tarkin* sailed past the fighter and buffeted the port-side wing. Vader wrestled with his flight controls, struggling to keep the fighter from straying far beyond Hockaleg's orbit. He spiraled for several seconds before he managed to activate a single thruster and brought the fighter to a relatively dead stop before the thruster burned out.

Vader's eyes shifted behind the lenses of his black metal mask as he looked through his cockpit's damaged window. Wreckage was everywhere. Several kilometers beyond the *Tarkin*'s blazing remains, the *Executor* was apparently intact, but Vader took little consolation from this observation, because, due to the electromagnetic interference, he could not even signal the *Executor* to go after the *Millennium Falcon*. It occurred to him that even if he could get a signal through, the *Falcon* had probably already left the Patriim system.

And then he saw a white saucer-shaped blur speeding out of Hockaleg's orbit, and realized he had spotted the *Falcon*. He was about to use the Force to call out to Luke, but then the freighter vanished into hyperspace. And once again, Vader felt robbed.

He had to make Luke his ally. Luke had to yield to the dark side of the Force and join him. Unless that happened, Vader would never be able to overthrow his own Master, the Emperor Palpatine.

Vader saw a large piece of twisted metal moving toward his fighter, and he reached out with the Force to send the debris off in a different trajectory. He wondered how the Emperor would react when he learned of the *Tarkin*'s destruction. With the Emperor's far-reaching powers, it was possible that he was already aware of what had happened in Hockaleg's orbit. Although Palpatine would undoubtedly

The explosion's shockwave struck Vader's TIE fighter, knocking it away from the ice and sending it tumbling across space.

express his displeasure at losing the *Tarkin*, he had been lately more preoccupied by the construction of the second Death Star in the Endor system. Vader assumed the Emperor would likely send him to Endor to ensure that the new Death Star did not follow the *Tarkin*'s fate. Thinking of this prospect, Vader fumed. He was a soldier, not a building supervisor, and he had grown weary of working with scheming officers and incompetent bureaucrats.

He checked his comm system again and heard nothing but static on every frequency. The *Executor*'s crew had been aware that he was in his TIE fighter when the *Tarkin* exploded, and he surmised they had already sent out search teams to recover him. He also suspected that he could be in for a long wait. Unable to use their ship's sensors to locate his fighter, the teams would have to use their own eyes to find him amidst the scattered debris. Although he didn't entirely trust any member of his crew, he did trust that they would find him sooner than later. After all, they knew fear kept everyone in place.

But then he thought of the late Colonel Nord, who had most certainly feared him, too. Nord hadn't been the first Imperial officer who'd tried to kill Vader, and like most of the other would-be assassins, he hadn't had the courage to take on the Sith Lord directly. *The problem with such cowards*, Vader decided, *is that they're not more afraid.*

As Vader watched for any sign of the expected search teams, he wondered who or what might try to kill him next. He wondered about this with something resembling fervor, as he had become increasingly eager, over the years, to rid the galaxy of anything that threatened him or tested his patience. He welcomed the unexpected because he knew it could not kill him. He was confident that he would continue to survive because he always did. He sincerely believed his survival was the will of the Force.

He sighted a spacecraft moving toward his position. He was surprised to see that it was not a ship from the *Executor*, but rather a boxy shuttle from Hockaleg. He tested his fighter's running lights, then flashed them to draw the shuttle pilot's attention. As the shuttle drew closer, Vader looked to its main viewport, and was further surprised to see the craft was helmed by an Imperial Stormtrooper.

Vader switched on his fighter's interior lights so the trooper could see him clearly. He raised one black-gloved hand, pointed at the shuttle, then pointed above his head to the fighter's egress hatch. The trooper responded with a nod. Vader watched the trooper expertly maneuver the shuttle to position its starboard side as close as possible to the top of the fighter's cockpit.

Vader slid back the egress hatch above his black-helmeted head, rose from his seat, and launched himself through space to the waiting shuttle. The trooper had already opened the starboard airlock. Vader guided his body into the shuttle, and the airlock's outer hatch slid shut behind him. The chamber soon pressurized and then the inner hatch opened. Vader proceeded to the shuttle's bridge, where he found the armored trooper standing at attention. Vader gazed down at the trooper, and his deep voice echoed in the bridge as he said, "Why isn't an Imperial pilot in command of this vessel?"

The trooper replied, "I was stationed at the shuttle launching pad on Hockaleg when the *Tarkin* exploded, Lord Vader. I left my post to search for survivors."

Vader recognized the trooper's distinctive voice and clipped manner of speech. "You served in the Clone Wars." It wasn't a question.

But the trooper replied, "Yes, sir."

"And you are an experienced pilot."

"Yes, sir."

"Then *why*," Vader said, "are you in stormtrooper armor?"

"I was demoted, sir."

"Why?"

"I disobeyed an order and assaulted a superior officer twenty years ago, sir," the trooper replied, no trace of regret in his voice.

Vader was impressed by the trooper's strong composure. In fact, he did not sense any fear in the trooper. And although Vader lived and breathed to instill fear—especially in subordinates—he did not feel any compulsion to rattle this particular soldier, who exuded reliability as well as loyalty. Instead, Vader simply asked, "What was your operational unit during the Clone Wars?"

"Shadow Squadron, sir."

Vader's breathing apparatus made a small wrenching noise. "If you were in Shadow Squadron, you were trained by...?"

"General Skywalker, sir. Do you wish to return to your Star Destroyer?"

"Not yet," Vader said. He gestured at the shuttle's controls. "Leave a distress strobe with my fighter and then take me to the garrison on Hockaleg."

As the trooper deployed a beacon, he said, "Begging your pardon, sir, but when the search team finds your fighter empty, they may assume that you're adrift."

"So be it," Vader said as he lowered himself onto the copilot's seat.

As the shuttle descended through Hockaleg's atmosphere, Vader said, "I am curious about the details of your demotion."

"It's all on record, sir," the trooper said, angling the shuttle toward the spaceport.

"I would prefer to hear it from you."

"Permission to speak freely, sir?"

"Granted."

The trooper cleared his throat. "You are aware I'm a clone, sir?"

"Yes."

"Well, twenty years ago, after Shadow Squadron was disbanded, I had a new commanding officer—a non-clone. When he ordered me to kill my gunner—who had been wounded in combat, but not mortally— I refused. And when my commanding officer tried to shoot me for refusing, I broke his jaw. I spent a year in solitary."

Vader considered the details, then said, "What happened to the injured clone?"

"He recovered, although he was killed several months later during a bombing run."

"Do you regret your actions?"

"No, sir. Everybody dies. I'm just glad I helped a friend live a bit longer."

As the spaceport came into view, Vader said, "If you were to serve under my command, would you ever disobey an order?"

"Yes, sir, but only if it helped you live longer."

Vader was stunned by the aged clone's words and the implication that he might disobey one of his orders... or that he might consider the Sith Lord a friend. Before he could ask the clone for an explanation, the clone tested the comm and received a loud burst of static. Switching the comm off, he said, "I can't establish contact with spaceport control, sir. We don't have clearance to land."

Vader said, "Do you expect any troops will fire at the shuttle?"

"I don't know, sir."

"Take us down."

The shuttle landed beside the launch gantry. The shuttle's boarding ramp extended and the clone stepped out, carrying his blaster rifle. As he led Vader down the shuttle's boarding ramp, he tapped the side of his white helmet and said, "CT-4981 to TK-813, do you read me? TK-813?" He glanced back at Vader and said, "Just static, sir." At the bottom of the ramp, he looked around and added, "Where is everyone?"

Vader heard shouting in the distance, and then the sound of blasterfire. He turned to the clone, and could tell by the tilt of the clone's helmet that he heard the shots too. They looked toward an alley between two nearby buildings and saw a stormtrooper emerge, firing his blaster rifle behind him as he ran. He stumbled and collapsed, face down on the ground.

"TK-813!" The clone ran to the fallen trooper and rolled him over. Blood flowed out from under TK-813's chest plate. The clone hauled the younger Stormtrooper behind a small shack while Vader strode toward them, his eyes focused on the alley.

"What happened?" the clone said to the injured trooper.

"You were right about the laborers, sir," the trooper gasped. "They don't like... the Empire. After they saw the... *Tarkin* blow, they attacked the headquarters, and then..."

The trooper's body went slack.

"He's gone," the clone said.

"Stay with me," Vader said. He walked fast toward the shuttle, the clone keeping close to his back. They were halfway to the ship when five armed men in grease-stained coveralls ran out from behind the

> **Vader removed the clone's helmet. Although the clone still resembled Jango Fett, his face was more heavily lined with age and his hair was mostly white.**

gantry and started firing at them. Without breaking his stride, Vader raised his right hand and deflected the energy bolts with ease. He assumed the five men recognized him and were aware of his capabilities because they gaped and cringed as they lowered their blasters.

Keeping his gaze fixed on the men, Vader said to the clone, "Board the shuttle and prepare for—"

Vader was interrupted by another round of blaster fire, followed by a clatter of armor behind him. He glanced back and saw the clone sprawled on the ground, clutching at his left side. Another group of laborers had emerged on the launchpad and now faced Vader too. They all looked very afraid.

Ignoring the laborers, the Dark Lord dropped to one knee beside the clone. The clone was still breathing, but Vader could tell that he wouldn't last long. The clone said, "I couldn't just walk away and… let them hit you, sir."

Vader removed the clone's helmet. Although the clone still resembled Jango Fett, his face was more heavily lined with age and his hair was mostly white. Vader said, "Contrail, when we were with Shadow Squadron, at the Battle of the Kaliida Nebula, your call sign was Shadow Eleven. You flew well."

The clone did not seem surprised that Vader knew his name and details about Shadow Squadron. He smiled and said, "I had… a good teacher, sir." And then his eyes went shut and he died.

Vader rose and directed his gaze to the men who had shot the clone. One of the men said, "Lord Vader, please forgive us. We didn't know you were on Hockaleg."

"I was adrift," Vader said as he drew his lightsaber and ignited its glowing crimson blade. "Allow me to thank you all for bringing me back." ☻

FIRST BLOOD

WRITTEN BY **CHRISTIE GOLDEN**
ART BY **BRIAN ROOD**

S ith apprentice Vestara Khai stood beside her master, Lady Olaris Rhea, in the courtyard of the Sith Temple. Grand Lord Darish Vol was present, along with all the High Lords and Lords of the Sith Circle. There were too many Sith Sabers to include them all, so only a prestigious few had been chosen. Vestara's father, Saber Gavar Khai, was among that number. She watched him as he stood next to his friend, Ruku Myal, a Saber as fair-haired as Khai was dark, as animated as Khai was solemn. Vestara was the sole apprentice. Oh, the rest of the Sith on Kesh would be watching, of course. Holocams were set up all over the courtyard, and the event would be broadcast live all over the planet.

Vestara did not pay much attention to the speech Grand Lord Vol gave, and she suspected that, revered as Vol was, few others did either. Everyone was waiting for the Sith training sphere, Ship, who had told them to gather, as he had something very important to tell them.

And when he finally spoke, inside their minds, Vestara was stunned.

For long you have been isolated. Yet a well-established trade route closer than you know will open the galaxy to your conquest. We will find a vessel to take, and use it to repair the crashed warship Omen that stranded you here. And we will strike again

and again, until we have a fleet to breed fear throughout galaxy. Five of you will accompany me on this initial voyage. Come.

Murmurs of excitement arose, and then the names were placed in their minds. *High Lord Sarasu Taalon.* No surprise there, Vestara thought. Dark purple head held high, the Keshiri High Lord seemed unable to keep from smirking as he strode up to stand beside the Sith training sphere. *Lord Ivaar Workan.* Again, not unexpected. Both men, the Keshiri and the older human male, were powerful in the Force and, Vestara had heard, ruthless as well. Of course, Ship would choose them.

Lady Olaris Rhea. Lady Rhea exuded pleasure and confidence in the Force as she absently patted Vestara's cheek and lithely strode forward to join the two High Lords.

Saber Ruku Myal. Vestara felt a ripple of surprise in the Force. A Saber? When there were still Lords and High Lords from which to choose? Myal's chiseled features betrayed little, as did his Force aura. Nonetheless, he had to have been surprised at the choice.

Vestara Khai.

Vestara blinked, confused, thinking that Ship was speaking solely to her for some reason. *What is it, Ship?*

A brush of humor. *Come along, apprentice. Do not keep your betters waiting.*

Vestara knew she did a poor job of concealing her astonishment and delight

as she made her way to stand with a High Lord, two Lords, and a Saber. But in the end, the disapproval coming from the crowd members meant little to her. She was going with Ship, and they were not.

"Good thoughts, Apprentice Khai?" The voice was masculine and kind. Vestara smiled. If her father couldn't be here, at least her father's friend was.

"The best, Saber Myal," she replied. "I am thinking of how fortunate I am to be here on this historic occasion."

"Apprentice," growled Taalon, "you waste your energy and that of others. You should be meditating."

"No, Taalon. None of us should be," said Workan. And he was right. Vestara felt the change in Ship, a tension, a readiness. Part of the curving sides that formed Ship's interior wall became transparent. These five Sith, for the first time, beheld a spaceship other than the *Omen.*

They heard Ship in their minds: *This vessel is a Damorian s18 light freighter. It has a crew of six. It is en route from Eriadu, a major shipyard. Its cargo will help our cause greatly.*

"What do we do?" asked Taalon.

We must damage it so that it is forced to land for repairs, Ship replied. *Command me.*

Taalon, the leader of the group, responded immediately. At once, Ship— designed to obey a powerful will—sprang into action. Vestara and the others found themselves making use of the Force to press their bodies flat against the floor of Ship's interior as the vessel, eager for battle, dove toward his unwitting prey. Weapons appeared out of nowhere—laser cannons manifested from its belly and screamed fire at the freighter, a magnetic accelerator formed at its back to hurl devastating metallic orbs that punched holes in the freighter's side.

Vestara watched, wide-eyed. She had never seen Ship attack before, and it was a beautiful dance of destruction.

Doesn't it have any defenses? She thought to him.

It can carry up to six BDY crew skiffs, came Ship's response. *They would have launched by now if they were going to.*

And as Ship had said it would happen, so it did. The freighter was disabled and unable to make the jump into hyperspace. Instead, it headed for the planet. Elation rippled through the Force, as Taalon directed Ship to follow.

The planet was pleasant and temperate. Ship had done perhaps too good a job on the vessel; there were gaping holes in its side... and even at a distance, Vestara saw footprints in the soft mud.

"They have fled already," said Taalon as he and the others stepped out of Ship's interior. Vestara let the other four precede her, as was proper.

"Of course they have," said Workan, in a tone of voice that was almost a sneer. "Did you think they would sit around and wait to be caught?"

"Look there," said Myal, pointing. "Humanoid tracks going off in two separate directions."

"They will have weapons," warned Workan.

"So do we," smiled Lady Rhea, patting the lightsaber clipped to her belt. They had more than that, of course. All of them carried small, handheld blasters and parangs. The parangs, sharp-edged glass tools that, when thrown, returned to the thrower, had originally been designed merely to clear fields. Now, they were useful and deadly weapons. And of course, they all had the ultimate weapon.

The dark side of the Force.

Vestara had been extending herself in the Force as the others had. The fear exuded by the fleeing crew was rich and satisfying, almost overshadowing something—

"Come, Vestara," Lady Rhea said. "We will go with Lord Workan."

Vestara opened her mouth to say she thought she had sensed something, but out of the corner of her eye she caught the movement of a small ground-dwelling mammal scurrying out of sight. She was grateful for her hesitation. She was already being scrutinized as the only apprentice on the mission; she didn't want to make a single misstep. Vestara closed her mouth and nodded, moving to follow as instructed.

"*You* will come with me, Lady Rhea," Lord Taalon commanded. "Lord Workan will take Saber Myal and *Apprentice* Khai." The smooth voice brooked no disagreement. Lady Rhea inclined her fair head as if she didn't care either way.

"Do me proud, Apprentice," she said to Vestara.

"Yes, Lady Rhea. Of course," Vestara replied.

The hunt was on, and Vestara could feel the excitement building inside her. The terrain—open, grassy plains with patches of brown soil here and there—was far from ideal for concealment. There were clearly marked footprints here, flattened grasses there, and only one place that might offer any shelter—the gentle rise of forested hills.

"We're fortunate they are not Force users," said Myal.

"We are even more fortunate that they had no chance to hide their path," commented Workan. Vestara remained silent—she only spoke when spoken to. Both the High Lord and the Saber were right. The frightened Force auras were like beacons, and the trail was obvious.

"Should we take them alive?" asked Myal. "They might be able to help us repair the freighter."

"No," Workan said. "You think too small, Myal. Ship will know how to repair it, if it is not too damaged. If he cannot, we will salvage what we can and return when we have more vessels. It is best to eliminate all witnesses."

Vestara expected as much. She only hoped that she would be permitted a kill. She knew that Workan and Myal, who outranked her by a considerable amount, would be eager for this sort of kill themselves. It was new for the Sith, to openly attack an enemy. Normally, in her society, murder and assassination

The freighter was disabled and unable to make the jump into hyperspace. Instead it headed for the planet.

were almost… genteel. One's opponent was eliminated either by oneself or a hired killer. Vendetta killings were honorable, and one bragged by snapping off the recognizable blade of the shikkar. But this—openly chasing a foe, dispatching them like beasts—was new. They were not Sith. They did not deserve any elegance or sophistication in their deaths.

There was movement in one of the trees, and it was not caused by the wind. Workan paused, unfastened his parang, took aim, and let it fly. Emitting its unique whirring sound, the weapon struck home. The leaves of the tree shook slightly, and a body fell. It was short and squat and appeared to be male, wearing what Vestara knew to be a

pilot's outfit, with an overly large head that was—unfortunately for the pilot—cloven in two. The huge black eyes were wide and staring, the folds that encircled his mouth flapping in his death throes. Vestara wrinkled her nose.

"Sullustan, I think," said Workan. "So ugly."

Vestara's danger sense tingled. She opened her mouth in order to warn her companions, but they had sensed it as well. All three of them drew their lightsabers, batting back the blaster bolts that did nothing other than reveal the shooter's location to his killers. "You flushed his friend," said Myal.

"You take this one," said Workan. Myal inclined his head, drew his blaster, and fired while Vestara and Workan almost effortlessly defended him. This shooter, a human, also dropped, dead before he hit the ground.

Myal sighed, disappointment furrowing his brow. "Too easy," he murmured. Vestara agreed. Apparently there was more challenge in planning and carrying out the murder of a fellow Sith than there was in killing these beings.

Workan's comlink chirped. It was Taalon. "We have found the rest, holed up in a cave. I thought you two would wish to see them before we dispatched them."

You two? Vestara fought to keep her expression motionless. Workan and Myal exchanged glances. "Indeed," said Workan. "What do you wish Vestara to do?"

"She will return to the frigate and begin cataloguing its contents," said Taalon. Vestara felt her cheeks start to burn with embarrassment and used the Force to hide it. Workan clicked the com and looked at Vestara expectantly. She bowed and turned around, breaking into a trot as she returned to the frigate. Ship sensed her unhappiness but she did not respond to his inquiries.

Vestara was used to unquestioning obedience, but this time, the dismissal stung. Taalon had deliberately denied her a chance for a kill and had added insult to injury by assigning her a menial task that had no urgency whatsoever. As she approached the grounded freighter, though, she sensed another presence in the Force—and this time, she was sure it was not an animal.

Vestara drew her lightsaber and activated it with a fierce snap-hiss just as someone stepped out of the hole blown in the freighter's hull.

The human girl was barefoot, wearing only a single garment that covered her from shoulder to knees. It was stained, tattered, and oft-mended. Pale flesh showed old and new scars. A fresh gash on her head suggested that she had been injured in the crash. *That's why her Force presence felt so faint to me*, Vestara realized. The girl had been unconscious, and Vestara, like the other Sith, had focused on the fear of the known prey.

"Please don't hurt me!" The voice was young and frightened. The girl flung up her hands in a pleading gesture, her face—too old and haggard-looking for the age Vestara suspected she was—filled with fear. "I don't care about the cargo! You can have it!"

Intrigued, Vestara lowered her weapon slightly, happy to seize another chance to learn something about this vast galaxy that her people would soon conquer. "You are not a member of the crew. Are you a stowaway?"

The girl hesitated, and Vestara lifted her lightsaber. The other girl shrank back. "The pilots were helping me escape from B'nish. I am—I was—a slave. Are you bounty hunters? Pirates?"

Were they pirates? As good a name as any. "Pirates," Vestara confirmed. "We wanted the cargo."

"The others—"

"Are dead, or will be soon."

She swallowed. "I have nothing you could want," she said. "Take the cargo. Leave me here. No one will find me."

"It... doesn't work that way," Vestara said quietly.

"Please... the others won't even know. I wasn't on any crew roster. Just let me go, say you never saw me. I just... I just want to be... to live as a free being. I've never known that. No one will know!"

No one would. No one except Vestara. No one except Ship, whom she could feel in her mind, quietly observing her behavior. This girl, slave or no, harmless or no, was not Sith. And therefore she had to die.

"I can make it quick and painless," Vestara said, wondering why she said the words even as they came unbidden. Why should she care what pain she caused? "Kneel down, I will—"

The girl's blue eyes, hopeful a moment ago, now went hard even as tears sprang to them. "No," she said, her voice firm and surprisingly strong. "No more kneeling. No more obeying. You are not my master. No one is. I *will* die free!"

And quick as a sorumi doe, she took off running. Vestara was just as fast. Her parang was in her hands in an instant. She gathered the Force to guide her aim, then let fly.

The glass weapon could not know pity. It went through her with the same ruthless efficiency as it had once sliced through tangled undergrowth. The impact of the blow knocked the girl off-balance in mid-stride.

Red, the world was *red*, hot and vital and piercing. Vestara swayed for a moment. No one had warned her... she hadn't expected... quite so *much*...

She had died resisting death, embracing life with a fierce passion that Vestara had never before encountered, and the sensation in the Force as that life was ripped away stopped Vestara's breath as her heart slammed against her chest. She felt her own knees buckle and her world swirl around her. For a merciful instant, the grayness dimmed the urgent violence of the *red*, long enough for the Sith apprentice to gather herself and remember the power of her will.

Only the Sith were to survive. This girl would never have been one. Vestara had done exactly as she should have.

So why do you still tremble, apprentice?

I—I don't know, Vestara thought, not bothering to wrap a lie around herself. Ship knew how to see through those. She was still recovering from the feel of the wounded Force, from the sight of so much... too much... red. She walked up on uncertain legs to stand over the body, and wondered what the girl's name had been.

Name her yourself, Ship said.

Vestara swallowed, then reached out in the Force to calm her own beating heart. She took a deep breath of the copper stench of fresh blood.

I will name her First, Vestara decided, letting cold dispassion settle upon her. For she will be the first of many. And she was. ☸

BUYER'S MARKET

WRITTEN BY **TIMOTHY ZAHN**
ART BY **BRIAN ROOD**

The sign over the huge junkyard said "Blackie's," and the man who'd emerged from the booth beside the narrow entrance had a flowing cascade of black hair. By the usual standards of logic, Lando Calrissian decided, that should be the yard's owner.

Except that he didn't act like an owner. There was hesitation in his step as he strode toward his visitor, an uncertainty in his face that didn't fit a man his size. The much smaller man trailing diffidently behind him looked far more at ease.

Still, Lando was a stranger here in Vorrnti City, and the post-Endor stage of the war against the Empire was still raging across this sector. Maybe Blackie just didn't like strangers.

"Afternoon," Lando said amiably as the two men came up to him. "Blackie?"

"Yeah," the big man growled. "You?"

"Name's Calrissian," Lando said. "I'm looking for some hard-to-find merchandise and heard you were the man to see."

"Got that right," Blackie said, pride momentarily eclipsing his animosity. "Third largest yard in the—"

"What exactly are you looking for?" the smaller man interrupted.

Something in Lando's gut warned him to hold back on the specifics. "Won't know until I see your stock," he said instead. "Shall we?"

He started forward. Blackie courteously stepped out of his way, but the smaller man didn't move. "The yard's pretty big," he warned. "We could walk around the rest of the day and still not see everything."

"No problem," Lando assured him. "I can get the kick-sled out of my ship, Master—ah—?"

"Cravel," the other said. "And if you'd bothered to read your landing documents, you'd know repulsorlift vehicles are banned everywhere in the district."

"It's the scrap rats," Blackie explained. "Repulsorlifts attract them like crazy. That's why the spaceport has that two-meter-high thorn hedge you went through on your way out—they don't want the vermin swarming in and chewing on someone's landing gear."

"That could be a problem," Lando agreed. He *had* read the landing documents, of course. But it never hurt to look stupid when walking into a bargaining situation. "Well, time's a-wasting. Let's head in and see what you've got."

Reluctantly, Cravel finally stepped aside. "Fine. After you."

The yard was every bit as impressive as it had looked from above when Lando had brought his new ship, the *Lady Luck*, into the spaceport a kilometer away. It was also incredibly secure, far more so than any of the warehouses or repair service shops scattered around outside the port's hedge.

Surrounded by an eight-meter-high wall topped with shred wire and an arching network of spider mesh to keep out any snooping airspeeders who might be willing to risk a violation of the repulsorlift ban, the place was more impressive even than many of the new military outposts the freshly-minted New Republic had opened up.

And there, no more than fifty meters from the entrance—standing like a frozen sentinel among a group of rusty harvesters—was the exact item Lando had come all this way to find.

An Imperial All Terrain Armored Transport.

"Whoa!" he said, pointing like a kid seeing his first tricker snake. "Is that an *AT-AT*?"

"It's not for sale," Cravel said quickly.

"Not working, anyway," Blackie added. "Someday I need to sit down and take a good look at its engines."

"Oh, I wasn't looking to buy it," Lando hastened to assure him, shading his eyes as he peered up at the massive war machine. There was a net scaffold hanging over the machine's head, with three men standing beside the chin and the two Taim & Bak MS-1 heavy laser cannons mounted there. "I was just surprised to see it, that's all," he continued, lowering his eyes and looking around them. "Is that a Corellian half-tread over there?"

He let them walk him around for another half hour, listening to Blackie's sales pitch with half an ear, noting how much calmer Cravel seemed now that they were away from the AT-AT.

And as they toured the yard, he thought. Hard.

By the time they came to a pair of dilapidated Huttese marsh crawlers, he'd come up with a plan.

"Ah—*now* you're talking," he said, gesturing to the crawlers. "Those up and running?"

"Do they *look* up and running?" Cravel retorted.

"Afraid their engines are shot," Blackie said. "But either would be good for spare parts."

> "Yeah, I've dealt with my share of big shots," Lando commiserated. "Pains in the neck, all of them."

"Right you are, and I'll take 'em both," Lando said, doing a quick visual measurement. The larger of the two was about three meters high, twenty long, and—most important of all—eight wide. It would clear the junkyard's narrow entrance but with less than half a meter to spare on each side. Perfect. "You got a tractor-hauler I can borrow to pull them out and across to the spaceport?"

"I've got one," Blackie said, his earlier wariness back on his face. "But you should probably hold off for a couple of days."

"Why?" Lando asked. "Customs fees about to go down?"

"There's some kind of big shot coming in day after tomorrow for a major real estate transaction," Cravel said. "His people have already taken over the whole customs building, and they're not going to look kindly on someone who wants to start filing datawork on something else."

"Yeah, I've dealt with my share of big shots," Lando commiserated. "Pains in the neck, all of them. Fine, but I'm not going to just sit here and let someone else grab those crawlers. Let me have them now, and I'll rent one of those warehouses down the street to stash them in until the air clears."

"Well… sure," Blackie said hesitantly. "Sure. Let's go back to the office and do the datawork, and then I'll get the hauler and pull them out of the yard for you."

An hour later, Lando took up position just outside the junkyard, watching the hauler's treads churning up the dirt as Blackie dragged the first of the crawlers through the yard toward the entrance. He reached the gap and slowed, and Lando could see the man's head turning back and forth as he checked his mirrors, making sure he wasn't about to scrape the crawler against the entrance support posts.

Lando let him get the crawler about a third of the way through the gap. Then, with a startled shout, he snatched out his blaster, crouched down, and opened fire on the hauler's underside.

Blackie shouted something Lando couldn't hear over the roar of the engine and the screaming of the blasterfire. But the interference didn't last long. The engine seized up on Lando's third shot, the roar becoming a howl as the power regulators began cascading, and even that faded away on Lando's fifth shot. He gave it three more shots, just to be sure, before ceasing fire. Blaster in hand, he peered under the hauler, watching out of the corner of his eye as Blackie came boiling out of the hauler's cab, swearing like a Corporate Sector sabacc player. "Calrissian!" he snarled. "What in the—?"

"Did you *see* them?" Lando cut him off, putting a mixture of disbelief and revulsion into his voice. "They must have been half a meter long, with teeth the size of gyv knives—"

"What's going on?" Cravel's tense voice came from behind Lando. Lando turned to see him running toward them from the office booth, a blaster clutched in his hand. "Who was shooting?"

"He was," Blackie said in disgust. "Saw some scrap rats and lost his head. Brilliant, Calrissian. Just brilliant."

"Can you fix it?" Cravel asked, crouching down to peer under the hauler.

"Yeah, with enough time," Blackie said, his voice suddenly tight. "But…" He trailed off.

For a moment no one spoke. Then, Cravel straightened up. He looked at Blackie, then at Lando, and finally holstered his blaster. "Then I guess you'd better get to it," he said, a forced lightness in his tone. "Hang on a second, and I'll help you collect your gear."

"What can I do to help?" Lando asked.

For a moment he thought Cravel was going to say what he was obviously thinking. But the other merely nodded toward the spaceport. "Go back to your ship," he said. "It's going to take a few days to fix this mess."

"Sorry," Lando apologized. "I'll pay all the repairs, of course."

"We'll talk about that later," Cravel said. "Go on, get lost. Blackie, you come with me."

Fifteen minutes later Lando was back inside the *Lady Luck*, keying his comm board. It had been horribly risky, but he'd pulled it off. More importantly, he'd pulled it off without getting shot.

Now if only the man he needed could get here in the next two days.

"Coruscant Military Command," a brisk voice came from the comm.

"This is Lando Calrissian," Lando identified himself. "Former General Calrissian. I need you to connect me to Lieutenant Judder Page of the Katarn Commandos."

The big shot Blackie had talked about came in right on schedule, settling his ship as close to the customs building as possible and striding the rest of the way surrounded by a wedge of heavily-armed bodyguards. The people he'd come to do business with were already there, having casually drifted in over the previous few hours.

But it wasn't real estate they were going to be buying and selling. Not by a long shot.

"Well?" the nondescript man standing beside Lando asked.

"It's glitterstim, all right," Lando confirmed sourly, taking one last look at the customs building and then moving around the corner of the warehouse they were skulking beside. "No matter how carefully they package the stuff, some of the odor always gets out. Probably being grown in secret chambers out in the woods—it's a pain to recreate the Kessel environment for the spice spiders, but if you can pull it off there are huge profits to be made."

Judder Page grunted. "I don't want to know how you even know that, do I?"

"Probably not," Lando agreed. "Your men ready?"

"*Mine* are," Page said. "Question is, are yours?"

"I think so," Lando said. "Now that the buyer and his money are here, they should be showing themselves any minute."

The words were barely out of his mouth when, inside the junkyard's wall, the AT-AT clumped its way into view, heading for the marsh crawler still sitting in the exit.

"I'll be skrimped," Page said, sounding as awestruck as Lando had ever heard the man get. "And they got it working in *two days?*"

"Two days," Lando confirmed. "I'm guessing all Cravel originally wanted were the heavy lasers, probably with an eye toward mounting them and a generator on one of Blackie's treaded vehicles. I've seen that approach before: a gang takes over a junkyard near a target, cobbles together just what they need for that one job, and then just leave everything but then loot behind."

"Until you forced them into Plan B."

Lando nodded. "Amazing how the smell of big profit brings out the best in people."

"Or the worst," Page said. "Come on —time to make ourselves scarce."

They slipped around one more corner, putting the AT-AT out of sight. But not out of hearing, and Lando winced at the sound of the AT-AT's big feet crunching down on the crawler he'd blocked the yard's exit with. The crunching stopped, and the

ground beneath them began a rhythmic shaking as the walker headed toward the spaceport. Page touched Lando's arm, and together they wove their way between the buildings toward the spot Page had calculated would give them the best view of the upcoming drama.

As usual, he was right. They reached their vantage point just as the AT-AT came to a halt across the thorn hedge from the customs building and opened fire.

AT-ATs weren't the kind of war machine that could sneak up on anyone, and the bodyguards were already outside the building, pelting the massive intruder with fire of their own. But even heavy blaster rifles were of no use whatsoever against AT-AT armor. The machine's chin laser cannons raked the customs building with fire, calmly and systematically laying it open and killing everyone in sight.

The visiting big shot was one of the last to die, making a desperate race across the spaceport toward his ship and leaving

> [The AT-AT's] chin laser cannons raked the customs building with fire, calmly and systematically laying it open.

a trail of dead bodyguards behind him. The AT-AT's gunners nailed him with a laser shot, then hit him once more just to be sure.

"There they go."

Lando looked up at the AT-AT's side. The boarding hatch had opened and two men on droplines were winched rapidly to the ground. With the walker's lasers still firing on the scattered survivors, the men unhooked from their lines and raced toward the scene of destruction. They disappeared into the smoke and dust, emerging a minute later lugging two large containers each. Running more slowly now under their burdens, they headed back to the AT-AT.

"Page?" Lando prompted anxiously as the thieves started fastening their stolen containers to the lines.

"Patience," Page advised. They had to see what the thieves were wearing and then change into something that more or less matched.

And then, with the thieves still bent over their task, two men wearing similar outfits emerged from one of the buildings and raced silently up behind them. They reached the thieves, there was a double flash of hold-out blaster

stunners, and the now unconscious men were unceremoniously shoved out of sight beneath the AT-AT's body. The newcomers grabbed the lines and one of them waved, and both men and containers were winched rapidly upward. Lando held his breath as they disappeared inside...

It was decidedly anticlimactic. One minute the AT-AT's lasers were firing at stragglers from the carnage. The next minute the weapons went suddenly silent.

"And that," Page said, straightening up, "is that."

"There's still their ship," Lando pointed out.

"Don't worry, it's covered." He eyed Lando curiously. "You want to tell me now why you insisted we wait until they attacked the spice dealers before we moved in?"

Lando shrugged. "Blackie told me the AT-AT wasn't functional," he said. "I figured that as long as Cravel had a crew here that was clearly up to mischief, I might as well let them get the thing in working condition for me."

"And you want a functional AT-AT *why?*"

Lando smiled tightly. "Come and visit me on Nkllon in a few months and you'll see."

"*Nkllon?*" Page echoed, frowning. "I thought that place was way too hot to do anything with."

"You'll see," Lando said again. "So will the whole New Republic."

Page shook his head. "If you say so. Oops—time to get back to work. See you later."

He headed toward the AT-AT, where one of his commandos had reappeared in the side hatch and was winching the money and glitterstim containers back down.

Lando grimaced. Yes, the Nomad City project was an ambitious one: an old surplus Dreadnought balanced atop forty surplus AT-ATs, matching Nkllon's slow rotational speed so as to stay continually on the planet's cool dark side while they mined the planet's incredibly rich metal ores. If he could pull it off.

One AT-AT down. Just thirty-nine more to go.

Mentally, he shook his head. The smell of big profit did indeed bring out the best in people. The best, and the worst.

And the craziest.

Giving the AT-AT one last look, he turned and headed for the junkyard. Time to see how good a deal Blackie would be willing to cut him. ☙

GREG & TIM
HILDEBRANDT

AND LEEBO MAKES THREE

WRITTEN BY **MICHAEL REAVES** & **MAYA KAATHRYN BOHNHOFF**
ART BY **GREG** & **TIM HILDEBRANDT**

The Rodian glanced around *The Nexu's Den* as if looking for someone he desperately hoped not to see. Sitting across from him at the dimly lit corner table in the seedy port bar, Dash Rendar absently wondered why he even bothered trying to see—the air was a bilious pall of deathstick smoke and other inhalants, all designed to make the present more interesting and the future less attainable. His lungs protested in spite of his shallow breathing.

Aside from the smoke, the place smelled like stale droid lube and fermented fruit. He'd been in worse. It didn't seem anything to be particularly proud of at the moment.

His Nautolan partner, Eaden Vrill, endured it the way he endured everything—with silent stoicism. Nautolans as a species tended to be unemotional. Add to that Eaden's few decades of training in the teräs käsi martial arts discipline, and the result was a *very* inscrutable alien. They'd been working together for over four months, and Dash still found it hard to fathom what was going on much of the time behind the amphibian's large, maroon eyes.

"Awright, look," Kood Gareeda said at last, his vocal organs giving the Basica whistling, rubbery sound that made comprehension dicey. Once again, Dash marveled at the alien's choice of occupations. Stand-up comedy was hardly the best choice for someone whose sibilants and fricatives all sounded alike. Not that most audiences stayed around long enough to be annoyed by this. Put bluntly, Darth Vader probably did better *shtick*. But concern about Gareeda's financial future would have to take a back seat to concern about their own. As far as Dash was concerned, it was all over bar the counting. He doubted that Eaden wanted to spend the money, but a mech-of-all-trades would be useful aboard the *Outrider*.

"Remind me again what he's programmed for," Dash prompted the Rodian. He'd swear the guy was sweating, and Rodians didn't even have sweat glands.

Gareeda ticked off the droid's features on his scaly digits. "Navigation, piloting, and weapons, as well as da usual repair capabilities standard in da LE series."

"And you're selling him because...?"

Another glance at the door. "'cause I was misinformed. I was told his safety protocols been hacked. Dey *lied* ta me." The Rodian glowered at the dormant droid. "He's a mopak bodyguard. He'll shoot *at* sentients, but he won't *hit* 'em. What good's dat?"

A heavy *thump* from the door's direction once again drew the Rodian's attention. Dash decided it was time to wrap up this palaver.

Comedian or not, Gareeda's behavior suggested he was expecting something decidedly *un*funny to happen at any second. It was even making Eaden jinky, judging from how the heavy cilia on his head twitched whenever Gareeda's nervous gaze swept past the entrance.

Besides, if the Rodian *was* under some sort of time pressure, that could only work to their advantage. "Fifteen hundred," Dash offered.

He got a baleful look from Gareeda's black, insectile orbs. The comic's fleshy proboscis worked angrily for a moment. Then—

"Fine. Gimme da creds. I gotta get off

dis rock." "Well, if you need a boost off world, we can offer that, too."

The Rodian's bulbous eyes seemed to protrude even further. "No, no. I, ah, I c'n find 'nother passage..."

"You don't need to. You got us. Ten hundred—and a lift."

Gareeda made a slurping sound that approximated a human's gnashing of teeth, then stuck out a scaly hand. "Fine. Done. How soon d'you—we—space?"

Dash, suppressing a grin, handed over a one thousand credit note. "One hour. Dock Eighty-Four Twelve. Mid-Town facility."

Gareeda nodded and stood up to leave. Eaden halted him. "It's got a restraining bolt installed. What's wrong with it?"

The sharp, bitter odor of rank fear again pervaded the air. "Nuttin'. Jus' wanted ta make sure it didn't... wander off, dat's all."

"Great!" said Dash. "Let's fire it up."

The Rodian looked like he might cry. Dash had never seen such a sight; in fact, he wasn't even sure if Rodians *could* cry. "Look, if I'm gonna make it t'your ship inna hour, I *gotta* get my gear."

He was so obviously desperate that Dash gestured for him to be gone; there was no fun in torturing someone in such dire straits.

Gareeda fled like a mynock out of Mustafar. He didn't use the front entrance; he headed out the back.

"Well," said Eaden, "there he goes. Leaving us a thousand credits lighter with what's probably an inert piece of junk."

"At that price, who cares? Even if it doesn't work, the chassis alone is worth half again as much." He flipped the droid's master switch, and was pleased to see its photoreceptors light up.

"Optic circuitry works," Eaden said. He addressed the droid. "Are you functional?"

"Who's asking?" the droid replied tartly, then scanned the noisy, smoky chamber. "What's wrong with this reality? Where's my boss?"

Dash rolled his eyes. Wonderful. The Rodian had given the droid a personality substrate. Fairly easy to embed, and almost impossible to remove, because the more it interfaced with those around it, the more ingrained the substrate became. It was probably almost firmware by now.

Well, nothing to be done about it. "Your boss took off."

The droid's optics fluttered. "He... *left* me?"

"Sold you. Took a thou of my hard-earned creds."

"*One thousand*? I'm worth five times that!"

The droid's voice carried such indignity that Dash grinned in spite of the situation. "Got a pretty good opinion of yourself."

"Believe me, you don't want to know my opinion of *you*."

Before Dash could reply, the bar's front door slammed open. Four beings entered. Two were large, brutal-looking humans, followed by a Barabel. The last was a Trandoshan. They looked exactly like what they undoubtedly were: trouble. One of the humans zeroed in on Dash's table and pointed. The others looked. Then, all four moved with a purpose —right at them.

Eaden stood. Cracked his knuckles.

Dash turned to the droid. "What do you call yourself?"

"None of your business. I—"

"Stow it. Emergency nomenclature override. New name: Leebo."

"Integrating data. New name: Leebo."

"Okay, Leebo, let's move back. We don't want to get hit by flying thugs."

> ## Dash canted the ship to port but not fast enough—a beam splashed against the rear deflectors, rocking the *Outrider* and jolting her crew.

As Eaden had anticipated, Kood Gareeda was a no-show; they lifted off without him. No sooner were they clear of the planet's gravity well and entering deep space than they were hailed.

"Heave to," came a raspy voice over the comm, speaking Shyriiwook, Dash noticed with surprise.

"Says who?" he asked.

"Says Kravengash, business associate of Hox Bilan."

Dash blinked at the comm. Neither of the names meant anything to him, but the phrase "business associate" did. It meant "Trouble" with a capital Blaster. This far Rimward the ubiquitous crime syndicate Black Sun was little more than a name; even so, it was still a name that inspired caution. Even the Empire stepped lightly around the interplanetary criminal organization. Dash had run afoul of them more than once and he hated them with a passion; an emotion many rank-and-file

criminals heartily echoed, although Dash's loathing went quite a bit deeper. He didn't have time to dwell on that now, though.

Out here in the Deep it was the dream, he'd heard, of most small-time organleggers, spice runners, and purveyors of other ill-gotten merchandise, to someday pull off something of such audacious criminality as to become noticed by the galactic underlords of crime—to become a "made sentient," as it were.

Dash gritted his teeth. He'd thought— *hoped*—that by heading this far out he'd finally be rid of that whole noxious crew of cutthroats, at least for awhile. That maybe he could at least let some memories settle before going back to the more "civilized" center.

Apparently not.

"It would seem that we now know why Kood Gareeda was so anxious to consummate his deal with us," Eaden said mildly.

"You think?" Dash flipped the comm off. "Time to go. Stand by for lightspeed."

But the Wookiee was impatient; he started blasting before they could make the jump. Charged-particle beams sizzled past them, close enough to burn paint.

Dash canted the ship to port, but not fast enough—a beam splashed against the rear deflectors, rocking the *Outrider* and jolting her crew. A sizzle of sparks erupted from the console.

Eaden looked at Dash. "Hyperdrive is—"

"Offline again, yeah, I noticed." He hit the thrusters, pulled the ship into a tight parabola and started looking for cover.

There was nothing save the flat blackness of space, with a few stars twinkling...

Very few, he realized.

Somewhere close by was a light source big enough to wash out the starlight. Dash looked at the mass indicator and quickly homed in on the source—a huge gas giant, over 200,000 kilometers in diameter. He didn't stop to think. He slewed the ship to port and up.

"I need calculations, Leebo! Plot a slingshot orbit around that gas giant. If we can get enough speed, we can kick-start the hyperdrive."

"Just what makes you think I can do that?" Leebo asked. "And if by some chance I *could*, hull integrity would be at risk, and—"

"Getting shot by that gunship will risk hull integrity a lot more, bolthead! Gareeda said orbital navigation was part of your

package. So get me those numbers or I start ejecting mass—and guess what's first out the airlock?"

"Your point is persuasive," Leebo said. A moment later, the droid rattled off a complex calculation.

"Implement," Dash said tersely to Eaden.

"No time to check the sequence," Eaden objected. "If he's off by so much as a decimal point—"

"Just *do it*!"

The Wookiee's cruiser hung close behind them as if tethered by a tractor beam as Dash plunged the *Outrider* into the far reaches of the huge planet's atmosphere.

Behind him, Leebo rattled off coordinates, velocities, and vectors.

"Optimum perigee in twelve-point-nine-seconds....increase thrust by point eighty-one....ninety-seven degrees vertical, thirty-seven degrees starboard roll on my mark," the droid said. "Four... three... two... one—*now*!"

Eaden made the corrections while Dash engaged the thrusters. The *Outrider* shot out of the gas giant's gravity well like a laser lancing off a durasteel mirror and rocketed into vacuum—close enough to the cruiser that they could see their distorted reflection in its fuselage.

"*All right!*" Dash yelled. The ship vibrated from the combination of speed, gravity, and the thrust of her own engines. It rattled his teeth, but the hull held together.

"We have hyperdrive," Eaden said, his eyes on the instruments.

"Fire 'em up. Let's ditch this system."

The cruiser was turning, but there was no way it could complete the maneuver in time. Eaden threw *Outrider* into hyperspace. The stars blurred, and a moment later they winked out of normal space.

"My previous master wouldn't have yelled at me," Leebo pouted.

When Dash glared at him, his temper slowly building, the droid added, "I'm just sayin'..."

The cruiser was turning, but there was no way it could complete the maneuver in time. Eaden threw *Outrider* into hyperspace. The stars blurred, and a moment later they winked out of normal space.

"Back to the cantina, where those four thugs were obviously looking for something they thought we had."

Dash turned to look at the droid. He didn't like where this was headed. "They might have had a perfectly legit reason—"

"And I suppose it's a coincidence that Kood Gareeda is not on this vessel, though he desperately wanted to flee Rodia. And also that a local crime boss tried to stop us as soon as we lifted."

Dash blinked. Yeah. It didn't take an astrophysicist to plot *that* course intersection. "Put it on autopilot. You and I and Leebo are gonna go down to the common room for a little talk..."

"He *sold* me. I *still* can't believe it."

"Yeah, yeah, we've established that. Moving on. Why would this Hox Bilan be looking for you? Seriously enough to send muscle *and* a cruiser?"

"Not a clue. I've done nothing to justify such action... that I recall."

"What about Gareeda? He do anything?"

"Other than irritating audiences by being painfully unfunny?" The droid rattled its shoulders in a shrug. "Although probably he wasn't bad enough to score a deathmark from a career criminal. Probably not."

"I'm curious," Eaden said. "Why are you so fond of him?"

Leebo hesitated. "He programmed me to like him."

Dash laughed. "*That's* funny."

"Your *face* is funny." Leebo's tone was decidedly sulky.

Eaden had been studying the droid intently. Now he said, "That restraining bolt's pulling too much power."

Dash looked at him. "And you know this how?"

"I once worked security in a droid factory on Coruscant. That is not a standard design."

"Get a wrench and let's have a look."

Eaden removed the bolt. When he turned it over, a short, thin rod fell onto the table. "Hmm. That appears to be a micro-datastick."

Dash picked up the tiny device, which was as long as his thumbnail and one-eighth as wide. He looked at Leebo. "Got a reader slot?"

"Of course." Leebo took the proffered datastick and pressed it into the tip of one finger. There was a short pause. "It's encrypted."

Of course it is. "Can you break the code?" Dash asked.

"Eventually."

Dash swore softly. He'd bet the *Outrider* and everything on her that the datastick belonged to Bilan and that the criminal wanted it back. A lot.

This was bad... but maybe not *all* bad. Maybe they could swing a deal. If they could convince Kravengash they neither knew nor cared what was actually on the datastick...

Hey, we acquired this by mistake, don't know what it is, don't care, happy to give it back, and if you want to, you know, give us a little something for our trouble, we're okay with that, too.

That these crooks were more of the penny-ante nature could actually work in their favor. Most of them were little more sophisticated than space pirates. Surely he could smooth-talk his way out of their bad graces.

Could be worse...

An hour later, Leebo was back in the cockpit. "I've decoded the information on the datastick."

Dash said, "And....?"

"It's a list of Black Sun Vigos in the Third Quadrant, along with data records of their transactions for the last six months, profits and losses, along with names of those on their payrolls— including police, military, judges, and politicians."

Dash stared, speechless. "All *that*...?"

"For starters."

Okay, it *couldn't* be worse.

"Let's pretend we didn't hear this." He looked at Leebo. "And you forget you know it."

"Kind of hard without scrubbing my memory."

Eaden cleared his throat.

Dash swung about. "*What?*"

"It appears that we lost Kravengash," the Nautolan said, his voice maddeningly mild.

"Yeah?" Dash tripped both scanners, close- and long-range. No hyperdrive signatures detected. "Still think Leebo was a bad investment? If he hadn't been here, we'd be plasma."

Eaden didn't say anything.

"What, too stubborn to admit you were wrong?"

"Not at all. I was merely wondering what this Hox Bilan fellow wanted with us."

Dash shrugged. "Where are you going with this?"

Dash felt like his scalp had been given a knuckle-burn by a wampa.

He was quite literally stunned, speechless. "How—how did —"

"Doesn't matter," Eaden said.

Dash stared at him.

"Most likely the Rodian needed cash and agreed to ferry—or let Leebo ferry—the data." He looked at the droid. "Did you have any idea of the stick's ultimate destination?"

"Sorry. My boss was fond of the phrase 'Need to know.'"

Eaden stated the obvious: "Knowledge of this makes us a danger to both Black Sun and the Empire. The Imperials would move planets to get this data. With it they could wipe out a major portion of the criminal organization in the Third Quadrant. Black Sun wants this, obviously, and anybody who might have learned what it was *will* be vaporized."

Dash looked at the droid. "There's probably a transponder of some sort in the datastick. That's how they tracked you."

"Oh, I feel so loved. Can't we eject it into space and let them find it?"

"They could tell it's been decoded, and we don't want that," Eaden said. "The only hope we have of surviving is to make sure, somehow, that they—Bilan, Black Sun, the Empire, whoever finds it first—think we never knew it existed, much less what was on it."

"Would it help," Leebo asked, "if we could suddenly be halfway across the galaxy?"

"Sure couldn't hurt. What have you got in mind?"

They were approaching a binary star system, where an old Hutt jumpgate, though officially out of commission, was still in operation, maintained by a cadre of smugglers who offered passage for ships in a hurry—at a price, of course.

As they drew closer, they noticed two things: First, the com was silent; the gate crew weren't responding. Could be the com was out, or it could be the crew weren't around?

Or something worse?

"Odd," Leebo muttered. His optics momentarily defocused, which Dash knew, was the droid equivalent of deep thought.

Dash was temporarily distracted by a *ping!* from the aft sensor.

Kravengash was coming up fast from behind.

"Captain Rendar, we have a problem," Leebo said.

"I know. The gate crew is gone and the Wookiee's on our tail again."

"Those are the least of our problems." The droid pointed at a holoschematic of the star system. "The secondary star in this system is a white dwarf."

"So?"

"My sensors show it's accreted enough degenerate matter from the primary to put it near critical mass."

Dash stared at the forward screen, which showed an awe-inspiring view of the binary system. A list of alphanumerics curtained down the screen. "How near? Millennia? Centuries? Years?"

"Closer to eleven—"

Dash felt a rush of relief. "Eleven years? That's not so—"

"—*minutes*."

Dash was speechless. *Eleven minutes* until the star went supernova, producing, for a few moments, more energy than the

The Imperials would move planets to get this data. With it, they could wipe out a major portion of the criminal organization in the third Quadrant.

You *might've* mentioned the star that in—" he glanced this chrono "—*nine minutes* will reduce this ship and us to clouds of quarks!"

"Well, how was I to know? A star exists for billions of years—the odds were literally *astronomical* that—"

"Enough. We *have* to get through the gate," Eaden said. "And we can't do that with Kravengash blocking our route. They'll nail us when we decelerate for transition."

Dash was thinking fast and furiously. "Maybe he doesn't know. If we tell him, than maybe we can both get out of—"

"Oh, he knows," Eaden said. "No doubt he's been told he can look forward to a lingering and painful demise if he fails to recover the datastick. So for him, it's a choice between protracted torture, or annihilation so swift he'll never feel a thing."

"Doesn't help us," Dash said. "In four minutes we're all gonna be gamma rays."

"I'll distract them," Leebo said.

Dash blinked. "How?"

"Take a life pod and harass 'em. Are the pods armed?"

"Yes, but—"

"You can make the gate transit while I keep the Wookiee occupied. After a few more minutes, he won't be around to follow."

"Neither will you," Eaden pointed out.

Leebo's servos whined as he shrugged. "You've shown me more kindness in a few hours than my previous owners ever did. I owe you."

When the Wookiee came in for the kill, Leebo's escape pod zipped in from above and started firing. The blasters on the pod weren't much, but they were enough that Kravengash had to deal with them.

Dash watched the viewport. "So, long, Leebo," he murmured.

He looked at the datastick in his hand. Considered keeping it... for about three seconds. He ejected it into space. Good luck on finding *that* after the star blew up.

Dash aimed the *Outrider* at the gate and Eaden triggered the entrance code.

Dash hoped it still worked—otherwise they were going to be caught on the wrong side of the gate in the deadly sphere of a supernova.

With a minute and ten seconds to go, he triggered the thruster...

...and felt the familiar jolt of the energy transfer as the gate lobbed them into another part of the galaxy.

"Too bad about the droid," Eaden said when they were safely on the other end of the jump. "I was beginning to... that's peculiar."

"What?" Dash followed Eaden's gaze to the viewport.

The gate was dilating again.

No. Not the Wookiee.

There was a flash of light and the life pod shot through.

No way. Dash activated the comm. "Leebo?"

The droid's face appeared in the heads-up display that overlaid the forward viewport. "You were expecting someone else?"

"*How—?*"

"Beats me. I was between the ship and the gate, battling nobly for your lives—"

"Yes," Eaden said. "And was the cruiser by any chance eclipsing the star system when the star went nova?"

"Maybe...."

"Ah," Eaden said. "The supernova energy interacted with the hypermatter in both ships' drives to create a protective local space-time hyper-fold. It only required that the cruiser's bulk shield the pod for a fraction of a second."

Dash stared at him as if he'd grown a second head.

Eaden shrugged. "Elementary hyper-physics—to a droid with the proper programming."

Dash regarded Leebo wryly. "So you knew about that stunt all along. And you had me believing you were gonna sacrifice yourself."

"I'm insulted," Leebo said. "I take on this dangerous mission—loyally, selflessly, with no thought for my own safety..."

"Banthaflop." Dash grinned. "Come aboard. And welcome to the crew, Tin Man..."

rest of the hundred billion stars in the galaxy combined? They couldn't outrun that! No wonder the gate crew weren't around. This operation was about to get shut down for a long, *long* time...

"You said nothing about this! All you said was there was a jumpgate near a binary system!"

"And I was right."

"Yeah," Dash said, seething. "Kudos.

A FAIR TRADE

WRITTEN BY **CHRISTIE GOLDEN**
ART BY **JOE CORRONEY**

The inside of Khedryn's mouth tasted like he'd taken a long lick of one of Farpointe's packed-dirt roads. A pounding headache felt like someone was twisting screws into his temple. He stepped gingerly into *Seeker*'s cockpit and slid into his seat.

"How do you feel?" Marr asked, plugging a complicated formula into *Seeker*'s navicomp. Even without the hangover, Khedryn couldn't have followed the formula. The numbers on the screen swam and he swallowed down a bout of nausea.

"Not as bad as I smell." He took a tentative whiff of one armpit and winced, the nausea rearing anew. "Are these the same clothes I had on last night?"

Marr, intent on his data, murmured something too unintelligible for Khedryn to decipher.

He looked out of the cockpit. *Seeker* streaked into the black, away from Fhost's gravity well. The swirl of stars through the window made Khedryn sick.

"There's caf in the galley," Marr said. "Might help."

"Thanks. Later. So… remind me of last night again."

Marr tapped a final key and looked over to him, the wall of his tan forehead creased in a question. The top of his head stuck out of the ruff of his light hair like the peak of a cloud-swathed mountain. "You played sabacc, drank, and talked—the latter two more than you should. There were ears all over the cantina."

The disapproval in the Cerean's tone irked Khedryn. He tried to think of a snappy retort, but the overindulgence in pulkay had left him too muzzy-headed to come up with anything. Instead, he sagged in his chair and acknowledged the reality.

"I need to slow it down some. It's affecting the work. But no harm done this time, right?"

Marr had the good grace to say nothing.

As *Seeker* cleared Fhost's system, Khedryn attuned her scanners to the frequency of the subspace salvaging beacon they'd left on a derelict. The scanners picked up the sound almost immediately—a satisfying, regular chirp that announced the presence of credits floating free in the black. Hearing it salved Khedryn's headache. A tractor beam malfunction had prevented them from towing the derelict back to Fhost when they'd first discovered it, and Khedryn had not wanted to risk reactivating the damaged derelict's engines. But now *Seeker* was squared away and they could pull the salvage home.

"There's the beacon," Marr said.

Khedryn eyed the blip on the scanner's screen. "No getting away from us this time, m'lady. Let's go get her," Khedryn said, and Marr activated the hyperdrive.

The black of Fhost's system gave way to the blue swirl of hyperspace, and *Seeker* burned its way deep into the Unknown Regions. Khedryn hurriedly darkened the cockpit's window. The churn of the blue roiled his already shaky stomach.

He put a hand on Marr's shoulder to steady him. "Time for that caf, I think."

"I'll mind the store."

By the time Khedryn had swallowed down two stomach tabs and three cups of caf, he felt more or less himself again. Carrying a caf for Marr, he wound his way back to the cockpit. Seeing Khedryn, the Cerean took the caf with a nod of thanks, and checked the instruments while he sipped.

"Good caf and good timing," he said. "We're about to come out of hyperspace."

Khedryn slid into his chair and disengaged the homing beacon. "Then let's make some credits."

Marr adjusted the radiation shields, disengaged the hyperdrive, and the blue gave way to black. The system took shape before them—a distant pair of dim, red binaries, the chaotic swirl of a thin asteroid belt, and, closer, two orange and red gas giants swarming with moons.

Marr input the coordinates for the derelict, Khedryn engaged the ion engines, and *Seeker* speared the system, swinging toward one of the large, barren moons orbiting the closer gas giant. Khedryn felt a brief rush of concern—that someone else had found the derelict, that Marr's math had been off and its orbit had decayed faster than they thought—but as they came around to the far side of the moon, the dim, red light of the dying binaries glinted on the hull of the derelict. He smiled and exhaled.

"Hello, beautiful."

A military heavy-equipment transport had been converted for standard hauling and hung in a low, decaying orbit over the moon. Its appearance was that of a large beetle, and a closer inspection showed the ship was minus its two escape pods and was structurally undamaged except for one of its engines, which looked to have blown wide open. Khedryn and Marr had already examined the interior—cargo bay empty, a conspicuous absence of logs.

A smuggler's ship. A life support malfunction had forced the crew to evacuate and they'd never returned.

"I think I could get her to fly, given enough time," Marr said.

"I don't doubt it. But with no life support, we'd have to fly her in hardsuits. Easier just to pull her home."

"Any concerns about the crew?"

"If they lived—a large if—this ship'll be scrap and her electronics refurbished and gone before they ever find it—or us. You worried?"

"Not at all," said Marr.

"Then get us into tractor range and let's hitch her up."

Seeker devoured the kilometers, closing in on the derelict. In moments, the ship filled their field of vision.

"Big girl," Khedryn said, eyeing the hauler's hull.

Marr nodded and maneuvered *Seeker* around for a tractor latch.

Before he engaged the beam, though, a proximity alarm started to trill.

"What's that?" Marr said, leaning forward to eye the instruments.

"A malfunction. Has to be. There's—"

"Another ship coming out of hyperspace," Marr said.

"*What*? Who?"

Khedryn leaned forward to examine the scan signature of the unknown ship when an explosion rocked *Seeker*, nearly knocking him from his seat. Alarms screamed.

"That's cannon fire!" Marr said.

Khedryn cursed. "Rear deflector at full."

"Fire in cargo bay two," Marr announced, his hands moving rapidly over the instruments. "We're leaking pressure out of bay one."

Khedryn grabbed the stick. "Seal it off. Going evasive."

A flashing light and the change in pitch of the alarm announced the loss of engine power. Khedryn cursed.

"Get them back online, Marr. We're floating dead. Who the hell is firing at us?"

His shoulders bunched in anticipation of the next shot, but it didn't come. Instead, a chime sounded.

"They're hailing us," Marr said.

Khedryn would have to buy time. "Put them through, but keep working on auxiliary power for the engines."

The hollow sound of an opening channel carried over the cockpit speakers. Khedryn winced when he heard the voice on the other end.

"Khedryn Faal, always and ever in my way."

"Reegas," Marr said.

Khedryn's fists curled into white balls. Reegas flew a highly modified YT-2400 freighter, armed to the teeth, and crewed by five thugs. He ran a criminal syndicate on Fhost. And hated Khedryn.

"You're wondering why I'm here," Reegas said.

"Because you're a murderous thief, is my thinkin'," Khedryn muttered, but did not transmit.

"I'm taking that derelict," Reegas continued.

Khedryn's fist slammed on the transmit button. "That's ours—"

Comm squelch cut him short.

"And I'm taking *Seeker*, too. That engine shot was intentional. I could've just blown you out of space. Consider yourselves lucky. I'm coming over, Faal. You've got ten minutes to debark."

"Debark? Are you—"

Once more, the squeal of interference shut him up and resurrected his headache.

"If you're there when I board…" Reegas said. "Well, there's no telling what might happen then. My boys like shooting things, after all."

Khedryn felt the vein in his forehead pulsing. "Don't they know I have a hangover?" He muttered.

"I can't have the engines up in ten minutes," Marr said.

Khedryn rubbed his temple. "How'd they even find us out here?"

"You were chatty last night. They might have heard about the derelict and put a beacon on *Seeker*."

> # "That engine shot was intentional. I could've just blown you out of space."

"Dammit, Marr. You're supposed to get me clear before I talk too much."

"You *always* talk too much."

"Shut up, Marr." He took a deep breath, his mind racing through options. "All right. Listen, no questions, just answers. I want *Seeker*'s engines dead and beyond repair. Can you do *that* in five minutes?"

Marr considered, then nodded.

"Do it. And I need you to tune the deflector so they can't scan *Seeker* for life signs."

Marr looked as incredulous as his natural placidity allowed. "Anything else? Maybe chart a new—"

"Once all that's done, arm yourself and meet me at the hardsuit locker. Quick, now."

"What's the plan?"

"I don't know yet. I'm just putting tools at our disposal."

He hit the transmit button on the comm. "We'll be off, you kriffin' thug. But don't think I'll forget this."

Reegas was laughing when he replied. "Nine and a half minutes, Faal."

While Marr worked, Khedryn hurried through *Seeker*'s corridors until he reached the equipment locker. He took a hatch cracker and cabled it to his hardsuit.

"Where are you, Marr?" he asked over the comlink.

"Coming now. Engines are ruined. No one is fixing them."

"Good."

Khedryn started squirming.

Marr sprinted into sight, grabbed his own suit, and started pulling it on. They tested seals, the comm—all was five-by-five.

"Let's get to the pod," Khedryn said.

Marr grabbed his arm. "He'll shoot the pod down, Khedryn."

"I know. That's why we won't be in it."

Marr released him. "If he scans it, he'll know we're not aboard."

"Exactly."

"Right? And then what?"

Khedryn frowned. "Still working that out."

And then he winked his lazy eye at Marr.

Reegas and three of his crew stood at the hatch to the *Starhawk* shuttle attached to *Blackstar*. His men wore blasters, ablative vests, and habitual scowls.

"*Seeker*'s escape pod just launched," announced Marden over *Blackstar*'s comm.

Reegas answered into his comlink. "Scan it for life-forms."

A pause, then, "None."

"Blow it out of space, just to be sure. They could have a screen on it. Can you scan *Seeker*?"

"Deflectors prevent a clean scan."

Reegas eyed the hard faces of the men.

"Faal may be stupid, but he doesn't quit. They'll be waiting for us."

Snickers from the men.

"We kill them both and space the bodies," Reegas said. He hated Faal, and wasn't even sure why. Men of different polarities, he supposed. It happened sometimes. "I want the ship intact."

The men double-checked the charges on their blasters and boarded the

Starhawk. Reegas took position in the shuttle's small cockpit. Through the window, *Seeker* and the derelict floated against the body of the gas giant. Reegas could turn both of them into over a million credits. That Faal would die in the process was just a bonus.

"Coming to see you, boys," he muttered at *Seeker*.

The shuttle separated from *Blackstar* and shot across the kilometers. While it flew, *Blackstar*'s plasma cannons fired, long red lines that atomized *Seeker*'s escape pod.

Khedryn's breath sounded like a bellows inside the hollow confines of the hardsuit's helmet. He blinked away the spots left over from the escape pod's explosion. He and Marr hugged the port side of *Seeker*, opposite her starboard docking ring.
They watched the shuttle disengage from *Blackstar* and accelerate toward them.

Khedryn glanced across space at the

derelict and, more importantly, its engines. Marr said he could get them online.

"They'll blow their way in through the docking ring," Marr said.

"Yes. We wait until they get closer."

The two friends clung to the side of the ship they were about to lose, waiting as the shuttle approached. When it was close to *Seeker,* but at an angle oblique to Khedryn and Marr, the former tapped his ship farewell and said, "We go."

Both of them engaged the anti-grav propulsion systems in the hardsuits and shot out into space.

The shuttle bumped hard against *Seeker*, clamps seizing the docking ring, and Reegas's men went to work. Two covered the door with blasters while the third affixed the shaped charges to the hatch.

"Blow it," Reegas said.

The explosion blew the hatch from its mounts, filling the area with smoke and the acrid tang of thermite. Reegas's men poured through the opening, blasters raised. To Reegas's surprise, though, he heard no blaster fire. Weapon drawn, he followed his men onto *Seeker*.

"This ship is not that big. Find them. You and you, with me. You two, that way. Sound off if you see or hear anything."

Khedryn and Marr slammed into the side of the ship, both of them grunting at the impact. They maneuvered themselves crabwise over to an external airlock door.

"Quick now," Khedryn said, and handed Marr the hatch cracker.

Marr affixed it and started working on the hatch's security code. Numbers blazed across its surface, reflected in reverse on the face-plate of Marr's helmet. The indicator light on the control panel stayed red.

Khedryn bit his lip with frustration. He glanced back at *Seeker*, wondering when Reegas would find the missing hardsuits and put two and two together.

Marr's intense stare drank in the cracker's failed formulae. He stopped the device's routine, pushed a few buttons, and started it down a different path.

"Got something?" Khedryn asked.

"Nothing certain. It ran the hexidecimals and got nothing, so it's something else. I tweaked it to run a base eleven run, then a twelve, and so on. The problem is the spaces."

Khedryn had no idea what Marr was talking about. He looked through the hatch's tiny window to the dark interior of the ship, then across the gulf of space to *Seeker*.

"Marr, we're running out of time."

"I know," Marr said. "I'll have it soon."

Khedryn stared at the unlit light of the hatch's control panel and tried to will it green.

Reegas and his two men prowled *Seeker*'s narrow passageways, blasters leading. They encountered nothing, heard nothing. The ship felt like a tomb. When they reached the central axis and the ship's locker, the lead man looked back and said, "Hardsuits are gone, Reegas."

And all at once it clicked for Reegas. Faal and Marr weren't aboard. The escape pod had been a diversion to make Reegas think an ambush awaited him on *Seeker*.

"They're on the derelict! They're going to try to fly it out of here!" He activated his comlink. "Marden, disable the engines on the derelict! Just the engines! Right now!"

"Why?"

"*Just do it!*"

"Yes, sir."

Marden locked *Blackstar*'s cannons onto the derelict's engines, reduced the energy output of the beams, and

fired. The engines exploded, rocking the entire ship out of its orbit. Pieces of metal pelted *Blackstar* and the blast wave made it roll gently.

The soft beep of an alarm drew his eye. The external airlock door facing the derelict was acting up. It had probably taken some debris from the explosion.

"Blast it."

He hopped out of his chair and hurried to the rear of *Blackstar*.

Khedryn's mouth went dry when he saw a light go on beyond the interior airlock seal. "Marr, someone is coming! Hurry!"

"Got it," Marr said, and the light on the external airlock turned green.

Khedryn pulled himself inside the airlock while drawing his blaster. He slammed a gloved hand to close the outer door.

"Come on," he said as it closed. "Come on."

> ### *Blackstar's* cannons lit up space and turned the shuttle to debris.

The moment he heard it seal, he threw the lever to open the inner door, which slid up with a hiss. He caught a flash of a movement from down the corridor, the discharge of a blaster bolt, and heard Marr's shout of pain.

He fired blind as fast as he could while throwing himself against the wall.

"Marr!"

The Cerean lay on his back on the deck, a smoking black furrow in the shoulder of his hardsuit. O2 leaked out with a soft hiss.

"I'm all right," Marr said, waving a hand.

Khedryn nodded, relieved, and poked his head out. A body lay down in the corridor—a human, blaster hole burned in his chest. Khedryn had seen him before, in the cantinas on Fhost, but couldn't remember his name.

"Damn, damn, damn," he said, unsealing his helmet.

"What is it?" Marr asked, as he climbed to his feet.

"Killed him."

Marr put a hand on Khedryn's shoulder.

Khedryn shook his head. "Come on. Stay sharp. There could be more of them."

He grabbed the comlink from the dead man and they hurried to the cockpit. A ship wide scan by Marr showed no one

else aboard. The dead man's comlink started to ping.

"Verra," Reegas called over the comlink. "Verra, report."

Verra. That had been the dead man's name.

"Verra's dead, Reegas," Khedryn said over the comlink. "And I'm sitting in your cockpit."

He would have paid ten thousand credits to have seen Reegas's face when he said those words.

A long pause, then, "We can deal, Faal," Reegas said. "Don't do anything rash."

Khedryn imagined Reegas and his men running for the shuttle.

"If you've got any men in that shuttle, get them out now." Khedryn counted to ten. "Shoot it, Marr.

Blackstar's cannons lit up space and turned the shuttle to debris. The explosion sent *Seeker* lurching sidewise. It pained Khedryn to damage his own ship, but it was worth it to hear Reegas's curses and the ship's wailing alarms carrying over the open comm channel.

"You're stuck there, Reegas. *Seeker's* dead in space. We killed the engines." He looked out the glass at the derelict, noting the fires still burning in the engine section. "So's the derelict, thanks to you. You'll be out here a long while, I wager."

Reegas's curses filled the comm.

"You remember that I could have blown you from space," Khedryn said.

"Oh, I won't forget anything."

Khedryn tsked. "You be nice now, and maybe I'll send someone back from Fhost to find you." He hardened his tone. "Let me be clear. You cross me like this again and I won't hesitate to kill you. And don't try to get this ship back. She's mine now. I think that's a fair trade after what you did, right?"

Silence.

"*Right?*"

"Yeah. A fair trade. You send someone back for us, Faal. You send someone."

"There's caf in the galley. If that's not enough to keep you warm, you can always cuddle."

Reegas let loose with another string of expletives while Marr programmed the navicomp for a course to Fhost.

"This *is* a nice ship," Marr said, running his hands over the instrumentation.

"Agreed," Khedryn said, looking around. "Let's call her *Junker*. Suit you?"

Marr smiled. "Suits you and me, if not the ship. Junk she is not. But maybe you mean it ironically?"

Khedryn eased back into the pilot's seat, smiled, and played dumb. "I don't know what you're talking about half the time, Marr. Light up that hyperdrive and let's see what she can do." ☻

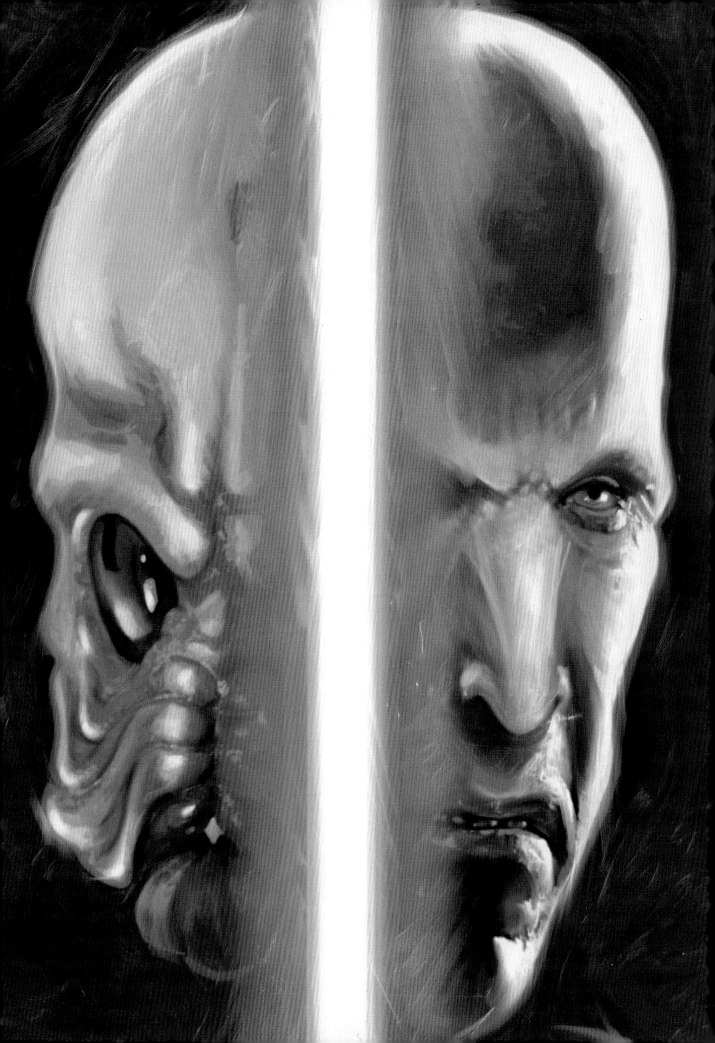

THE TENEBROUS WAY

WRITTEN BY **MATTHEW STOVER**
ART BY **BRIAN ROOD**

Dying, Tenebrous observed with mild surprise, was turning out to be not only pleasant, but wholly wonderful; had he ever suspected how much he'd enjoy the process, he wouldn't have wasted all these decades waiting for his foolish apprentice Plagueis to do him in.

So, even as he lay gasping around the icy barbs that pierced his lung, Tenebrous smiled. Even with the jerking and convulsing in his body's last reflexive rebellion against the fall of eternal night, even as organ systems shut down one by one to maintain the last shreds of light and life within the vast intricacies of his brain—massive beyond even those of other Biths, a people justly legendary for their intellectual prowess—Tenebrous found himself particularly enjoying the incremental disappearance of his own midi-chlorians. His Force-perception was even more acute than the magnifying powers of his enormous eyes; in the Force, he could feel each individual midi-chlorian wink out in turn, a spreading wave of darkness, like stars eclipsed by the silhouette of an approaching ship.

Or falling through the event horizon of a black hole.

Ah, darkness. Darkness at last. The darkness he had dreamed of. The darkness he had planned for. The darkness that was his one true love. The darkness he had taken as his name.

Was he not Darth Tenebrous?

His vision dimmed. His hearing became a rush of wind like static on an electrovoder—and then silence. The sole sensation registered by his quivering flesh was the rip of shattered bone and slow suffocation choking his consciousness, as his shredded lung could supply only a fraction of the oxygen required by his massive brain.

It hardly mattered. Shielded from suffering by his command of the Force, Tenebrous observed the death agony of his physical form with appropriately Bithan dispassion. And now his impossibly refined perceptions detected the brush of Plagueis' mind, as the apprentice probed the vanishing midi-chlorians of his dying master with his own use of the Force, as Tenebrous had known he would. Tenebrous had spent decades making sure that Plagueis would be unable to resist doing exactly that.

Everything was proceeding according to plan.

Foolish, pathetic Plagueis... Tenebrous' Muun apprentice would never comprehend his own limitations. These limitations were only peripherally due to the unfortunate tendency of Muuns, as a species, to measure every interaction as a transaction to be manipulated for maximum profit. No, Plagueis' real weakness was fear. Fear so deep and all-pervasive that the fool did not even register it as emotion—again and again across the decades of his apprenticeship, Plagueis had insisted that his fear was not fear at all, instead claiming it to be merely rational prudence. But Tenebrous knew the truth. Had always known it. Tenebrous had chosen his apprentice specifically *because* of it.

Plagueis was afraid to die.

Were Tenebrous the sort of individual who could experience pity, he supposed he might feel some for his apprentice. Crippled by dread, Plagueis would never know the freedom of an unbounded will that was the true legacy of the Banite Sith. And were Tenebrous the sort of individual to be fair-minded about such things, he would have accepted much of the blame for Plagueis' incapacity. As both pity and fairness were entirely alien to his nature, though, Tenebrous instead pleasurably recalled the relentless needling of his apprentice across their long, long years together. He had pricked constantly at Plagueis' sore spot, to make certain it could never heal.

Not even animals fear death, Plagueis. The lowliest beast in existence exhibits more "rational prudence" than you ever have. They fear only pain and injury. Bright lights and loud noises. You are less than a beast. You fear a mere concept—*and one you do not even understand.*

Thus was the ground carefully prepared. Thus did the seed of Plagueis' fear sprout and blossom into obsession. Thus had Tenebrous skillfully re-directed his apprentice's unparalleled aptitude for midi-chlorian manipulation away from the deepening of insight, from the intuition of the future, and from the amassing of personal and political power—away from any and all pursuits that might have proven inconvenient for Tenebrous' ultimate plan—toward a single goal. A goal Tenebrous had chosen for his own purposes.

power with a level of analytic precision simply beyond the capacity of any other species. The future was always in motion, and while other Sith struggled to foresee the faintest, least specific hints of what was to come, Tenebrous had no need to see the future.

He could *calculate* it.

While still merely an apprentice, his analysis had shown him the inevitable end of the Banite Sith and its preposterous Rule of Two. His calculations plainly indicated the coming of a shadow so vast it would darken the galaxy entirely—so vast it would mark the end of both Jedi and Sith as the universe had known them heretofore. The rise of the shadow would be the *end of history itself.*

Tenebrous had not the slightest doubt that the entire galaxy would measure time according to its arrival. Events would be marked by how far they had preceded the shadow, or by how long after it they followed.

Though the exact nature of the great shadow remained occult, the remorseless

Shielded from suffering by his command of the Force, Tenebrous observed the death agony of his physical form with appropriately Bithan dispassion.

The mastery of life and death.

More than a century before, when Tenebrous had been but a Sith apprentice himself, the magnificent computational power of his Bith brain had led him far beyond the simplistic Force studies imposed on him by his Master. He had always been far too intelligent to be seduced by the traditional Sith metaphysical twaddle of dark destiny and the witless fantasy of endless war against the equally witless Jedi Order. Soon he had confirmed to his own satisfaction that the dark side of the Force, far from being some malevolent mystic sentience bent on spreading suffering throughout the Galaxy, was in truth merely an energy source, and a tool with which he could impose his will upon reality. It was a sort of natural amplifier he could use to multiply the effectiveness of his many useful abilities.

None of which was more useful than his matchless intellect.

Like many Sith before him, he had turned his powers toward knowledge of the future. But unlike any Sith before him, he had the enormous brain of his people, which combined sheer brute processing

logic of his extrapolation detailed the coming destruction of the Banite system, and the rise of what would become known as the "One Sith." One Sith! The conclusion was so obvious as to require no confirmation: one single Sith Lord would arise of such power that he'd have no need of any apprentice nor fear of the Jedi. He would take and hold the galaxy by his own hand alone. Without an apprentice—or a Jedi Order—to destroy him, the One Sith would rule *forever!*

A heady prospect, with only a single drawback: Tenebrous was not to be that Sith Lord. His own death was clearly foretold, entirely inevitable, and it would precede the rise of the shadow by decades. His fate was explicit in the numbers, and numbers do not lie. However—as Tenebrous came eventually to realize over his many years of research, contemplation and calculation—it might be possible for the numbers in question to be, well, *deceived...*

The key, he'd discovered, lay in an obscure legend obliquely referenced in the *Journal of the Whills,* about a hero fairly typical in most cultures—the sort

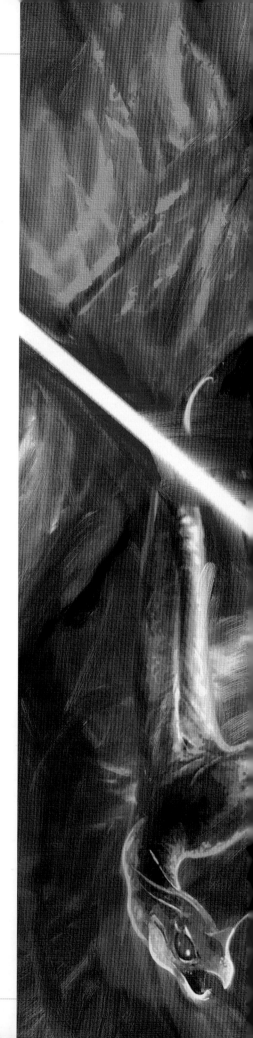

of promised future savior who appears in the foundational myths of nearly every developed society. What distinguished this particular savior from his run-of-the-mill equivalents was that he, according to four of eleven possible translations, was to be "born of pure Force." After three standard years devoted specifically to exploring all possible permutations of the interpretation, Tenebrous determined that such a birth was indeed possible, at least metaphorically—"born of pure Force" could be read as indicating the creation of a living being through direct manipulation of midi-chlorian processes in an already living being.

And further, as Tenebrous discovered with rising excitement, such a being's Force potential might be limited not by its creator's *own* midi-chlorian count, but instead only by its creator's level of discipline and attention to detail. Indeed, his calculations indicated a range potentially far beyond his own. With proper execution, the "savior" might have a midi-chlorian count as high as *fifteen thousand*! Perhaps even more. It might be possible to create a being with the greatest Force potential ever recorded!

And—by the application of his own suitably subtle variation of the ancient Sith brute-force essence transfer—Tenebrous could ensure that his own consciousness would be present at the creation of this being, this savior, this Chosen One. And, at the moment of creation—long before the Chosen One could hope to resist—Tenebrous would seize it. Would *become* it.

With this single stroke, decades after his body's death, he would become the most powerful Force-user in the history of the galaxy.

It was all there in the numbers. He could not possibly fail.

Once his analysis had been parsed to its *n*th degree, polished into a gem perfect beyond the possibility of flaw, Tenebrous had devoted every second of every day of his life to fulfilling his plan. Nothing would be left to chance. He had exterminated his doddering Master with his customary efficiency, and had embarked immediately on a decades-spanning quest for an apprentice of his own. And not just an apprentice, but *the* apprentice: one possessed of a very specific combination of particular skills—primarily surrounding the direct perception and manipulation of midi-chlorian activity—but also a range of weaknesses, from short-sighted concern

with personal profit to an unconquerable dread of the unknown realms beyond the walls of death.

An apprentice whose sole purpose was to create the being Tenebrous would finally become.

Thus would Darth Tenebrous, the greatest mind in the history of the Sith, be reborn to rule the galaxy.

Forever.

Now that his body's physical senses had altogether perished, Tenebrous found his perception of the Force to be proportionately heightened. With glorious precision, he could trace the slightest wisp of Plagueis' clumsy Force-probing as his apprentice sought to record and analyze every detail of Tenebrous's death. He could feel Plagueis himself: crouched nearby, his eyes closed, the long spiderish fingers of one hand stretched forth as though to snatch Tenebrous' disappearing midi-chlorians from mid-air.

This was Plagueis' customary technique: a close examination, through the Force, of the midi-chlorian decay that accompanied

> ## While other Sith struggled to foresee the faintest, least specific hints of what was to come, Tenebrous had no need to see the future. He could calculate it.

the physical death of his victims. Tenebrous was by far the most powerful Force-user whose death Plagueis had the opportunity to observe, and he had known all along that his apprentice would apply all his physical, mental, and Force capabilities—pitiful as they might be—to witness each slightest detail.

As though midi-chlorians somehow embodied the principle of life itself, they vanished as life fled. Plagueis had more than once speculated that they somehow migrated from dying cells and returned to rejoin the Force from which they had sprung–more evidence of the apprentice's muddy thinking and pathetically romanticized mysticism, but no matter. The delusion of the student had proven an inspiration to the teacher, and the concept of midi-chlorian migration—flawed though it was—became the key to Tenebrous' master stroke.

Amidst the billions upon billions of individual midi-chlorian deaths in Tenebrous' cells were a tiny fraction of midi-chlorians that were not dying. That

would not die so long as they inhabited a living host. These especially tenacious midi-chlorians—Tenebrous had privately labeled them with the jesting sobriquet *maxi-chlorians*—had been altered. Improved. It would not be an overstatement, in Tenebrous' opinion, to use the word *perfected*. These maxi-chlorians would indeed migrate, but not into the Force.

They would migrate into Plagueis.

To detect this infinitesimal percentage would require the precision of a Bith; it was far beyond his apprentice's limited perceptions—and indeed, Tenebrous had gone to considerable trouble to ensure it would always remain so.

Instead of actually training his doltish apprentice, Tenebrous had flattered Plagueis' mysticism while pricking his insecurities, sending him off on one useless, doomed-to-fail mission after another. In turn, Tenebrous had invested every available second of the freedom this afforded into designing, creating, and deploying the one weapon that Plagueis would never suspect. *Could* never suspect. His own prejudices about the Force ensured Plagueis wouldn't believe such a thing was possible.

Tenebrous created a retrovirus that could infect midi-chlorians.

Midi-chlorians were, after all, merely symbiotic organelles that contribute to the organic processes of the living cells they inhabit. Due to their role in Force interactions, altering them was singularly challenging—they had an unsettling tendency to spontaneously express unexpected and unfortunate side effects—but by applying the full analytic prowess of his vast Bith brain and the preternatural power of his Bith senses to detect and resolve sub-microscopic structure, he eventually succeeded in creating a retrovirus that would transform normal midi-chlorians into long-lived maxi-chlorians.

But that was only the beginning.

With the patient, painstaking attention to the slightest, most insignificant detail that was his hallmark, Tenebrous had encoded his custom retrovirus with his most potent weapon: his own consciousness.

Once completed, Tenebrous had released the virus into his own bloodstream. It had spread throughout his body, infecting midi-chlorians in every one of his cells with gratifying alacrity. Not *all* his midi-chlorians, though, as the infected maxi-chlorians no longer fully functioned; to infect them all would have cut off his own connection to the Force.

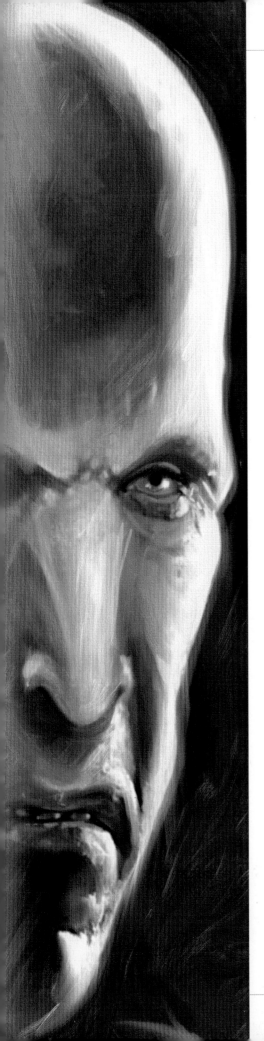

A partial severance of this connection was a necessary sacrifice, however, and through an extended process of trial and error, he was able to fine-tune the effect and confine it to the one sector of his Force powers he no longer needed—his ability to sense the motion of the future.

Of what possible use was the ability to see a future he already knew?

Now, dead at last, he could begin to enjoy the fruits of his lifelong labor. In the Force, he could feel that his body had already suffered irreversible brain-death, yet his consciousness remained, fully aware, fully functional, and connected to the Force in a manner more intimate than he had ever believed possible. Freed now of the crude biological processes that mark the passage of time, Tenebrous found he could perceive the measured tick of each individual nanosecond while simultaneously comprehending the entire sweep of galactic eons.

Beside Tenebrous' corpse, as Plagueis carefully observed the vanishing of Tenebrous' midi-chlorians, maxi-chlorians were being subtly and invisibly carried

Hmm—perhaps he should have invested some time in actually training the foolish Muun. Tapping Plagueis' Force powers would be more entertaining if they weren't so stunted from disuse. And yet...

As he continued to explore, Tenebrous gradually became aware of the full range of his apprentice's connection to the Force, which was considerably deeper, broader, and more powerful than Tenebrous had ever suspected. He reflected, with a twinge of uncomfortable premonition, that perhaps Plagueis had been right when he contended that Tenebrous had always underestimated him.

Now Tenebrous touched upon his apprentice's powers of foresight, which were also vastly more developed than Tenebrous had believed. For a moment, Tenebrous found his perception cast far forward in time— to Plagueis' own death at the hands of his apprentice, who was himself visible only as a smear of darkness...

A shadow!

For an instant, Tenebrous felt the death anguish of Plagueis... and felt the searing

Now Tenebrous touched upon his apprentice's powers of foresight, which were also vastly more developed than Tenebrous had believed.

across the intervening space to settle in Plagueis' eyes and mouth, on his skin and into an open wound on his back, where they entered the apprentice's bloodstream and slipped into his cells, releasing their viral cargo of Tenebrous' mind.

Perfect. And what made it even more perfect was that his apprentice would never comprehend the ironic pun of the name Tenebrous had given him: Plagueis.

The diseased one.

Driven by the dark side-powered will of the Sith Master, the retrovirus propagated with incredible speed. As it carried his consciousness throughout his apprentice's body, Tenebrous found himself becoming pleasurably aware the he was gaining access to Plagueis' sensorium. He could literally feel what Plagueis felt, both the coldly clinical satisfaction at having successfully engineered Tenebrous' murder... *and the* Force-perception that let Plagueis monitor the last vanishing remnants of Tenebrous' uninfected midi-chlorians.

Full access to his apprentice's Force-perceptions! Delightful. Better than Tenebrous had allowed himself to hope.

agony Plagueis felt.... at his *failure* to have ever created *the Force-user Tenebrous was to become*! He would allow his own apprentice to kill him too soon...

This could not be. It could not be *contemplated*, much less allowed to come to pass. Fury competed with panic as Tenebrous threw his mind at the future, seeking to understand how it was Plagueis could be so complacent, so foolish...

So blind.

The searing truth was driven home by the gathering darkness that clouded his borrowed foresight. Soon all he could see of the future was a hazy smear of shadow... as the retrovirus he had become infected Plagueis' every cell. The retrovirus he had allowed to sacrifice his ability to gaze forward in time... and had thus robbed his apprentice of his power to sense the future.

Which would seal his own doom as well.

His single-minded pursuit of eternal life and supreme power had accomplished only this. He would be destroyed by his own triumph.

Now wholly giving himself over to panic, Tenebrous turned his will upon undoing the damage he had done. With all his multiplied power, he yanked his maxi-chlorians back out from Plagueis' body in a spray of Force energy from his eyes, his mouth, the wound and every other cell. He had to *think*—he had to find a way *out*—or perhaps he didn't. Perhaps there wasn't one.

Perhaps the best he could hope for was the slow, inevitable extinction of his consciousness as his maxi-chlorians too faded and winked out. Then, at least, he would no longer have to squirm in the agony of his self-inflicted defeat....

If his maxi-chlorians were going to fade.

Because it dawned on him that he wasn't sure exactly how long the process should take, but he certainly didn't seem to be losing consciousness. He reached out with the Force—perhaps he could sense something. Anything. Or even contact Plagueis, somehow make his presence known, as his apprentice would never allow him to survive, no matter how reduced his powers might be...

But Plagueis wasn't here. Not only had Plagueis somehow vanished, Tenebrous could sense no trace of him ever having been here at all... what was happening? How could this be?

The only trace of organic life Tenebrous could sense were some ancient mummified remains...

Of a *Bith*.

How long had he been here? How long would it take for every trace of Plagueis to vanish? Those remains were years old—decades, perhaps *centuries* old.

Tenebrous wondered, with dawning horror, if his retrovirus might have somehow *mutated*, if its effects on the maxi-chlorians might go somehow deeper than excision of foresight?

What if his eternal life would be... *this*?

Or worse: what if his foresight hadn't been eliminated, but had been somehow *twisted* in upon itself? What if his remains were ancient because this was the thousandth time he had relived his death and the shattering revelation of his life-long self-deception... what if this was the millionth time he'd relived it?

The *billionth*?

Then he knew, and at that moment he wished he still had a mouth, because he really, really needed to scream.

Dying, Tenebrous observed with mild surprise, was turning out to be not only pleasant, but wholly wonderful; had he ever suspected how much he'd enjoy the process, he wouldn't have wasted all these decades waiting for his foolish apprentice Plagueis to do him in...

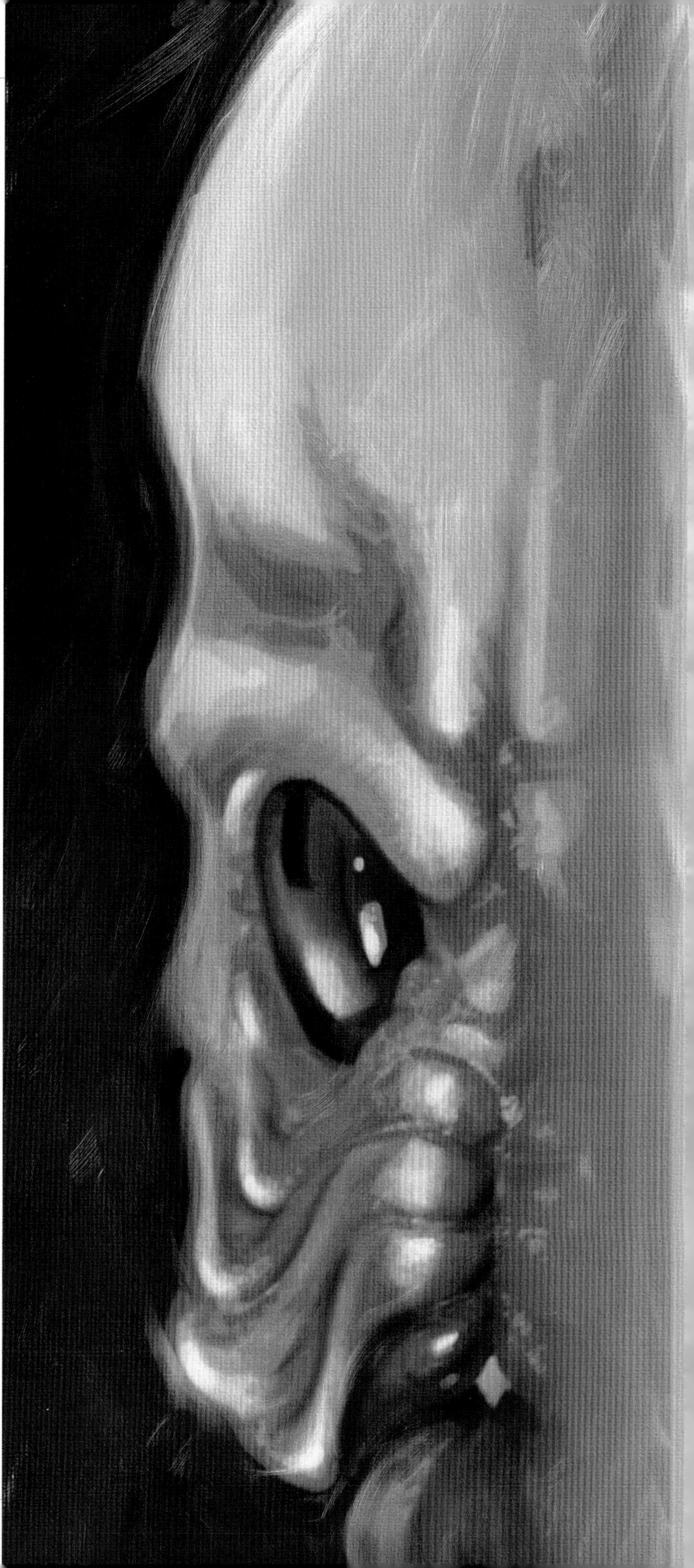

MAZE RUN

WRITTEN BY **DAVID J. WILLIAMS AND MARK S. WILLIAMS**
ART BY **BRIAN ROOD**

It was the mother of all lightning storms. Huge jets of relativistic plasma surged from the polar regions of the black hole, lighting up the dark with tendrils of shimmering fire. There was only one direction for a sane pilot to go: far away, as quickly as possible.

The *Millennium Falcon* gunned its engines and headed in.

Nor was this black hole an ordinary specimen. Every galaxy rotates around a supermassive vortex, but this particular one was the hub of the dwarf galaxy known as the Rishi Maze. Vast fields of gravitation, energy, and debris stretched out on all sides. Perhaps that labyrinth of death was the reason the galaxy was called the Maze in the first place. Perhaps.

Han Solo didn't care.

What he cared about was angles and vectors and flight paths. As well as the fact that he'd been presented with a challenge of the first magnitude, for only the very best pilots stood a chance of getting through the Maze. That was what Solo cared about.

And payment. That, too.

The truly annoying part was that so far this undertaking had already cost him the highest price of all: a girl. While carousing at his favorite space bar back at Mos Eisley, he'd been *that* close to getting with that minx Jenny. They'd flirted and flitted around one another for months and he'd finally managed to peel her off from her throng of admirers, when the broker approached him. Norund Tac—fixture

at the Merchants Guild and a longtime glitterstim smuggler—said he had a run that required a cool hand on the stick... somebody who could handle not just the Imperial Blockade of Hutt space but who could get through to the very center of the Rishi Maze. Tac was fronting for a group of spacers running an illegal energy farm deep in that maelstrom and who badly needed supplies of every kind: phase-loop generators, ramscoop coils, reserve shielding, the works. The Empire had the vertical space trade lane shut down, so the only way to reach the customers was via a run through the radiation fields dangerously close to the galaxy's black hole. Which was all the more reason to drive a hard bargain—or else walk away entirely.

As it was, Han balked right up until the moment Tac laid half the payment on the table and promised a tidy little bonus at the delivery point. By the time they'd sealed the deal, Jenny had wandered off with Tork the Bouncer and another night of potential bliss went up in smoke. By the morning, Han and Chewie were aboard the *Falcon* and running from an Imperial cruiser hell-bent on preventing them from jumping out of Hutt space. But giving the Imperials the slip was the *Falcon*'s speciality and in the chase that followed, she more than lived up to her reputation... albeit with a few hits to the aft shielding.

Of course, that was the easy part. Now they had to thread the maze. Han watched while the *Falcon*'s computer spat out the

initial parameters of the run, calibrating a whole host of variables to plot the optimal way through the legion of obstacles. Han spread his gloved fingers over the holo-deck and began to shift the various indicators around for the tasks ahead. He'd learned his lesson long ago: reconfigure the deck as needed and never get locked into anything. Flexibility was the key, and Han had made sure that the *Falcon* was the most flexible ship he'd ever piloted. To most, she was just another beat-up old freighter, barely capable of carrying a load big enough to support her operations—but to Han she was better than having your own personal Star Destroyer. He'd put enough special tweaks and one-of-a-kind modifications into her to make the *Falcon* the match of any smuggling vessel on the Outer Rim.

On the screen, the radiation levels were climbing, and on the speakers so was the volume of Chewie's growls.

"Nothing to worry about," drawled Han.

Chewie's barbed retort resonated through the cockpit. He was down in the access corridors, still running the post-hyperflight checks. They'd hoped to have some time between exiting hyperspace and entering the Maze, but with Imperial ships in the vicinity, they'd had to forgo that luxury. But what Chewie *wasn't* forgoing was conducting the checks manually. He was a stickler for caution.

This was fine by Han. Given that he liked taking extra risks, he and the Wookiee balanced each other out. Great partnerships

had been built on far less. Han grasped the stick and throttled the *Falcon* in, dodging past the photospheres of some of the stars caught in the black hole's outermost orbits. A few of those stars even had planets that the black hole had yet to tug loose from their grip: chunks of rock hewing close to their suns, any atmosphere long since swallowed by the maw that filled half the sky. Chewie's face appeared on the screen— he tossed back his head and growled to indicate that everything was checking out from the hyperspace jump and they could proceed as planned.

"Good," said Han, "because we already have." The Wookiee protested, but Han just kept talking over him: "I'm taking us in now; we can't waste any more time if we want to catch that directional beacon when it goes off." *That* had been its own argument, of course—Chewie wasn't too happy with the fact that they didn't even know the precise location of the rogue energy-farm, and that instead, the station would signal to them once they'd navigated enough of the Maze to be reachable on the comlinks. Even though Solo had replaced the *Falcon*'s stock sensors with a military grade package years ago, finding the beacon amongst all the energy distortions would be no easy feat. He throttled the *Falcon* up to half speed and eased the ship into the gaps between the radiation fields. Those fields were shifting quickly enough that the *Falcon*'s computer was working hard to plot the optimal flight vectors—and working overtime to factor out interference on the instrument readings. Han gazed out of the cockpit as he eased between gigantic lakes of high-energy clouds. The ship shook as the gravitational forces increased—and then suddenly the radiation levels were spiking. Chewie's questioning growl reverberated through the com system. All Han could do was shrug agreement.

"Getting a little hot up here," he said, and put the *Falcon* into a slow roll, flipping the craft belly up to where her shields were at maximum. For a moment, the rad-readings held steady—and then they kept on climbing, reaching steadily toward the red, becoming intense enough that the cockpit was in growing jeopardy. Han let out a curse. Given the damage to the aft-shields, he'd expected this kind of development, just not so soon. If he stayed where he was, the radiation would boil him from the inside out. He flicked off the auto-pilot and proceeded to power down some of the ship's more fragile systems.

"Chewie, prep the engineering station. I gotta close up the cockpit."

Which took only another ten seconds. Han lowered the cockpit's blast shielding and proceeded to get the hell out of there,

making for the auxiliary flight controls at the engineering station. Departing from the cockpit left a bad taste in his mouth because he'd have to fly the ship entirely by instruments and holo-display. He thought back to his flight training days and remembered how the words of his old instructor Alexsandr Badure and the infamous tactician Adar Tallon meshed.

When all else fails, you've always got your eyes.

But now he was blind. A light sweat broke out on his brow. It became just that little bit heavier as he reached the engineering station to be greeted by Chewbacca's mournful howl.

"What do you mean the navcom's out?" Solo stepped back, gave the casing a well placed kick, and was rewarded with the holo-screens flaring to life. "See? The old girl loves me." Ignoring Chewie's skeptical grumble, he keyed the 3D nav display's resolution to maximum. The astrogation displays centered on the black hole as they scrolled myriad data on the rising gravity and energy fields. Solo's fingers danced across the touch screens, making micro adjustments to the ship's course and speed while Chewie coaxed ever-greater performance levels from the engines. As always, the *Falcon*'s navcom anticipated moves and fed course corrections as needed. The computer was so attuned to his piloting that Solo had long since come to regard it as a third crew member. Now that trust was paying off. For the next twenty minutes, man and machine and Wookiee ran the galaxy's most lethal gauntlet without incurring any further damage. As they emerged from another gap in the radiation fields, Solo resumed scanning for that beacon.

Only to find something else entirely.

The whole screen was alive with data. There were so many mass-signatures that for one crazy moment Solo thought they were in the middle of an asteroid field. And then the holo-display crystallized: he was looking at a massive cluster of debris caught in a gravitational pocket. Chewie's inquisitive rumble echoed up from the engine-room.

"Copy that," said Solo. "It's a ship's graveyard—" But even as he said that, he realized it wasn't quite true. Chills went up his spine as he realized what he *really* was looking at: not pieces of broken ships, but rather pieces of a *single ship*... a battlecruiser, thousands of meters long, its spine long snapped by the impact of the gravitational fields. Yet the ship's huge axe-shaped aft seemed to be mostly intact, blunt and menacing. Strangely, there didn't appear to

be any listing of this type of vessel in the *Falcon*'s records, though Solo had been assured that the last system update was the most comprehensive ship overview one could get on the black market. It certainly wasn't any kind of craft Solo had ever encountered, and there were few ship designs he *hadn't* seen during his time on the Outer Rim.

"You ever see a ship like that?" he asked Chewie as the Wookiee emerged from the ship's engine room wearing his welding goggles, a power-torch in one paw. Chewie leaned in and took a closer look—then let out a series of short barks.

"You really think it's that old?" Han frowned. "It's one hell of a piece of engineering, that's for sure. Some of its systems are still functioning..."

Han trailed off as the threat computer flashed on, displaying half a dozen contacts peeling out of the debris and moving in fast. He let out a low curse. His active scans had probably set them off. But they were too small to be fighters. Which meant...

"This ship's got some kind of automated defense system," he muttered. But Chewbacca had already put two and two together and was sprinting off to the quad laser. Solo

more data. The computer had decoded the transmissions among the defense drones.

And between those drones and the derelict ship.

Solo swore under his breath. The ancient starship's power plant and main engine systems were still active! The sensors showed the bright lines of microwave energy flowing from the starship, powering the drones. The computer was busy trying to disable those energy signals, but wasn't making any headway. Still... a crazy idea came into Solo's head. So crazy he didn't even dare tell Chewie. He patted the *Falcon*'s nav-computer like a beloved pet.

"Don't let me down, baby"—and then he turned the *Falcon* sharply, sent it hurtling past the huge ship. The drones turned to pursue him while the *Falcon*'s computer went into overdrive, its signals wending their way ever deeper into the starship's systems, searching for the behemoth's engines. As the *Falcon* shot past the huge craft's rear, the drones opened fire at a range that was all too close; Han's chair shook as the *Falcon*'s shields went into the red. He heard Chewie's howls of anger sounding from the quad-laser turret.

But as the drones closed in for the kill, the *Falcon*'s computer found what it was looking for—

"*Do it*," Han said through gritted teeth.

—and ordered the giant starship's engines to ignite a full burn. White heat surged across the pursuing drones, detonating them in

> ## Han recalled another of his tutor's key rules: never mind the fancy maneuvers—just go straight at them!

throttled the ship into high-gear; as he tracked the incoming drones he realized that even a crack shot like Chewie would be hard-pressed to destroy them. Each drone radiated a shield much more powerful than any machine of that size ought to boast. He recalled another of his tutors' key rules: never mind the fancy maneuvers—just go straight at them! It wasn't like he had any other choice. He pulled the *Falcon*'s nose up and punched it.

As he did so, the drones rolled into attack position and unleashed a withering barrage of blaster cannon fire at the *Falcon*. Solo felt the ship buckle as he spun the craft on its axis to present the rear shields to his attackers. He heard the unmistakable sound of the *Falcon*'s quad lasers answering back. As Chewie scored a direct hit, blowing one target to pieces, the remaining pods broke off and angled for another line of attack against the *Falcon*'s weakened front shielding. They were going to bring him down through sheer numbers, Solo realized. Like wolf cats harrying prey. But even as he braced himself, the holodisplay caught his attention with

a series of flashes. Next moment, the burn ceased, the long-derelict reactor exhausted. All that was left of the drones was more debris. The momentum of the starship's engine-block carried it forward into the next piece of wreckage, which in turn slammed against the forward section. A nasty chain reaction was underway, but Han wasn't waiting around—he punched the *Falcon*'s afterburners and roared out of the gravity pocket, back into the fields of energy. They were moving much faster now with the boost. That black hole was getting closer with every moment, a backdrop against all the stars and radiation, the hub around which it was all turning.

And then Solo heard a loud beeping.

At first he thought it was another of those drones. But Chewie's yell of triumph said otherwise—

"Pay-dirt," yelled Solo. They'd found the beacon. Its syncopated rhythm echoed through the corridors of the *Falcon* as the computer ran extrapolations back to its source: a rock orbiting a star that in turn was orbiting less than 1.5 tera meters from

the event horizon of the black hole. The energy readings indicated a substantial base there—easily large enough to harness energy from the black hole that stretched over it like some kind of demented sun. Solo let out a sigh of relief—and stopped as the base's defense weaponry locked onto the *Falcon*. The comlink began flashing. A disembodied voice reverberated through the cockpit.

"Unidentified vessel, identify yourself."

Solo took a deep breath. "Epsilon zero-five-six-eight-Z," he said. The code phrase he'd been given back at Mos Eisley, the sequence upon which this entire mission depended...

"Affirmative," said the voice. "This is Firebase Alpha. We read you, *Falcon*. How was your trip?"

A grin spread over Solo's face. "Just fine, Alpha. No problems." His voice took on a sardonic tone. "Apart from Imperial starships on the way in and some kind of half-dead starship in the middle of the Maze."

"Sounds like you met our Sith relic," said the voice.

"Your *what*?"

"Most of the routes skirt the wreckage. Sorry you got the one that didn't."

"You and me both," muttered Solo.

"Well... congratulations on keeping your hide intact. We're clearing you for landing on approach vector 1.3 Zeta."

"Roger that, Alpha," said Solo. "Think you could have a couple of a glasses of T'lil T'lil ready for us?"

The voice chuckled. "We'll see what we can do Alpha—over and out." As Han switched off the comlink, Chewie's rumbling baritone sounded over the ship's speakers. Han frowned.

"What do you mean power surge?" Han scanned the internal sensors and saw that the forward cargo was indeed showing a weird energy reading. It looked like it might be some kind of feedback from the just-received beacon—an echo in the system. But even as Solo suggested this to Chewie, the Wookiee cut him off, grunting that he was heading forward to the hold.

"Oh for the love of..." Solo activated the autopilot and raced to the forward holds to find Chewie already inside, pointing a hand scanner at one of the huge oblong crates that constituted the *Falcon*'s cargo. Solo's eyes went wide.

"It's coming from *inside that box*?" he asked.

The Wookiee nodded. Han was getting a sinking feeling

about this. He grabbed a charged pry-bar and unceremoniously popped the cargo container's magnetic seal, revealing a two-meter long canister covered in what looked like Imperial markings. At the top of the canister was a device that could only be a detonator. And as for the canister itself...

Han snatched the hand scanner from his friend's gigantic paw and shoved the device up close. The result flashed onscreen:

"Baradium," he said.

Chewie snarled with anger. The scanner rattled off more specs, but Han didn't need to read any of them. He'd spent enough time as an Imperial cadet to know all about baradium and the disintegrating wave its fusion reaction unleashed.

And there was enough here to fracture a small moon.

Solo slammed his fist against the bulkhead. It all fell into place like getting dealt the perfect hand in a rigged card game. There was only one type of man insane

enough to hide on the lip of a black hole mining energy: Kriffin' *Rebels*. And what better way to wipe them out then to send in a couple of dupes unwittingly carrying a bomb on a supply run? Chalk one up to the Imperials' department of dirty tricks. The hand scanner told him the rest of the story: the beacon's signal must have inadvertently played havoc with the bomb's electronic detonator, activating it prematurely. Undoubtedly, the plan had been for it to go off when the *Falcon* reached the base. Now it was on a countdown. But how much time did they have?

There was a beeping noise on the speakers.

"Thirty seconds until touchdown," said the autopilot.

Han and Chewie started moving at the same instant, scrambling to close the bomb in its container and get out of the hold. As Chewie sealed the compartment, Han activated the sequence to vent the outer hatch and dump the cargo into space.

But Chewie's next growl turned Solo's blood to ice.

"What do you mean the doors won't open?" Han pushed Chewie out of the way and frantically hit the overide button. The hatch still refused to cycle. Apparently, the controls to the hold had been damaged—whether by radiation or by hits from the drones or the Star Destroyer no longer mattered. Chewie was already racing back to the cockpit, and Han dashed after him. He found the Wookiee trying every possible sequence and combination to get the hatch open. Out the window the massive superstructures of the base rose from the darkness as the *Falcon* made its final approach...

"Chewie, get us the hell out of here." Chewie slid into his acceleration chair and turned off the auto pilot. The ship bucked and jumped as Chewie shut down the landing approach and spun the *Falcon* away from the base. The speakers crackled.

"Alpha to *Falcon*, you're off the approach course. What's going on?

I repeat—"

"*Falcon* to Alpha, we're having a little bit of problem. Over." Han shut down the com and made for the door. Chewie's quizzical grunt stopped him for a second.

"What do you think I'm going to do? Somebody's got to get that cargo hatch open. And if we can't do it from the inside—" Chewie's eyes widened as he realized what Han was saying.

"This will be easier than selling water to dirt farmers on Tatooine."

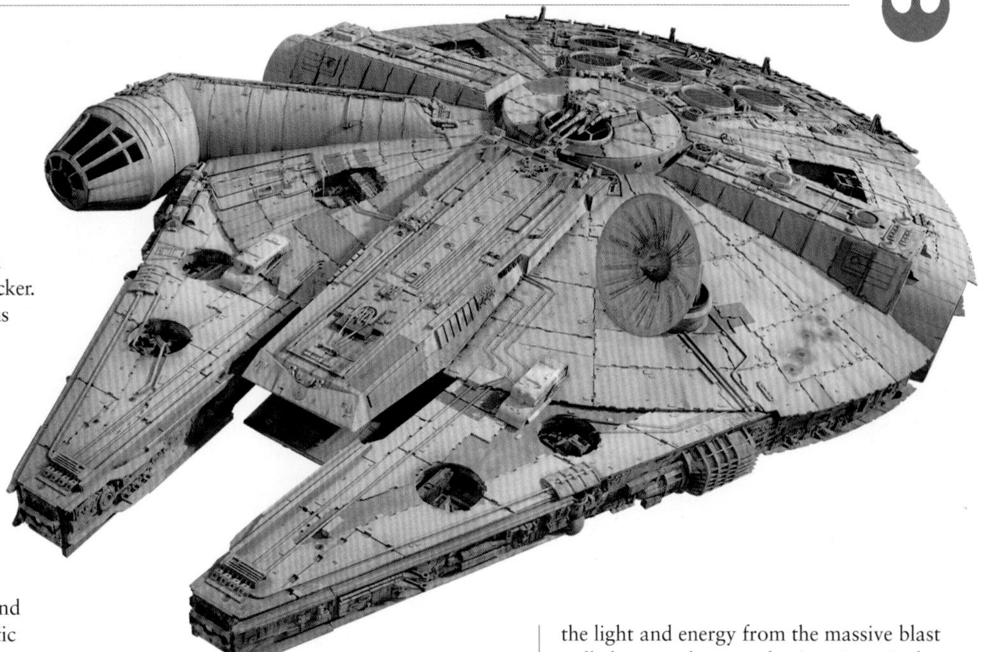

"What do you mean the doors won't open?" Han pushed Chewie out of the way and frantically hit the overide button.

The Wookiee let out an ear-shattering roar. Han looked his friend in the eyes and smiled the smile that would one day be known across the galaxy.

"Trust me."

Chewie's mournful wail followed Solo all the way to the equipment locker. Han retrieved the old military surplus spacesuit, then jogged to the central hatch access and proceeded to strap it on. The ship shuddered and the walls shook as Chewie continued to veer away from the approach vector, struggling against the gravity of the black hole. Han engaged the hydraulic lift and felt its reverberation under his feet as he rose toward the ceiling and went through his checklist: magnetic boots engaged, blast visor down, helmet sealed. He took a deep breath.

"Get it together, Solo," he muttered, "or this is going to be a short walk."

And then the dorsal hatch slid open above him and he was out in the vacuum. The black hole filled most of the sky, impossibly huge and menacing. Off to one side was Firebase Alpha, structures clustering over that rock—and now he could see the giant energy siphons stretching down toward the black hole, crackling with enough energy to fuel a thousand warships...

Han took in the view in an instant, and then he forced himself to look only at the *Falcon* as he made his way across her surface. He felt the hull rumble beneath him as Chewie fought the black hole's pull to buy Han time to get to the manual hatch controls. But the readouts in Han's helmet showed him he wasn't going fast enough. That bomb was going to detonate before he could get it away from the *Falcon*. He wasn't going to make it. Unless he did the one thing he'd always been best at.

Cutting corners.

Solo turned off his mag boots and fired a quick blast from his suit's thrusters. The ship's hull passed rapidly underneath him as he honed in on the cargo hatch. At the last minute, he re-activated his boots and managed to catch himself a meter away from the cargo doors before reaching for the first of the external locks and pulling with all of his might. To his relief, the lock slotted into its open position. As his hands closed on the second and final lock, the ship's hull surged beneath his feet like a living thing. He held on as the *Falcon* accelerated in—straight *toward* the black hole. Han nodded. Chewie had started his run. Now Han had to do his part. He pulled against the last lock.

It wouldn't budge.

He shifted, positioning himself so he could use both hands. But just as he started to apply the pressure, the ship shook so violently it felt like it was breaking apart. In fact, several pieces of the landing gear ripped free and flew toward him like shrapnel. Han went flat against the hull as the metal shards skipped past him—except for one, which struck him a glancing blow on his rear-pack. He opened his eyes to see the suit's power meter draining rapidly to zero. *Damn.* He pulled himself back to his feet, grabbed the controls of the door with both hands and pulled. The lever came loose and the hold door opened as the light went green. Even as Solo's suit's energy was going into the red...

Suddenly, he was floating off the hull—no power to his boots. The maw of the black hole was drawing him inexorably in. As he spun through the darkness, he saw the *Falcon* hurtle away—and then suddenly flip, its nose coming up hard as the contents of the hold shot out. The *Falcon* turned away from the black hole as the jettisoned containers reached its edge, the bomb exploding even as they did so, all the light and energy from the massive blast pulled across the event horizon in a single instant and vanishing into darkness.

Han smiled.

It was getting hard to breathe.

At least Chewie had made it. He wondered if he'd get to that event horizon before he ran out of air. He hoped so.

It would be one hell of a way to go.

But then he saw another light reflected in his visor—the bright flash of the *Falcon*'s engines. Chewie had turned the ship around and was bringing her back toward Solo, coming in at an angle so as not to veer across that deadly horizon, spinning like a top to increase momentum and maneuverability. For a moment it looked like the *Falcon* would smash right into Solo... But at the last moment, the ship stopped its spinning and activated its tractor beam, pulling Solo directly toward the still-open cargo doors. Solo curled into a ball as he shot through. And then the exterior doors sealed.

The interior doors opened. Han pulled off his helmet as the *Falcon* accelerated away. He couldn't stop laughing. He'd always thought he was an amazing pilot, but once again his Wookiee partner had shown there was more to him than met the eye. Han was still laughing as an anxious Chewbacca ran into the room, scooping Solo up in a Wookiee hug.

"It's all right pal. I'm all right—thanks to you." Chewie put him down, but still held the somewhat woozy Solo upright. Solo stepped back, stretched.

"So... I guess after we drop off what's left of the cargo, we go back and have a word or two with Tac. How does that sound?"

Chewie's barking laughter echoed through the ship.

THE GUNS OF
KELRODO-AI

WRITTEN BY **JASON FRY**
ART BY **JOHN VAN FLEET**

*S*teniplis Sector, Outer Rim
Territories, 17 BBY
　　All things considered, Shea
Hublin didn't like the planet
Kelrodo-Ai very much.

The volcanic world's thin soil was
broken by outcroppings of black rock
pitted with holes, the air left an acrid taste
on the tongue, and the light was yellow
and harsh.

Then there were the Separatist clankers
salvaged and reprogrammed by their new
masters. The Empire had taken control of
the galaxy's central systems in a quick and
orderly fashion, but out here in the spiral's
Western Reaches, troops had been few and
authority almost nonexistent. Separatist
diehards had fled here to make common
cause with pirate kings and slave lords,
bringing a wealth of hardware with them.

Now, too much of that hardware was
here on Kelrodo-Ai, tucked beneath a
planetary shield.

Shea and the rest of his squadron had
dug in at a hastily assembled forward air
base beneath that shield. Their mission was
to bring down the generators that powered
it—generators hidden in the heart of the
mountain that loomed across the plains.

The Kelrodoans called the fortress

the Citadel of Axes, and claimed it had been their masters' stronghold for millennia. Now, it was the key to the sector, protected by innumerable cannon emplacements and fighters. Fifteen of the Imperial 77th Wing's pilots had already died on Kelrodo-ai. Shea knew more would do so.

No, Shea Hublin didn't like Kelrodo-Ai at all.

But he wasn't going to say that now. This moment demanded a different message.

He turned and nodded at the holocam operator and the pretty reporter from Eriadu News Service.

"Ready when you are," Shea said.

The reporter stood beside him, squinting in the sunlight, and turned to face the holocam. Behind them, the squadron's V-wing fighters waited on the scrubby Kelrodoan turf, traces of Republic insignia still visible on their fuselages.

"This is Eris Herro of ENS, embedded with the 77th Air Wing at Kelrodo-Ai," she said. "And this man needs no introduction— Captain Shea Hublin, the hero of Deepspace Cimarosa and Feather Nebula."

Shea waved that away, embarrassed.

"Captain Hublin, the resistance here has been unexpectedly fierce. Can you update us on your mission objectives?"

Shea pulled at the bottom of his tunic as the holocom operator turned and panned the distant mountain.

"Ma'am, I'll leave assessments of the overall campaign to Moff Tarkin. I won't deny that Kelrodo-Ai is proving a difficult target, but let's remember this: The Western Reaches Operation has restored security and the rule of law to eight sectors so far, with successful liberation operations on 95 worlds. We are the best-equipped and trained military force in galactic history. And we are the Emperor's justice. We may face setbacks, but we will prevail."

"The Emperor's justice? What do you mean by that, Captain?"

"This has been a lawless region for far too long," Shea said. "I've seen terrible things here: Separatist gulags, slave camps—things that exist because of Republic corruption and Separatist rebellion. We're here to shut them down. Because we believe in the vision of men like Emperor Palpatine and Moff Tarkin —in Imperial authority and prosperity."

"Some note there are no humans on Kelrodo-Ai, Captain. They say reclaiming this alien world is a waste of valuable Imperial lives and resources."

"Ma'am, those people need to remember that we are one Empire," Shea said. "One Empire in which every species has a role to play, to the extent that its capabilities allow."

"My goodness, Captain—you're starting to sound like one of those alien rights activists we've interviewed recently!"

Shea smiled.

"Don't worry, Mom—I'm not going to be bringing any alien girls home for dinner! But no matter what shape we are, Miss Herro, we all love our children. The Kelrodoans may not have sophisticated technology. They may have primitive customs. But they deserve to contribute to the Empire while enjoying its security—and that's what we're bringing them."

"Inspiring words, Captain Hublin," said the reporter, turning back to the cam. "This is Eris Herro, reporting from Kelrodo-Ai."

The ENS crew had departed and Shea found a stool, staring across the plain at the mountain and its hidden fortress. Lieutenants Kaal and Starks, his fellow flight leaders, ambled over as one of Sword Squadron's Kelrodoan grooms shuffled forward, keeping his eyes on the ground.

"Thank you, Fara," Shea told the alien, extending his foot. "Excellent job shining these."

The Kelrodoan grunted, black eyes fixed on the ground. Kaal—Scimitar Flight's leader—eyed Fara with barely concealed distaste, then clapped Shea on the back.

"Good show, Hublin!" he said. "You actually sounded like you believe that One Empire poodoo."

Shea looked around, worried one of the minders from the new Imperial Security Bureau might be nearby. Kaal was too careless about what he said— and too certain that he knew what Shea thought.

"I *do* believe that poodoo," he said. "Did you know Fara here was a warrior chieftain? Maybe he's never fired a blaster or been aboard a Star Destroyer, but he got to be a chieftain *somehow*. Doesn't that suggest he has something to contribute?"

"We've got enough problems without handing blasters to the likes of him," Kaal grumbled.

Before Shea could reply, Starks jumped in to keep the peace.

"After this next hop, I'm gonna be the holostar," he said with a grin. "You know, I think that Miss Herro likes you, sir. And she's not the only one—any more heroics and you'll be up for a commendation from Moff Tarkin himself."

"Not likely," Shea said. "We're a small part of a very big operation. Moff Tarkin has a lot more to worry about than us."

"Oh, I bet he's watching," Starks said. "And others too. I could see Imperial Center making you a clone template, sir."

"Don't even say that," said Shea, scowling.

"You'd refuse?" Kaal asked. He looked genuinely surprised.

Shea looked around, and was relieved to see that none of the squadron's clone pilots were nearby. Only then did he answer Kaal. "They did something to their brains—made them more obedient," he said. "It's creepy. Or maybe there's just something about the idea of other me's out there that I don't like."

Kaal frowned, but Starks was grinning.

"Imagine a whole squadron of Starks!" he said. "Hey Fara, you making that porridge for lunch?"

"You don't even know what's in that alien slop," Kaal said.

"Whatever it is, it's good," Starks said with a shrug.

"Eggs," the Kelrodoan said. "Fara must harvest more."

Before Starks could say something, klaxons started wailing and the pilots looked up.

"Look sharp, gentlemen," Shea said. "Briefing in five minutes. Fara—"

The Kelrodoan was already bringing Shea's boots, scuffing irritably at a theoretical spot of dust.

"I hope Kaal didn't offend you, Fara," Shea said.

"Fara did not listen," the Kelrodoan said, fitting a boot onto Shea's foot. "You Empire-men are strange warriors."

"How's that?"

"You kill without looking your enemy in the face," Fara said, looking at the sky. "It is a new path to honor."

Shea frowned, but the Kelrodoan had turned away, and the briefing awaited.

"**B**andits incoming!" crowed Starks to his wingmen. "Dibs! Rocket! Time to bump!"

As Sword Squadron's nine remaining V-wings roared across the parched plains of Kelrodo-Ai, Starks couldn't resist a gleeful barrel roll.

"Don't go fangs out now, Dagger Leader—you can flat-hat on the way home," Shea said from behind the gargoyle mask of his flight helmet. "Scimitar Leader, does your flight have objectives logged?"

"Copy that, Blade Leader."

Kaal sounded annoyed. Shea knew Kaal had been at the briefing and read the intel, well aware that knowing it backwards and forwards could save his life and those of his wingmen. Still, as squadron chief, it was Shea's job to make sure no one had missed something obvious. Repeating the objectives so they wouldn't be forgotten once the shooting started was one way to ensure this.

"Intel pegs the emissions source as a near-vertical pipe behind the dorsal weapons emplacements," he said. "Confidence level that it leads to the main reactor tops 82 percent. The pipe is 25 meters wide—not much room to maneuver. Scimitar Flight, you're in rotation for first sortie. You good with that? My flight's happy to take it."

"Afraid I'll steal your close-up, Captain?" Kaal asked.

"You can have it," Shea said. "Okay, boys, we're going in—and we're going in full throttle."

Shea's astromech, Cutie, squalled a warning and Shea's board lit up with the red dots of incoming fighters.

"I count 30 bandits," Starks said. "Dagger Flight, let's latch!"

"Remember we're flying in goo, so maneuverability will be hampered," Shea warned.

Laser blasts streaked past his cockpit as the first wave of bandits shot overhead. Shea's heads-up display showed a motley mix of craft—Vulture droids rebuilt for organic pilots, battered Z-95 Headhunters, and snubfighters he'd never seen before. Sword Squadron's pilots vaporized four of the enemy craft on their first pass. The others turned sluggishly, wobbling as they pursued the streaking Imperial craft.

"Dagger Leader, splash this vapebait while we cover Scimitar Flight," Shea said.

"Copy that," Starks said gleefully. He and his wingmen peeled off to port, racing back to engage the bandits, while Shea and his wingmen drew alongside Scimitar's trio of fighters.

"Three klicks and closing," Shea said. "Check your telemetry, Scimitar Flight."

As Sword Squadron's nine remaining V-wings roared across the parched plains of Kelrodo-Ai, Starks couldn't resist a gleeful barrel roll.

"It's all good," Kaal assured him.

Ahead of them, the guns of Kelrodo-Ai opened up, the concussive blasts of heavy laser cannons shaking the V-wings' hulls.

"Dial up your SA, boys," Shea said. "Those are anti-capital-ship cannons—they track slow but they'll melt your shields in a nanosecond. Take it down to the deck."

A moment later Shea and his wingmen were meters above the grass, the exhaust from the fighters ripping the thin soil from the rock and leaving massive plumes of dust in their wake. The vertical face of the mountain rose up before them, then shot past in a blur as the V-wings banked sharply upwards. They rocketed past the pinnacle of the Citadel of Axes, then corkscrewed back down through a withering pattern of laserfire. Shea's life-support systems pumped air into his flight suit to keep him from blacking out, and he grunted with the effort to keep his hands on the stick.

"Objective dead ahead," Shea said. "Looks like there's some kind of grating over the shaft. Take it out, Blade Flight."

"Copy that, Blade Leader," said Blade Two—a clone whose callsign was Amp.

Shea opened up with his wing cannons and the grating vanished in a blinding flash. So did Blade Three, who'd strayed into the sights of one of the tower's heavy guns .

"Lost Ahrens," Shea said with a grimace. "Scimitar Flight, target shaft is clear. Stay with me Amp—we're their covering fire."

"We're inbound, Blade Leader," Kaal said.

Shea shoved his protesting V-wing through a tight loop, raking the citadel's gun towers with fire. He had no hope of doing any real damage, but wanted to keep them busy. Below them, Scimitar Flight's three fighters arrowed through the web of defensive fire and vanished into the open mouth of the shaft.

"We're in the pipe," Kaal said coolly. "Any bandits on our six?"

"That's a negative," Shea said. In fact, his scope showed a quartet of enemy fighters pulling up and away from the shaft. "What are they—"

And then Kaal screamed. LOSS OF SIGNAL, reported Cutie.

"Could it be a sensor gripe, sir?" asked Amp.

Shea cycled grimly through his scans.

"Negative," Shea said. "They're gone."

A pitted Vulture cut across his field of vision, forcing Shea into a loop that ended with the bandit disintegrating.

"Blade Two, Dagger Flight: abort," Shea said. "Scrub the hop."

An hour later Shea, Amp, Starks, Dibs, and Rocket were crowded around a datapad, staring at the recording from Kaal's prow camera. Nearby, Fara sat atop a outcropping, slowly lowering a sharp stick into the rock.

About 30 meters into the shaft, Kaal's recording showed the gray walls of the tunnel changing to a mottled pink and red, spotted with black dots.

"Rewind," Shea said. "And slow down the playback."

Now he could see it clearly. The walls were covered with long, ropy appendages —appendages that erupted in a sudden spastic fury, filling Kaal's viewscreen before the transmission terminated.

"Some kind of biological entity," Shea muttered. "Amazing reaction time."

"Can't we drop bombs down the shaft, sir?" asked Dibs. "Or send missiles?"

Shea shook his head.

"It takes pretty precise shooting to crack a reactor even when you *can* see it," he said. "As for missiles, what if it's a nonstandard reactor? Or there are jammers?"

"So we land ground forces," Starks said. "Take it from the outside."

"That will take forever," Shea said. "And we don't have forever." He looked at the other pilots. "Right now it's a stalemate.

We can outfly most everything they've got, but we can't breach their defenses."

Starks, he realized, was looking off to one side.

"Say, Fara, what have you got there?" Starks asked.

"Amp, play it again," Shea said, annoyed at how easily Starks got distracted. "Maybe we'll see something. Those black dots on the walls, could they be—"

"Eggs," said Fara.

"Exactly—wait. What did you say, Fara?"

The Kelrodoan had pierced a row of lumpy black spheres with his stick, and was using his long fingers to transfer them to a bowl.

"Eggs," he said. "For porridge."

Shea's eyes leapt from the outcropping to the distant mountain.

"Where did you get those eggs, Fara?" he asked. "I need you to show me— *right now.*"

Fara blinked and pointed to the outcropping. Shea clambered on top, followed by Starks, and shined his light down one of the holes. It was lined with pink and red flesh, studded with black dots.

"Stang," Starks said with a whistle.

"To harvest, you must be slow," Fara said. "To not disturb the colony."

"How slow?" Shea asked.

Fara poked the stick into the rock, moving very deliberately. The pilots crowded around him. Fara looked up and suddenly the tube's lining shivered. A moment later Fara was holding a broken stick.

"Slower than that," the Kelrodoan said with a shrug.

Shea nodded. "Prep for immediate launch," he said.

FIGHTER SLANG

BANDIT: a hostile fighter or starship

BUMPING: engaging in aerial combat

FANGS OUT: eager for a dogfight

FLAT-HATTING: showing off or engaging in dangerous maneuvers

GOO: a planet's atmosphere

GRIPE: a technical problem

HOP: a mission

LATCH: get into position to destroy an enemy fighter

ON YOUR 6: behind you

SA: situational awareness

SPLASH: shoot down

VAPEBAIT: a poorly skilled pilot

"Starks, you're with me and Amp on the insertion," Shea said as the mountain loomed ahead once more. "Dibs, Rocket—splash any bandits who try to follow us."

Shea yanked on the joystick, stone and sky trading places as he spun the starfighter up the cliff face.

"Once we hit the pipe, kill throttles and fire brakes," Shea said. "Repulsorlifts only, all the way down. We'll have to crawl—best estimate is it's about 250 meters."

"Sir, what if there are defenses besides the colony?" Amp asked.

"That's why we have guns," Shea said. "Insertion point's coming up."

Their astromechs cut the engines and fired retro-rockets a split-second after the V-wings passed through the pipe's fringe of twisted, ruined grating. They crept forward on repulsorlifts at a half-meter per second. The eerie silence was unnerving, but the agonizing pace was worse—Shea felt like he was bracketed in a dozen enemy gunsights.

The edge of the colony crept closer. Ahead of them, gelatinous black eggs nestled among pink tentacles. Shea heard Starks murmuring a prayer, and realized he himself was holding his breath. The nose of his fighter passed the first strands. Shea waited for them to whip forward and kill him.

Nothing happened.

He forced himself to exhale. Sweat was running down his face, impossible to reach inside his helmet.

"Cutie, anything so much as twitches, kill the repulsorlifts," he said. "I've got the reactor's central matrix. Starks, hit the north power regulator. Amp, hit the south. After impact, the overload spiral should reach criticality in two and a half minutes."

"We're gonna have to crawl back out," Starks objected. "What if that takes more than two and a half minutes?"

"Let's hope it doesn't," Shea said.

The three V-wings crept farther down the shaft.

"I can see the colony's edge!" Amp said.

"Make sure you're clear before you throttle up," Shea warned. "Cutie, how long did it take to transit the colony?"

All three pilots saw the response: 137 SECONDS.

They were silent for a moment. Then Starks sighed.

"One Empire," he said.

"One Empire," Shea agreed. "We're clear—punch it!"

Acceleration shoved him back in his seat as the engines propelled his V-wing into a low chamber hewn out of the rock, its floor cris-crossed with conduits. To Shea's relief, they converged on the familiar bulb of a hypermatter reactor, twin towers bristling with circuitry on each side.

"There she is—hit it and quit it!" Shea yelled.

Alarms began to wail in the chamber, and Shea saw battle droids gesticulating in confusion. He activated his proton torpedoes, bracketed the center of the reactor, waited for target lock, and thumbed the trigger. Before the torpedoes even went home he was banking to port and racing back the way he had come.

"It's away!" Starks yelled, as Amp's fighter turned to follow him.

"Cutie, give me a 150-second countdown to criticality," Shea said as shock waves buffeted his fighter.

Then they were back in the pipe, crawling towards that curtain of pink and red.

Shea activated his proton torpedoes, bracketed the center of the reactor, waited for target lock, and thumbed the trigger.

120 SECONDS, Cutie reported.

Shea could see each tentacle, could count each egg.

His V-wing climbed with horrifying slowness. He tried to tamp down his panic, force his foot away from the throttle.

"Captain!" Starks cried. "In 100 seconds this kriffing mountain is going to be a cloud of vapor!"

"I know," Shea said. "*Don't touch your stick.*"

50 SECONDS.

A low rumble began behind them. Shea stared at the tunnel walls, teeth clenched.

"Shea!" Starks wailed.

"Don't touch *your stick.*"

30 SECONDS.

Sweat stung Shea's eyes.

"Ambient temperature's climbing," Amp reported.

Shea realized he was mumbling: "Come on baby come on baby come on come on..."

20 SECONDS.

Shea thought the walls were dark gray ahead, but decided that was wishful thinking. He looked again. It was true.

There was a muffled thud somewhere below them. Then another.

10 SECONDS.

The V-wings drew even with the final row of tentacles. Shea ignited his engines and stomped on the throttle, savage acceleration slamming him back in his chair. His vision blurred, he saw blue sky—and the mountain exploded.

His fighter was tumbling end over end. He clung to the stick, watching chunks of rock and machinery whip past the cockpit, hesitate at their apogee, then fall back out of view. Cutie was screaming and his instrument panel was solid red... but he was alive—as were Starks, Amp, Dibs, and Rocket.

"You thought you were a holostar before!" Starks crowed. "Wait till they get a load of Shea Hublin—the Slowest Gun in the Western Reaches!"

Back at the base, Shea decided that the pillar of smoke rising from the plain greatly improved the view. He extended a stocking foot towards Fara. The Kelrodoan had kept his boots immaculate.

"We couldn't have done it without you, Fara," he said. "No way I'm letting you go now—you're the most valuable valet in the whole Empire."

"The Empire-man is too kind," Fara said, turning away and spitting on Shea's boot. After a moment he began to scrub at a scuff mark.

"No, you earned the compliment, Fara," Shea said. "And now you're going to see the galaxy—or at least the rest of the Western Reaches."

Fara glanced briefly at Shea, then turned to gaze at the plains and skies of his homeworld, as if he were trying to memorize them. Then he blinked and returned to cleaning Shea's boots, face expressionless.

"Sir!" Starks yelled. "You have a priority incoming holomessage!"

"Patch it through," he said—then sat up, startled.

He'd never met the man whose image flickered before him, but the hawklike features were unmistakable.

"Sir, I'm honored," he stammered.

Moff Tarkin smiled. "The honor, Captain Hublin, is entirely mine." ☻

HUNTING THE GORACH

WRITTEN BY JEFF GRUBB
ART BY JOE CORRONEY

arella the Hutt, hunter extraordinaire, reached out with a heavy, soft arm and stroked the activation sigil on his ship's holorecorder. "Expedition Log 2435—I am on the planet Lowick, on the hunt for the elusive Gorach. My prey is a brutal and wily creature, and even now I find it hard to believe that its ancestors once ruled this cluster of worlds. I have greased many pseudopods to track this specimen down, and now in the great rain swamps of this world, look forward to a challenging hunt before delivering the beast to its inevitable fate and hanging its head on my trophy wall. I will report again upon my success."

Parella switched off the holorecorder, slipped out of his hisp-silk robe, and retired to the ship's armory, where his droids already had his armor ready. The Gorach was reportedly both strong and quick, so the Hutt chose a full-body armor consisting of overlapping plates of Ruusan copper, running from the nape of his fat-swathed neck all the way to the tip of his tail. A heavy helmet nested snuggly into its fittings at the armor's neck, its HUD flickering to life on the inside.

His fingers stroked a toggle and an interior wall of the ship slid away, showing all manner of blaster pistols, carbines, and rifles, along with a selection of close combat weapons. This was to be a traditional hunt, one that tested both wits and brawn. He chose a blaster carbine with a long vibrobayonet attached, in the style of the Taloron Hunters.

Parella secured the ship, activated its passive defenses, then lowered the landing ramp and stepped out on the planet's surface. The ground was soft and mossy and gave slightly as his heavy armored form slithered forward. His official guide, provided by the closest settlement in this Ardos-forsaken wilderness, waited for him. It was a Pa'lowick of course, a mottled, spherical, body resting on stilt-like legs, its eye stalks raised in curiosity and its snout-like mouth pursed in apparent disapproval.

"I am Kashina Furt," said the Pa'lowick. "I assume you are Parella the Hutt."

"Parella the *Hunter*," corrected Parella. "When I am on the hunt, I prefer that sobriquet."

The Pa'lowick made a noise that sounded like a kloo horn with a cold. "I am your official representative for your hunt. You seek our legendary swamp ape?"

"Yes," said Parella, "Though I know the beast by another name. He is a Gorach. He will be found here."

Again the kloo horn-sniffing noise. "Are you certain? This part of our world is mostly unpeopled, save for the occasional duck snarer."

Parella nodded, "Yes, but those trappers have spread the legend of your swamp ape. Four-armed, hair like hanging moss, luminous yellow eyes, greenish pallor, twice your size. It is a Gorach."

Kashina Furt made another noise, and Parella was sure that it was disapproval. "Our swamp ape is described as such, but that does not mean that it is your Gorach. The Gorach themselves are a legend."

"A great legend," said Parella. "They were mighty warriors, brutal star barbarians that moved from planet to planet, demanding tribute and subduing entire populations in their wake. At the end, they held a dozen systems in their grip, before they fell apart in civil war and their subject species rose up against them. It is a lesson for all rulers—at the first sign of weakness, the lesser species will rebel." The Pa'lowick said nothing, and Parella realized that the Pa'lowick were one of those "lesser species" described in the legends. The Gorach had ruled here. Parella continued, "The location is good, the descriptions are apt; we will find the Gorach here."

"The time of the supposed Gorach ascension was millennia ago," said the Pa'lowick. "I don't think a community of would-be conquerors would remain hidden."

"I did not think there would be a community," said the Hutt. "The stories of

the Gorach said that they did not age, and met their end only by violence. I think it is a single beast you have been reporting for centuries. I will bring him to heel, and place his stuffed and preserved form in my hall. He will be a piece of art for my fellow Hutts to admire as I regale them with the tale of the hunt." The Pa'lowick made a noise to complain, but the horizon behind him exploded in a flash of light. He turned to see the fireballs rise up above the banyak trees and mangroves, and the wave of thunder swept over them.

"What was that?" managed the Pa'lowick. "Those," said Parella, "are my beaters, driving the prey to us. Come. The hunt begins."

There was a screeching rasp as Parella's beaters—drones armed with incendiary darts—screeched overhead and returned for another pass. They flew in an arc, driving the wildlife within towards Parella and his ship.

"You're going to kill everything in the swamp!" shouted the Pa'lowick.

"Some things, yes," said the Hutt. "Maybe most things. Things that would be insufficient prey in the first place, unworthy of the hunt. But if the Gorach is here, and is the Gorach I seek, nothing so basic as carpet-bombing will defeat him. You will want to stand behind me."

The first of the fleeing wildlife was upon them. The winged ones arrived first —heavy Marlello ducks flapping madly to get ahead of the flames, pursued by green-scaled marsh hawks torn between the desire for prey and fear for their own lives.

Runner snakes coursed through the tall grass and Fleet lizards danced forward on their hind legs, hoping to attain sufficient speed to spread the rib membranes beneath their arms and sail forward. Then came the quadrupeds—meltfoxes and cattail deer. A huge muskwolf with a twelve-point rack of antlers broke cover to their right. Despite himself, Parella brought up his carbine, but restrained himself. He was waiting for other prey.

And suddenly it appeared, back-lit by the burning marsh. It was taller than the Hutt was long, and heavily muscled. It was bipedal, with four arms mounted on a broad torso. Thick strands of hair hung from its arms and legs, forming a woven matt over its broad chest. Braids whipped like serpents around its head. Its wide eyes

glowed like lamps, reflecting the flame
around it. The Gorach.

It saw them standing before the ship,
and its eyes locked with Parella's. The other
creatures parted before the hunters, less
worried about them than by the fire behind
them, but this one, the Hutt realized, knew
in an instant what was happening. That the
obvious safe path led to death. It spun and
headed to Parella's right, along the line of
the flames itself, its mossy braids snapping
in the hot wind.

Parella pulled his blaster and fired at
the moving form backlit by the flames.
He struck it once in the leg and the beast
stumbled, but the shot did not cripple it.
Instead the Gorach redoubled its efforts
and was soon wrapped in the smoke of the
beater's flames.

Parella brought up his blaster carbine, firing as he did so. The Gorach had been waiting, and flung its spears immediately. Parella parried one with his vibrobayonet.

Behind Parella, the Pa'lowick
whimpered something.

"Come along," said the Hutt. "This
promises to be an excellent hunt."

The Hutt's broad body pressed lightly
on the marsh grass, even with the heavy
armor Parella was wearing, and the shallow
pools did not impede him as he moved
after his prey, as graceful as one of the
runner snakes that had earlier fled from

the fire. The ground was soft and marshy,
and held the Gorach's prints for only the
briefest amount of time, but it was enough.
Parella found the trail and yes, he had
struck his prey in the right lower limb.
The footprints showed it was limping.

Parella frowned and thumbed the
discharge up higher on his blaster. The
shot he had given it would have downed
a Wookiee, but it only discomforted the

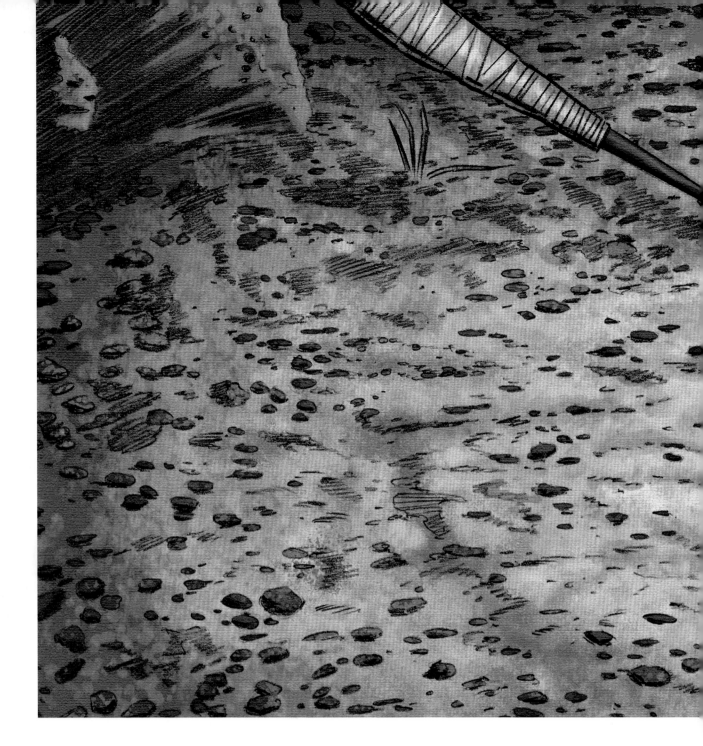

Gorach. The new setting would have a shorter range but a heavier punch.

In the Hutt's wake, Kashina Furt struggled to keep up. "The swamp is still on fire," he warbled, his prehensile mouth-snout flexing nervously. "We should wait for it to die down before we continue."

"If we wait, we lose it," said Parella. "The beast knows it is being hunted. It is finding a place to go to ground. Back to its lair, if it is close enough." "How…" panted the Pa'lowick. "How do you know?"

"Because that is what I would do." said Parella. "Once, a long time ago, the creature's ancestors ruled with merciless cruelty. Such rulers must be aware of potential betrayal at

The sky was smoky and black, and the air on Parella's tongue tasted of ash and exhilaration. Parella paused and examined the ground, then circled back.

any moment. The lust for survival is in their blood. This one knows now that it is being hunted, and every neuron of cunning is now aimed to self-preservation. It sees a superior foe. It will find a place to hide and hope that we lose interest in the pursuit."

"I've lost interest already," said the Pa'lowick, but if Parella heard him, the Hutt said nothing.

Already, the incendiaries of the beater drones had burned off, turning the hanging vines of the banyak trees into smoldering

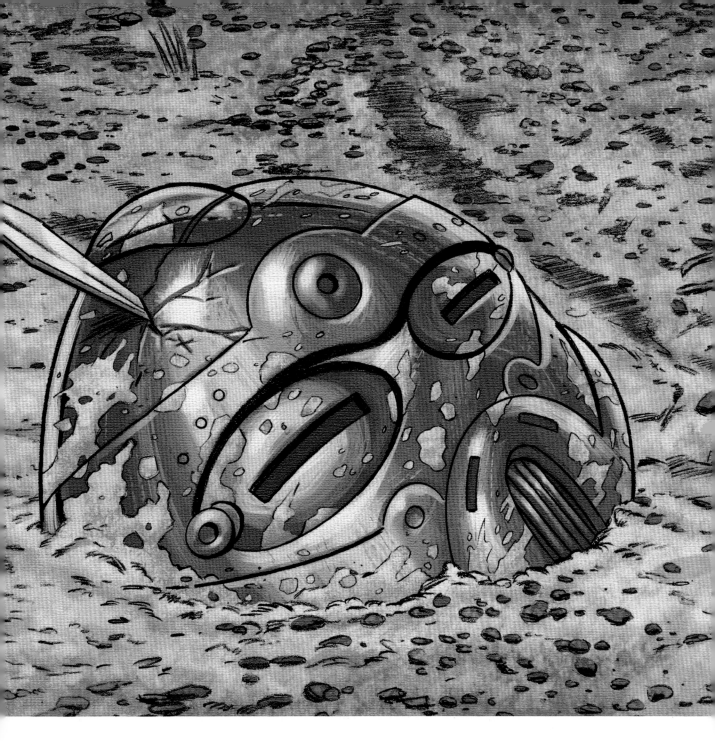

ropes of ash. The sky above was smoky and black, and the air on Parella's tongue tasted of ash and exhilaration. Parella paused and examined the ground, then circled back.

"It changed direction," said the hunter, pointing at the soft dirt. "Here. That's when the panic stopped. When it started thinking again. See, now it has moved across the stream here, the better to foil pursuers." He moved forward without looking to see if the Pa'lowick was following.

"Yes, it came this way," Parella continued. "Note that the reeds are getting thicker along here. We can see the path it took, but it has more cover. I would keep low and try not to offer a profile for a

blaster. Maybe even set up an—"

The next word was "ambush", and it was an accurate word. The hulking form of the Gorach rose from the weeds, a pole in each of its four hands. No, not poles. Spears—rude constructs tipped with sharp stones.

Parella brought up his blaster carbine, firing as he did so. The Gorach had been waiting, and flung its spears immediately. Parella parried one with his vibrobayonet, the spear's coarse bark rattling against the carbine's housing. Two more spears went wide to the right.

And then the prey was gone, hidden once more by the tall reeds which

whispered in his flight. It was then that Parella noticed that one of the spears was sticking in him.

Or rather, in the front plates of his armor. He looked at it with curiosity. The spear was tipped with what looked like a handmade flint tip, but chipped and sharpened to the point that it had cracked open the copper housing.

He pulled the spear from the armor, and it took effort. The spear point had nearly penetrated the armor itself. It was a marvel that it had done so.

"This armor provides near-insufficient protection," muttered Parella. "I will have words with the manufacturer at the close of this hunt. Perhaps full battle armor would have been more suitable."

"Does this mean we go back?" chirped Kashina Furt. It had taken refuge on the Hutt's armored back during the fight.

Parella gave a deep shrug and toppled the guide from his perch. "Quite the contrary. This savage remnant is well worth a decent hunt. What lies ahead?"

The Pa'lowick tapped his holomap and said, "There are some hills ahead. No inhabitants. I mean, no Pa'lowick inhabitants."

Parella grunted as he slid after his prey, as if Kashina Furt's statement made a difference. "We will find the creature's lair ahead. It is leading us to a battlefield of its choosing."

The terrain became an undulating carpet of hills broken by wide mud swaths thick with reeds. Water flowed here in thick, turgid streams that undercut the hills perilously at every bend. There were more banyak trees now, heavy with vines. They had moved out of the burned region, but the air still smelled of ash.

Parella moved slower now, stopping often by the mudflats to determine if the Gorach had passed through, approaching each stand of thick reeds with caution. For his part, the Pa'lowick guide kept close to the lumbering Hutt, jumping at every sharp snap of the underbrush.

"There," said the Hutt, motioning with the blaster carbine. "That would be its lair."

Atop the hill rested a large banyak tree, greater than the others, its gnarled roots twisted into a wide platform, exposed by erosion. Its vine-draped canopy blocked the sky and it loomed near a cliff overlooking a wide mudflat.

"Why there?" squeaked the guide.

"Commands the local approaches," started the Hutt. "It is dry and above the water table. Good drainage. Easy to secure."

The Hunter looked around, but there was no sign of the Gorach. Nor was there any sign of other life—the rest of the animals had fled the area.

Parella the Hunter moved slowly towards the tree, circling it from a respectable distance. Then he let out a deep, booming laugh. "There!" he said. "Its burrow!"

There was a large hole bored into the ground on the far side of the vine-strewn tree, disappearing into the darkness. Parella estimated that it would graze the shoulders of the Gorach as it entered and left. As it was, it would be tight fit for an armored Hutt.

Parella peeked around the edge of the Hutt. "Do you think it is down there?"

"Probably," said the hunter. "And it probably has all manner of primitive traps as well. Pits. Deadfalls. Maybe even poison-coated springknives."

"What…" Kashina Furt pursed its proboscian lips. "What are you going to do, then?"

"Send down the guide," said the Hutt, and reached out and snared the Pa'lowick's extended lips in a thick, meaty hand. He pulled the smaller creature off his thin feet and tossed him down the hole.

There was no snap of a trap, no sudden scream cut off by the sound of daggers piercing the Pa'lowick flesh. There was a soft groan down in the darkness, but nothing else.

Parella grimaced and shouted, "You see anything?"

Kashina Furt may have replied, but Parella heard something moving from the far side of the tree. Immediately, his weapon was up and ready, as the

> **The Gorach laughed now, and it was a powerful, hooting laugh. The Hutt could hear in the laugh echoes of its bloody past, of its gore-soaked, petty empire.**

Gorach appeared, wielding a new brace of flint-tipped spears. It unleashed two of those spears as Parella shot it. The bolts inscribed a deadly graffiti across the side of the tree, and Parella heard what he assumed was a scream as his shorter-range energy bolt found its home.

The Hutt quickly surged around the side of the tree, hoping that his prey would not try to flee again, back into the swamp. Luck was with him, because the Gorach had backed away, towards the edge of the cliff. It was still standing, but smoke curled from its furry hide and its thick, woven braids were now tipped with flame. It still had two spears in its right hands, but he noticed that one of the two left arms was badly scorched, and the Gorach was cradling it with its remaining good arm on that side. Parella smiled and leveled his blaster. "A good hunt," he said. "Not my best, but you will be a worthy trophy."

He pulled the trigger on his blaster…

… and nothing happened. It was then that Parella noticed a piece of flint,

sharpened to the point that it could crack metal, was jammed in the carbine's housing. The Gorach had hit its mark after all.

The Gorach laughed now, and it was a powerful, hooting laugh. The Hutt could hear in the laugh echoes of its bloody past, of its gore-soaked, petty empire. Even now, the creature refused to be cowed by its betters.

Parella laughed as well, and charged forward, putting all his weight behind the vibrobayonet. His carbine may have failed him, but the sharpened tip would still slip aside the defender's spear points and strike home.

If the Gorach chose to use its spears to receive the charge.

But it did not. Instead the powerful creature sprang upwards and grabbed the vines of the banyak tree. It swung itself into the foliage as the rampaging Hutt reached the edge of the cliff, which shifted and crumbled under his additional weight.

Parella cursed as he slid down the side of the cliff on a torrent of soil and lose rocks.

The Gorach had chosen its battlefield wisely. It knew the best place to confront a heavy-armored foe.

The Hutt, caught in the avalanche, splashed into the mudflats at the base of the cliff. Angry and embarrassed, the Hutt spun to reach the shore, but his armored belly plates could not find purchase in the soft mud.

Worse, he was starting to sink in the mire. He thrashed about, but could not maintain buoyancy in his heavy copper armor. He looked up at the banyak tree, and while he could not see his prey, he could hear the hooting laughter of Gorach. And then the mud covered his mouth and eye slits. The hooting lasted a long moment, then the vines of the banyak tree shook and the Gorach dropped nimbly out of the foliage overhead. It made its way carefully to the base of the cliff, favoring its wounded limbs. All that was visible now was the Hutt's armored helmet, poking like a stone from the surface of the mud pit. The Gorach raised its last spear and, with a great effort, threw it at the helmet with enough force to pierce it and the Hutt beneath it.

Instead, the helmet rang with a low, hollow sound. The mud bubbled and erupted with the mire-spattered form of the Hutt, naked now, his armor shed as a decoy. Parella had kept his vibrobayonet, though, and drove it deep into the center of the Gorach's torso. The surprised

creature fell backwards onto the bank, and the Hutt was on top of it in an instant, crushing its wounded legs beneath his bulk, holding it in place while he stabbed it a second time. The Gorach continued to flail about, and Parella stabbed it a third time, and only now did its spasms cease as the light died from its luminous eyes.

Parella pulled himself fully from the pit, scraping off the worst of the thick muck. He dressed the body of his prey as best as he could with the vibrobayonet and slung it over his shoulder. He reflected that he probably had not needed to stab it a third time, but that would be a problem for his taxidermist.

It was almost nightfall when Parella reached his ship with his deadly burden. He turned the jets of his personal shower up high, but the hot steam did little to remove the grit of the Lowickian swamp. He shrugged on a heavy robe, poured himself a strong herbal infusion, and curled up next to his holorecorder. "Expedition Log 2436," he began. And then he heard someone calling his name, from outside the ship. He lowered the landing ramp and saw the Pa'lowick guide standing in the gathering gloom.

"You're alive!" said Kashina Furt.

"The hunt is over," said the Hutt. "Your efforts will be rewarded."

"I passed out when you threw me down the hole," warbled the Pa'lowick, "but when I awoke, I found myself in its lair. It was gone, but its lair! Its lair!"

"What madness are you going on about?" grunted the Hutt."

"It is filled with art! Carvings made of stone and simple pottery and firegems! What I found there was a treasure trove! They were the most beautiful things I have ever seen!"

"So the Gorach stole shiny objects," said the Hutt, its eyes reduced to suspicious slits.

"No!" shouted the Pa'lowick, "I found the Gorach's tools! And his models! He created this art. This was no world-killing tyrant—this was an artist! The greatest artist I have ever seen! You—" the guide stammered, and looked up at the Hutt, "You didn't kill him, did you?"

Parella looked down at the small Pa'lowick. "The hunt is over," he repeated. "Your efforts will be rewarded."

The Pa'lowick stood there, unable to reply, and Parella raised the landing ramp once more. He returned to his cooling tea and touched the record sigil. "Expedition Log 2436," said the Hutt, and paused for a long moment, thinking of the inert form of the artist in his stasis chamber.

Then he said, "Nothing to report," and toggled the recorder off. ☺

GETAWAY

WRITTEN BY **CHRISTIE GOLDEN**
ART BY **JOE CORRONEY**

"I still think we could have had a nicer honeymoon on Hapes," Jagged Fel said. He and his old friend and new wife, Master Jaina Solo, were in a sleek little SoroSuub *Horizon*-class star yacht, and currently, the stars were their only companions. "Someplace...quiet, where we could relax. You know—that thing we never seem to be able to do."

"I'm letting you pilot, aren't I?" Jaina said.

"You don't find that relaxing."

"...not really."

"My point exactly. I don't know why I let you convince me that heading off to a hiking trek on a remote world was a better idea than sitting on a lovely beach in the moonlight with beverages in our hands."

"Don't worry, you'll get to be lazy," Jaina said. "We go hiking on this glorious, unspoiled planet for a few days—*then* we go to Hapes and do nothing."

"We could hike in unspoiled wilderness on Hapes."

"It's not the same. I thought you said you wanted to get away from it all."

"I meant away from *responsibilities*, not sanisteams."

"I promise you several days of lounging when we return."

"I'll hold you to that. I prefer to do most of my lounging with you *indoors*." He gave her a wicked grin.

Misdirection, finagling, and precise timing had been involved in this little "getaway." Karn Valenti, codenamed "Carved," and Lina Zek, "Curved," had once again been pressed in to serve as doubles for Jag and Jaina, and were currently on Hapes, staying just enough in the public eye to keep the illusion going and no more.

"I look forward to that," Jaina said. "But I have every confidence that Pharika will make sure we have a wonderful and memorable visit to the ruins."

Jag grimaced. "Two is company, three's a..." He paused. Jaina winced inwardly, realizing he was on to her. "Okay, Jaina. What's the *real* reason you wanted to go hiking on Sakuub?"

"Well," she began, "the hiking really *is* gorgeous. The back-country it's supposedly amazing. And... well..."

He was silent, waiting patiently.

It came out in a rush. "There's an ancient ruin there known as the Sky Temple of Karsol which as far as I can tell has never been explored by Jedi. I want to check it out and see if it could possibly be a lost Jedi ruin, or have more information about Abeloth for the future."

Jag emitted the sigh of the greatly put-upon. "Why don't I just drop you off and have drinks at the local watering hole till you're done?"

"Because I want to kiss you at moonrise."

"Oh. Okay. Do I get to kiss Pharika too?"

Jaina punched him playfully. Then, just to make sure, she added, "No."

Jag chuckled. Jaina left the co-pilot chair and climbed into his lap.

"Let's start lounging right now," she said.

"I'm piloting a ship," Jag said. She kissed him for a long moment. His voice was ever so slightly unsteady as he said, "Well, I suppose I could put it on autopilot."

"Wise choice," she murmured, smiling against his lips as she kissed him again.

The lone hangar in the single major city of Sakuub was one of the sadder ones Jag had ever seen. Their gleaming silver yacht stood out glaringly against the battered, patched-up, and aged vessels with which it now kept company. Some of these ships might even be antiques; most of them, however, were in that gray area between too old for fashion and too new to have other value. He noticed one vessel that jogged his memory, but he couldn't quite place—

"See?" Jaina said. "We really *are* getting away from it all." Jag started to say something about the ship that had caught his eye, but was interrupted.

"Excuse me?" They turned to see a young Sakuubian male approaching them. He was humanoid, his broad blue face bearing the distinctive ridges of his race. While his tunic was hardly the latest style, it was crisp, clean, and professional looking, and his four horns were neatly filed to elegant points.

"You are Ven and Kara Tumak?" he asked. They nodded, and he stuck out a three-fingered hand. He gave no sign that he recognized that the names were false. "I'm Dular. Welcome to Sakuub! Pharika sent me to greet you. I'm to take you to our local market, where she'll discuss your upcoming trek to our famous Sky Temple, help you select a few final items, and show you around the market, which has been in continuous operation for centuries and is a very popular tourist attraction."

He rattled off the information with the enthusiasm of one who had recently memorized something and wished to show

it off—and looked slightly disappointed when they gazed at him blankly.

"Oh, the *market*!" Jaina exclaimed finally. "Of course, we'd love to see it." Jag looked at her questioningly, as Dular turned to lead them to an old landspeeder. She shrugged and mouthed, *I don't know.* He stifled a grin.

Dular was pleasant enough, and chatted amiably as he ferried them through a section of the city as rundown as the port they had just left. The lanes began to narrow and grow more congested as they entered what was clearly Sakuub's historical district. It was tiny, quaint, and colorful.

And loud.

"I'll let you off here. Pharika will be waiting for you at Shuku's Fine Fungi, at the intersection of High Street and River Way, two of the Old Town's main streets, where all the food stalls are located. It's due north that way." He pointed down the street. "I'll be back in two hours to take you to your hotel. Enjoy your afternoon!"

He waved jauntily. They waved back. "Hotel?" Jag asked as they started walking up the stone-paved street. "So we get at least one night in a bed?"

"I thought you might appreciate that."

He pulled her to him and kissed her. "I do indeed. Now—to find Pharika."

They threaded their way through the crowd, which seemed as cheerful as it was noisy. As neither of them was particularly tall, spotting the food stalls up ahead proved to be a bit of a challenge. Jag had caught a brief glimpse of what he thought was a fungus cart when Jaina suddenly came to a dead stop beside him.

Her head was turned sharply behind her, and her face had gone still.

"What is it?" he asked, pressing his mouth close to her ear to be heard.

She shook her head. "I don't know. Just a bad feeling."

"With you, bad feelings aren't that simple."

"It's all right. We're not in any danger. At least not immediately."

"How reassuring." His tone implied anything but. "Let's find our guide."

As Dular had promised, standing beside "Shuku's Fine Fungi" was a tall, lithe Sakuubian who looked every centimeter the "native guide." Whereas Dular had seemed somewhat soft and proud of his relatively natty attire, Pharika wore functional, simple clothes and her arms were ropy with muscle.

She waved as they worked their way toward her. "You are Ven and Kara," she said, shaking their hands as Dular had. Her grip was so strong that Jag fought the urge to flex his hand afterward. "I trust Dular took good care of you."

"He did," Jaina said. "Nice to meet you, Pharika."

Pharika indicated the seemingly endless stream of stalls. "I thought before we embarked on our trip to the Sky Temple, you might enjoy seeing another part of our history. The market is famous in this sector. It is the perfect place to find a souvenir of your visit—and some delicious food we can consume as we hike."

Pharika spoke about the market's history as they browsed. Jag had thought he would be bored silly, but the market did indeed seem to have unique items, and the Sakuubians were a jovial people. He found that he was enjoying himself.

Jaina, however, never seemed to fully relax. He knew if she sensed danger, she'd tell him, plain and simple, so he wasn't concerned about an immediate threat. He was, however, aware that she seemed distracted, and often found her glancing around. At one point their eyes met, and Jaina jerked her dark head to the right. Jag turned just in time to catch a glimpse of an ugly, brown-gray tail slithering into one of the alleys.

Hutt. He nodded almost imperceptibly. Her "bad feeling" had now been explained. Pharika appeared not to have noticed the exchange, instead handing them a shawl of hand-woven phulla wool. They ran their fingertips over the soft, vibrantly-hued material.

"Thought I recognized a Dunelizard in the port," he said softly to her, recalling the ship he'd seen there. "We can still leave if you like."

Jaina shook her head. Jag smiled apologetically at Pharika. "I'm sorry, but I think the shawl is too expensive. I'd love

to see a scarf in this color, though."

Jaina's discomfort lingered through the ride to the hotel, which was a nice enough little place. They dropped their backpacks as they entered the room. Jaina began to thoroughly inspect everything, from the trinkets on the dresser to the sanisteam to the bed. "Wish I'd brought something a little more sophisticated than my eyes to search with," she muttered, sneezing at the gathered dust.

"You've got the Force. That's rather sophisticated."

Jaina got to her feet, turned to Jag, and planted her hands on her hips. "Why would a Hutt, who has extreme mobility difficulties, come to a planet where the two main attractions are a market with incredibly narrow streets and challenging backcountry hiking?" she demanded.

"We know the market is a draw," Jag said, sitting on the bed and taking off his boots. "The Hutt could be negotiating a trade."

Jaina sat beside him but made no move to undress. "Then why slither out of sight in such a suspicious way?"

"If he didn't recognize us, maybe his 'trade' isn't all that legal. And if he did, then three words: Leia. Chain. Jabba."

Jaina smiled, then leaned over and kissed him. "Sweet. Highly unlikely that Mom still inspires fear in an entire race all these years later, but sweet."

He grasped her arms and playfully tossed her back on the bed. "Let me see if I can take your mind off of worrying for the rest of the night." He kissed her. She wrapped one arm around him, placed her lightsaber within easy reach with the other, then for the rest of the night, neither of them worried about anything.

Jag had resolved to endure the four-day hike with stoic equanimity, as it was important to Jaina, but he was surprised to find himself actually enjoying the rigorous exercise. The path up the mountain to the Sky Temple wasn't quite vertical, but close to it. The air was fresh and clean, and the scenery was truly breathtaking. Pharika was a reassuring and insightful guide, and by the second night, Jag heard himself saying those extremely important three little words.

"You were right," he said. "It's nice to not have to think about anything but moving and looking at a gorgeous view."

Jaina beamed at him. "I'm glad," she said.

"You are not the first to find this to be true," said Pharika. "We do not have

> ## Why would a Hutt, who has extreme mobility difficulties, come to a planet where the two main attractions are a market with incredibly narrow streets and challenging backcountry hiking?

many tourists, but those who accept the challenge of the mountain seem to be restored by it."

"I still want to be lazy," he warned Jaina.

"You'll get your chance," she promised him. "In a few days."

They caught their first glimpse of the Sky Temple the following day. The steep path rounded a corner, and there it was, white stone against an azure sky. Jag knew that it was a ruin, but at this distance, it looked complete and magnificent. Maybe Jaina was right again—maybe this place *had* been a Jedi temple, a long time ago.

Jaina gazed at it raptly.

"Does it call to you?" Pharika asked. "Some say that even though it has crumbled to ruins, the Temple still sings to their souls."

"It does, in a way," Jaina said thoughtfully, then with her usual practicality, added, "Let's keep going!"

By nightfall, they had almost made it to the temple atop the plateau. Jaina wanted to push on, but Pharika shook her head.

"It would be both unwise and a disappointment," she said. "It is dangerous to climb in the dark, and you should see it for the first time bathed in the light of the morning sun."

Jaina reluctantly agreed, but her eyes lingered on the proud columns against the sky. As she lay next to Jag that night, he could feel the tension in her body.

"I think it *is* a Jedi temple," she whispered to him.

"You can feel it in the Force?" he asked.

She shook her head. "No, and that's puzzling. But Pharika's right. I do feel... drawn to it, somehow."

He kissed the top of her head. "Sleep now," he said, wrapping his arms around her. "Figure out ancient mysteries tomorrow."

Strangely enough, the road to the top was easy. Jag wondered why Pharika had been so insistent that it would be dangerous. She had, however, been right about the view. He slowed in appreciation and Jaina stopped dead in her tracks as they rounded a turn and, suddenly, the temple was *there*. It was small, as such things went, and the columns showed more wear up close than they had when glimpsed from far away, of course. But still—

Jaina staggered back, as if something had struck her. Jag caught her arm to steady her. Pharika came up, looking concerned. "Kara? Are you all right? The altitude does affect some climbers."

Jaina pressed a hand to her temple. "I'm fine," she said. "Please—could you give us a moment?"

Pharika glanced from one to the other, then nodded. "Of course." With a final concerned look, she walked off a discreet distance. Jaina turned a face lit with a huge smile to Jag, who was by now utterly confused.

"Jaina, what is it?" he asked.

"The Force!" she cried, pressing a hand to her heart. "This place is absolutely *soaked* in it! I have no idea why I didn't sense it before."

"If it is a Jedi temple, its founders might not want everyone knowing that."

Jaina nodded. "Makes sense. Especially if..." Her voice trailed off. With a glance back at Pharika, who had walked to the far side of a remaining column, Jaina approached the center of the ruins. She was still slightly unsteady, increasing Jag's

concern, but then she abruptly stopped her almost trance-like walking and looked down at her feet. He followed her gaze. She was staring intently at what appeared to be just another broken piece of stone, one of many littering the center of the ruins.

"There it is!" she cried.

"Congratulations, you found a rock," Jag said.

"No, it's not a rock. It's emitting a sort of distortion field that *disguises* it as a rock," Jaina said, all her attention focused on the object. Trembling, she knelt and reverently picked it up in both hands.

And then Jag saw it, too. It was a small octahedron, emitting a soothing, pulsing blue light from swirls and geometric patterns that danced joyfully along its surface.

A Jedi holocron.

"We knew you'd lead us straight to it... Master Solo."

The voice came from Pharika, but its hardness sounded nothing like the guide's former dulcet tones. Jag and Jaina whirled to see the Sakuubian pointing a blaster at them. Jag was about to break into a laugh at the thought of one lone woman standing against him and Jaina when suddenly a compact, sleek little ship emerged from the chasm below the temple. It was some sort of light, transatmospheric vessel, and Jag had never seen anything like it before. He didn't need to be a Jedi to have a bad feeling about it.

Jaina looked completely unruffled. "You won't harm me while I have this," she said calmly.

"No," Pharika admitted. "I wouldn't

harm you." She turned and fired a shot at Jag's foot without batting an eyelash. "But *he's* fair game."

Even as pain ripped through Jag and his leg buckled, a blur interposed itself between him and Pharika. In one swift motion, Jaina tossed the precious holocron to Jag, summoned her lightsaber to her from her open backpack a meter or so away, then turned to attack the woman who had dared to harm her husband. Jag caught the holocron in his right hand, tucking it protectively against his chest as he limped as fast as he could for cover. Every instinct told him to help Jaina, but he knew she would want him to protect the holocron. Besides, he was unarmed. The same could never be said of a Jedi Master. The best thing he could do was stay out of her way

for now and search for an advantage.

Jaina was beautiful in battle. She had long ago learned to master her anger and direct it well in a fight, and Jag did not envy either Pharika or her ally in the mysterious little ship. Jaina didn't appear to even be breaking a sweat as she leapt and dove, rolled, somersaulted, and batted back Pharika's well-aimed blaster bolts. Pharika was no slouch in the physical department either, continually tumbling to make sure a boulder or a ruined hunk of the temple was between them. Jaina moved inexorably forward, close enough now to—

Alerted by the Force, Jaina suddenly flung herself violently to the left. There came almost a shriek of energy from the vessel, and the ground burned where Jaina had just been. Without missing a beat, Jaina batted back

Pharika's fire with her lightsaber while using her other hand to levitate a huge chunk of fallen column with the other. It rose easily and Jaina hurled it toward the ship. The little vessel moved with astonishing speed, trying to dodge it, but the stone still landed a glancing blow that momentarily halted the ship's attack.

At that same instant, one of Jaina's returned bolts struck its target. It hit Pharika in mid-thigh and the "guide" cried out. That was all the invitation Jag needed. Placing the holocron down, he steeled himself against the pain and raced as fast as he could for Pharika, slamming into her and knocking her back to fall beneath him. She snarled at him, and he felt her trying to shove the blaster between their bodies. Jag shoved his knee firmly into her injured thigh and she cried out, her grip loosening. Jag grabbed Pharika's hand, pressed hard on a nerve cluster, and tugged the blaster away from her splayed fingers. Rolling well clear, he fired one quick blast at her other leg, rendering her no longer a threat, then turned to attack the hovering vessel.

It ceased firing and gained altitude. For a moment, Jag thought it was fleeing, but that hope was dashed an instant later.

One red blast disintegrated Pharika. Her "friends" clearly had no desire to risk her talking. Two more scarlet streaks came in rapid succession—but not at Jaina or Jag. Presumably, the pilot had no idea which of them had the holocron. Instead, the mystery ship fired directly at the towering columns of the ancient ruin.

Jaina could handle a lot, but Jag could see she was beginning to reach her limit. The human body, even when in harmony with and drawing upon the Force, could only do so much. Not even Jaina Solo could stand alone against a ship attacking both her and the ground upon which she stood. Still she tried, her body whirling and blocking. She turned a one-handed cartwheel, the other hand extended to stop a huge chunk of fluted stone from crashing down directly on Jag. The tactics had changed. The ship's occupants now seemed intent on burying them in rubble—and returning later for the holocron at their leisure. Jag didn't know a lot about holocrons, but one thing he did know is that they were designed to last through the ages. He was willing to bet something as ordinary as a rock wouldn't harm it.

This couldn't be the end. After all they'd been through? To die like this? Ridiculous. It couldn't happen.

Jaina, I love you—

She mis-stepped.

A huge chunk of rock came tumbling down. Jaina managed to roll away, but a sharp edge grazed her shoulder. Bright blood blossomed. She couldn't keep it up much—

The second ship was even more unexpected than the first. It was as familiar as the other was mysterious—the G1-M4-C Dunelizard fighter Jag had spotted earlier in the hangar. It announced its presence by firing a small laser cannon at the attacking ship, capturing its full attention. The mystery vessel stopped firing on the ruins and did a full turn, coming up attacking. It might have been sleeker and faster than anything Jag had seen before, but it was still no match for the inelegant but efficient laser cannon on the decades-old fighter.

With a final, well-aimed shot, the smaller vessel exploded. Jag shielded his eyes from the blast. When he opened them, it was nowhere to be seen. Any pieces that were left had fallen into the deep gorge below.

The Dunelizard hovered for a moment, then with a roar of engines that sounded as if they needed some tender loving care, it settled down a short distance away from the ruins. Jag got to his feet, gritted his teeth, and hobbled to Jaina, who seemed stronger than she had just a few moments ago, obviously calling again on the Force to bolster her strength. She got to her feet as he approached and reached to steady him.

"I have it. It's safe," He told her. She nodded, relieved. Leaning on each other, Jag still holding Pharika's blaster, they looked over at the Dunelizard.

The hatch opened, and an ugly, irritated Hutt stared out at them, blinking his slitted eyes.

"You!" Jaina said, as Jag brought his weapon to bear on the Hutt. "Who are you, and why did you help us?" The Hutt

> ## Jaina could handle a lot, but Jag could see she was beginning to reach her limit.

made a face. Jag hadn't realized such a thing was possible. "I didn't come here for that thing your husband is attempting to conceal from me," he said in Huttese, sneering and maybe just a little afraid. "Too dangerous for the likes of me. My name, I will keep to myself. As for why I did this…" He looked discomfited. Finally, he continued. "It is to repay you for your support at Klatooine, when you and your friend Lando Calrissian ruled that we upheld the Treaty of Vontor. It is no secret you are not fond of Hutts. Yet… you did this for us."

"I didn't do it for *you*, I did it because it was the right thing to do," Jaina said. "I didn't enjoy ruling in your favor. And it didn't even work. The Klatooinians rebelled anyway."

"That doesn't matter. My employer felt we owed you a debt. Now it is paid."

"Good," Jaina said. "Because that whole thing was really awkward."

"Indeed it was."

Jaina glanced at Jag. "We, uh… we thought it was you chasing us."

The Hutt grunted. "Of course you did," he said resignedly.

Jag looked over at Pharika's body.

"Whatever she was, she was not a simple guide. I wonder if she's even Sakuubian. You'll remember that Dular never saw her."

"I sensed nothing but good intent—until she started firing a blaster at you, that is."

"Do *you* know who she was?" Jag asked the Hutt. "Who she was working for? I've never seen a ship like that."

The Hutt, clearly at the end of his patience, waved his stubby arms. "All I know is that someone knew you were coming here and decided to use you like a Vadoorian sniffer rat to lead them to that holocron."

"Your employer clearly *also* knew we were coming here."

"You are less subtle than you think, Master Solo." Jag tried and failed to muffle a snort.

"You were not that difficult to find. I am done. The debt is paid. You are on your own." The hatch started to close.

"Hey," said Jaina. The Hutt paused. Their gazes locked. Jaina reached to touch the blaster in Jag's hand, indicating that he should lower it. He did so, and she said with quiet sincerity, "Thank you."

The Hutt grunted one last time, closed the hatch with too much pleasure, and powered up. Jaina didn't bother to watch it depart. She eased Jag down, retrieved an emergency medical kit from their packs, and began treating him.

"Hey, you still have a foot," she said, trying for levity. "Sort of. But nothing we can't fix."

"While that may be true, I won't be able to climb back down," Jag said matter-of-factly.

"So we take a shortcut," Jaina said. She helped her husband up, drawing his arm around her shoulder, and they made their slow way to the edge of the plateau, stopping and leaning against a boulder. They peered downward, seeing small bits and pieces of the destroyed black ship.

Once she was certain that Jag was securely resting on the boulder, she said, "Me first," flashed him a quick grin, and leapt off. She floated down, gracefully and slowly, landing gently several meters below on a lip on the otherwise sheer rock face. She looked up and held up her arms, her face soft with affection, offering to use the Force to bear him to safety.

"Taking the plunge indeed," he called down to her.

"You said for better or for worse."

"I did," Jag said, grinning, and jumped. ☙

ROLL OF THE DICE

WRITTEN BY **KAREN MILLER**
ART BY **DAVID RABBITTE**

*R*eally, on the whole, I could do without the bantha smell. It's a bit tricky trying to lose a game of pazaak on purpose without anyone working out that's what I'm doing, when all I can think of is how I'm going to stink of bantha for the next... forever.

So thought Myri Antilles, behind a carefully constructed expression of anxiety as she pretended to dither over whetheror not she should draw another card from her main deck.

Sitting opposite, her opponent—a Balosar man whose scarred, shriveled antennae and prematurely wizened humanoid features betrayed a tragic and probably terminal addiction to death sticks—drummed his not-quite-clean fingernails on the gaming table, whistling tunelessly. Around them, there were growing hints of impatience from the handful of onlookers who'd abandoned their own risky pursuits to drink searingly colorful cocktails and eat illegal appetizers and gawk for a while.

With a little gasp, Myri fluttered her outrageously enhanced eyelashes in a tell-tale sign of panic. Time to wrap this up. She'd learned all she was going to from her jittery fellow player.

The Balosar waved his antennae with ill-concealed bad temper. "Come on, doll, I ain't got all day."

Mutterings from the crowd commented on his breach of manners. Shoulders drooping, Myri shook her head. "I'm sorry." Up came her chin. "All right. I've decided. I'm going to do it!"

With breathless bravado she snatched the precise card she needed from her main deck and turned it over.

The gamblers gathered behind her, shamelessly ogling, let out an almost sympathetic groan.

"Six," said the Balosar, and revealed his chipped, stained teeth in a grin. "Pushes you to twenty-four, doll. I win."

It didn't take much acting for Myri to make the crowd feel her pain as the Balosar scooped credit-chips into his already laden basket. Losing always hurt, good cause or not.

"Oh, well," she said, looking around with a pathetic smile. "I did say I was no Mebla Dule, didn't I?"

"A gambler who wasn't kidding?" One of the oglers said loudly in Corellian-accented Basic, her voice ripe with amusement. "Somebody catch me. I think I'm gonna faint."

Ripples of laughter. A babble of conversations. Myri slid out of her chair,

gave a 'good luck' nod to the Rodian hustler who eagerly took her place, then threaded her way through the jostling, multi-specied throng of gamers, and the gaudy droids tasked to serve them, towards the females 'fresher on the far side of the gambling hall. Well. What Captain Oobolo, the treble-eyed Gran, liked to call the gambling hall. Really it was just the converted upper deck of his ancient light freighter. Sadly for him, though, not even curtains of Kashyyykian spider-silk and dangling chandeliers crafted from Manaxian amber and Fondorian crystal would fool a blind passenger into thinking the *Galactic Princess* was a cruise liner. And *nothing*, not even the overburdened air scrubbers, could counter the stink of corraled dwarf bantha in the cargo hold beneath her feet.

Still. Transporting the smelly little beasts around both galactic rims made for an effective cover... as did Captain Oobolo himself. *A Gran*, financing interplanetary political and corporate espionage? She'd scoffed at the idea when Commander Bilpin from Galactic Alliance Security

> **Myri had been careful to lose more than she won. Of course, if she'd be playing properly, she'd need an extra credit belt by now.**

had briefed her. But she'd swallowed her skepticism after hearing what he had to say. Security's evidence was only circumstantial so far, sure, but it was also compelling. And the situation was deemed urgent enough to warrant an in-person investigation.

So here she was, gambling again, only this time not just with money... but with her life. Because Oobolo might look like a mild-mannered Gran, and the *Princess* might seem like a harmless system-hopping freighter, but in this case looks—so Commander Bilpin had claimed with confident authority—were deceiving.

The 'fresher door groaned open at her touch. Gritting her teeth, Myri squeezed past the bevy of females—bald, skull-ridged Dresselian, and Twi'lek with their head-tails glitter-painted, insectoid Aqualish and leather-clad Dug, their large, square teeth spangled with gems—all fighting for space in front of the wall mirror and dived into an empty stall. Blessedly alone, she closed her eyes for a moment and resisted the urge to rub at the experimental recording crystals implanted in her face. Bilpin had assured her the ruby and emerald look-

alikes wouldn't cause any trouble.

"Guess what, genius?" she muttered, as the implants tingled her skin almost painfully. "You were wrong."

But she couldn't afford to fret about that now.

Suck it up, Antilles. It's not like you're gut shot in a downbelow Coruscant alley, or plummeting through atmosphere in a burning, out-of-control X-wing.

Uncoding the secured pocket in the leg of her slinky green jumpsuit, she checked how much Alliance money she had left after two days on board Gran's seedy gambling palace. Nearly four hundred in loose chits, and an untouched card worth a thousand. Plenty, then. She'd been careful to lose more than she won, but not look like a desperate no-hoper. Of course, if she'd been playing properly she'd need an extra credit belt by now, to hold her takings. For a heartbeat, pride stung. Ruthlessly she smothered it.

The noise level beyond her stall had dipped so she came out, freshened up at the tiny hand basin, then inspected herself in the equally tiny mirror. A stranger's face looked back at her: long silver hair intricately braided into loops, luridly green eyes, ridiculous swooping lashes, pouting aqua lips, and those extraordinary crystals, sparkling above her eyebrows and along her cheekbones' sculptured ridges. Inert until she fed them a biofeedback activation signal, to Captain Oobolo's security team and its scanners they'd looked like harmless body adornment.

Live and learn, Captain. Live and kriffing learn.

She was the first agent to use the crystals in the field. If they worked as well as the lab techs claimed, they'd give the Galactic Alliance a much-needed advantage over the enemies of peace.

Please, let them work. We need all the help we can get.

A headache was brewing behind her enhanced eyes, partly from the crystals, partly from the smoke and noise of the gambling hall and a little—just a little—from the stress of worrying that she'd not succeed in her mission. And she had to succeed. Not only because Security needed the intel she was after, but because—because—

I love my dad, I do. But it's not always easy being his daughter.

Wedge Antilles cast a long shadow. One of these days she'd have to sit down with Syal, ask her big sister how she dealt with filling his shoes.

Only let me wrap up this assignment first.

She squeezed her way back into the gambling hall, and swept her gaze around the games of chance on offer as a raucous tide of noise washed over her. Piped-in music, elated winners' laughter and heartfelt losers' wails, the irritatingly cheerful chatter of Oobolo's droids as they plied his customers with food and drink.

Today was turning into a replay of yesterday. Before spending an hour losing at pazaak, she'd stood for nearly that long feeding credits into a succession of greedy machines in the lugjack bar. No winnings, and no hint of illegal dealings either, or questionable conversations for the biocrystals to record. During that time, after cruising just past Malastare, they'd docked with a shuttle, waved goodbye to the gamblers who'd emptied their pockets, and picked up a few more hopefuls eager to throw their money at Captain Oobolo. Might be an idea to go for a leisurely stroll, check out the new arrivals.

So she wandered past the binspo players, furrow-browed and intense. Past the suckers losing their shirts and jewelry over games of Imperial Commander. Back through the lugjack bar, just in case. Played three rounds of dejarik for a loss, a win, a loss. Paused to eat a nerf-burger, then accepted a tall glass of fizzy from a passing droid, and kept wandering. All the while, she could feel the hot buzzing of Commander Bilpin's embedded crystals, recording faces, voices and vital signs. She didn't let her green gaze rest, swept it casually over every gambler in the hall. Found wild hope and misplaced confidence, elation and despair. Everything she'd expected to find in a gambling den... but nothing to make Bilpin bare his teeth in a hunter's smile.

At least not until she stopped at the sabacc table.

Danger-honed instinct woke, and she stared at the players: a Corellian, a Besalisk, two Dugs, two Rodians and a Kaminoan. All but the Corellian were new arrivals—and something about one of them had tripped her alarm. The Besalisk. There was something subtly *not right* about the Besalisk.

But what? A greenie might look at the jovial gambler, with her wide-mouthed, sharp-toothed grin, and gaudily sequined tunic and the flashy gold rings smothering the fingers of the two hands that by the rules were kept flat on the table and think *There's an easy mark*. Being no greenie, Myri looked past the distracting exterior, looked instead at the flamboyant Besalisk's deepset amber-colored eyes. Cold. Sharp.

Calculating. Cruel. Not gambler's eyes, those. They were the lethal eyes of a killer. She'd seen eyes like that too many times to be mistaken.

But it wasn't just the eyes that gave the Besalisk away. The glitz and glitter might be shouting *Don't mind me, I'm harmless*, but singing softly beneath that was a far deadlier song. Tension thrummed in the Besalisk's deceptively saggy body, a readiness to act with swift violence if violence was needed. Seeing it, sensing it, Myri felt her own muscles go taut with absolute certainty.

Gotcha.

Pretending to overbalance on her silly, spiky high heels, giggling apologies, she positioned herself at the front of the gathered sabacc spectators and activated a direct biofeedback pulse that would instruct the recording crystals to hone in on her quarry. The crystals buzzed in response. So far, so good.

The game of sabacc continued. As the stakes climbed to stratospheric heights and the other players started to sweat and

> "Droids with scanners." Wedge said, his familiar eyes intently serious. "Five of them, which is five too many. Time to go."

swear and slap their cards to the table with growing concern, the crowd of watchers grew until Myri was being pressed hard from all sides. Surreptitious bets broke out among the oglers, credits changing hands swiftly and discreetly before they were picked up by a surveillance cam and a security droid hauled them away to be evicted when the next shuttle docked.

An hour later, the Besalisk took everything with an Idiot's Array, one of the rarest and trickiest feats in gambling. Pandemonium ensued. Bells rang, streamers popped, sparklers ignited and showered the hall with bright, brief light.

'It's a jackpot!' the game's dealer droid announced, photoreceptors flickering in rainbow excitement. "The biggest win in *Galactic Princess* history. Huzzah!"

Myri watched, insides churning, as the Besalisk accepted her accolades from the droid, the chagrined defeated players and the crowd. She couldn't prove it, she couldn't even say for sure how it was done, but every instinct was screaming that the Besalisk had cheated. And she'd bet all the

credits in her pocket that Captain Oobolo's dealer droid was key to the swindle. Which meant—which *had* to mean—

"Congratulations, Hamajum!" Captain Oobolo boomed, his mottled skin flushed with pleasure, as the crowd parted as he approached. "A fine victory indeed. It's not every day we see someone pull off an Idiot's Array! Come, give me a few moments to tell me how you managed it. Everyone else? One drink on the house!"

Under the cover of noisy celebration, Myri followed in the two criminals' wake as they headed for the bar. Behind them, the dealer droid announced a new game of sabacc, another dealer droid drummed up trade for more pazaak, server droids began handing out the free drinks, and the bantha-scented air rang with the trilling of lugjack machines. The crowd broke apart only to reform elsewhere, and the gambling continued.

"I'll have a fizzy," Myri told the bar droid, handing over her empty glass. Taking its replacement, keeping Oobolo and the Besalisk in the corner of her eye, she wormed her way towards them, as close as she dared get. Close enough to see the Besalisk pass Oobolo a data crystal in a slick sleight-of-hand move worthy of a Jedi. If she'd not been looking for it she'd never have seen the exchange, never captured the moment with Bilpin's experimental crystals, and—

A jostle, an exclamation, and somebody's drink tipped down her back.

"Hey!" she protested, turning. 'Why don't you watch what—"

Then the words died, because she was looking into a face she'd never seen before... and eyes she knew almost better than her own. They belonged to the one and only Wedge Antilles.

"Sorry, sorry," her father gabbled. "All my fault. Clumsy. Let me help clean you up!"

With a last look at Oobolo, merrily slapping his Besalisk contact on the shoulder, the perfect picture of a gracious host and good loser, Myri let the skinny, bald, mauve-skinned man hustle her to the other end of the bar, and waited until a droid had given him a damp cloth.

"What are you *doing* here?" she whispered fiercely, as her father sponged her free of sticky, sickly sweet cocktail. "And don't you *dare* say watching my back because—"

"Mission's blown," he replied, keeping his voice too low for eavesdropping. "Bilpin's crystals aren't as secure as he thought. Or Oobolo's tech is better. Or both."

Stang. "I'm being jammed?"

"Both directions. With no way to reach you, I had to drop in."

Despite her jumping nerves, Myri felt a surge of relief. This wasn't personal, then. He'd have come to save whoever Bilpin had sent. But if she was being jammed, then chances were Oobolo's security team was even now looking for the signal's origin. She sent a biofeedback signal to deactivate the crystals, then risked a glance over her shoulder.

"Doesn't matter," she said, still whispering. "I got the intel hand-off."

"The Besalisk?"

"Right," she said, turning round. But the Besalisk was gone, and so was Oobolo.

Eyes warm, her father tossed the stained cleaning cloth onto the bar. "Good work."

There was no time to savor the compliment. Heart thumping, she made a sweep of the room, looking for trouble. "How long till the next shuttle, d'you know?"

Her father made a show of ordering her an apology drink. "Three hours," he said, handing her the glass of fizzy. "So we lay low, and stay close."

She quirked an eyebrow. "But not too close. I mean, you and I haven't been formally introduced!"

"Again, so sorry," he said loudly, eyes glinting, with both hands raised as he bobbed his bald head. "Good fortune, lady. Farewell."

Good fortune, yes. They were going to need it.

Myri let out a deep breath. Three hours wasn't that long. Besides, even if Oobolo's people did come looking, what could they find? With the crystals deactivated, she was as good as invisible. And it didn't matter that they were watching everyone on the secure-cam net, either. Provided she didn't do anything stupid, like win a jackpot, they wouldn't look at her twice.

We'll be fine. Just fine.

And they were… for two hours and twenty-six minutes. Then Oobolo's security droids crashed the party.

"Hey!" someone shouted. "Don't shove that thing in my face, I ain't done nothin' wrong!"

Startled, Myri fumbled the credit chit she was going to feed into her lugjack. When she straightened up after retrieving it, her mauve-colored father was standing in front of her.

"Droids with scanners," he said, his familiar eyes intently serious. "Five of them, which is five too many. Time to go."

She stared into the crowd, where a tall, physically imposing droid, uncomfortably reminiscent of a battle droid, waved a hi-tech sensor wand over one of Oobolo's gamblers.

"Yes," she agreed. "But go where?"

Before her father could answer, the public address system crackled to life.

"*Ladies, gentlemen, and gentle-folk all,*" Oobolo's voice greeted them. "*This is the captain. Apologies for the inconvenience, but our routine public safety sweep has*

revealed that someone on board is unwell. Now there's no need to panic, it's just a nasty rash, but I'm sure that whoever our afflicted friend is, he or she doesn't want to suffer needlessly or spread it around. So please remain calm and co-operative while my health team finishes up. And to take the sting out, have another drink on the house."

Agitated chatter, even some laughter, as the crowd reacted to Oobolo's announcement.

"Dad? Go where?" Myri asked again, leaning close. "And how? Don't tell me you've got a ship stashed in your suit pocket."

Her father grinned. "Nearly. There's a cloaked Alliance cruiser standing by. We eject in a lifepod and send up a flare, they'll come get us."

"Ha," she said, grinning back. "If you weren't mauve and bald, I'd kiss you."

"We've studied this ship's schematics," her father said. "Each 'fresher has an access duct leading to a maintenance bay. We'll meet down there and head for the lifepods. The duct panel in the females' fresher is on the back wall, third up, second from the left. See you soon."

Myri walked away from him without a backwards glance, neatly avoiding the droids. Inside the females' 'fresher she found a lone Twi'lek, her pale blue head-tails turned greenish from too many drinks.

"They want you outside," she told the muzzy-eyed gambler. Queasily compliant, the Twi'lek staggered out. Unhooking the slender, dangly earring from her left ear, Myri gave it a quick twist, activating its miniaturized laser scalpel core, sealed the 'fresher door then hurried to locate the access duct panel. Finding it, she used the scalpel again, swiftly severing the plate's bolts. Then, after lowering the plate to the floor, she tucked the scalpel in her jumpsuit's front pocket and wriggled feet-first into the access duct.

Just as she let go, a hard metal fist hammered on the 'fresher door…and the last thing she heard as she plunged into darkness was a droid's voice demanding to be let in, right now.

Her ride down the access chute was fast, bumpy and bruising. And when she shot out the other end she didn't land on hard decking…but on a warm, woolly mass of alarmed dwarf bantha.

"Stang!"

The stink of fresh bantha dung was a hundred times worse down here. Flailing about in the half-light, fending off wet, anxious muzzles and blunt, hairy foreheads, feeling the animals mill and shift, in danger of falling beneath their heavy feet, Myri struggled to find a way to safety.

"Myri! Over here!"

And that was her father. Using her knees

and elbows as bantha-prods, trying not to suffocate while holding her breath, she escaped the bantha corral.

"So much for studying the schematics!" she wheezed, as he took hold of her arm to help her over the corral's durasteel side. 'When was the last time you had your eyesight checked?"

Her father's teeth gleamed briefly in the gloom. "Everyone's a critic. Come on. The lifepods are this way."

"Are you sure?" she grumbled, following. "Because the last thing we need is—"

Blaster bolts stitched a line of red fire across the deck plating before them.

"Halt!" demanded the lead security droid. Four others loomed behind it, heavily armed and menacing. "On the floor, face down, hands where we can see them."

"Face down?" Myri echoed. "On *this* floor? You've got to be joking!"

Taken aback, unused to an argument, the droid stared. Not looking at her father, Myri slid her scalpel earring out of her pocket. "The more the merrier, I think."

He'd given her the earrings for her last birthday. Another gleam of teeth as he grinned. "So do I."

Before the droids could react, he unsheathed his own laser pen and in a perfect duet they loosed the banthas from their corral. With an added *"Sorry!"* Myri laser-blipped the nearest hairy rumps, sending the bewildered creatures into a panic.

"Run!" her father shouted, pointing. "That way! I'll drop us into realspace, you get the intel out of here."

Leave him? But –

"*Go!*"

No time to argue. The panicked bantha were as lethal as the droids, who were wasting no time in shooting anything that got in their way. Now the air stank of charred hair and meat as well as fresh dung. The bantha bellowed, blundering between herself and her father as blaster shots zinged off wall and ceiling and floor.

Summoning all her speed, strength and cunning, Myri broke for freedom. Felt her left shoulder pop as she crashed a droid aside, felt a crack in her right knee as she hurdled a fallen bantha. Sweat stung her eyes, blinding her. She couldn't see her father.

Never mind. Keep running. General Antilles can take care of himself.

Startled Chadra-Fan menials scattered as she sprinted through the freighter's dimly-lit engineering bay. Lifepods, lifepods, where were the kriffing lifepods?

There. Up ahead. Two of them. Heading for them, she felt the freighter shudder as its lightspeed engines cut out. *Way to go,*

Dad. She wanted to wait for him, but if she did he'd skin her alive. The mission mattered, nothing else. She knew that.

"Come on, Dad, come on!" she groaned, reaching the first lifepod and slamming open its hatch. One last look behind her—and there he was, bursting out of the engine bay with a droid on his heels. *Stang*, but the stinking tinny could run. Oobolo must've been tinkering.

Not waiting, no, she knew better, but before making her escape she opened the other lifepod's hatch. A few heartbeats' advantage was all Wedge Antilles needed.

She heard blaster fire as she slammed her own pod's hatch closed then hit the launch key. An explosion of propulsive gases and she was spat out into space, distant stars twinkling, the bulk of Oobolo's freighter looming large. But where was the Alliance cruiser?

A biofeedback surge reactivated Bilpin's crystals, so Alliance security would know it was her. A quick check of the lifepod controls revealed rudimentary steering and a comlink. She fed the link a secure ID code, started broadcasting, then pressed her face to the viewport. Looking for her father. Looking for help.

And there! There was the Alliance cruiser, almost close enough to kiss, its beautifully sleek lines rippling into sight as the cloak deactivated. And there was the other lifepod. Her father. But something was wrong, the 'pod was spinning, not drifting. Sparks spat before vacuum killed them. An unlucky blaster-hit. The other lifepod was crippled.

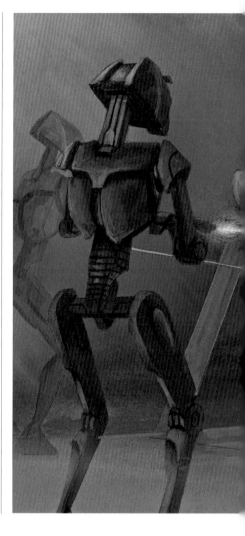

> "Come on, dad!" Myri groaned, reaching the first pod and slamming its hatch. one last look behind her and there he was, bursting out of the engine bay with a droid on his heels.

Blinding streams of light as Oobolo's freighter blasters fired—and missed. But next time? Myri struck her fist to the viewport. She couldn't sit on her hands, watch Oobolo blast her father out of the sky. Even as the Alliance cruiser leapt into the fray, answered the freighter's belligerence with its own lethal stream of plasma, she threw herself on the 'pod controls. Let the cruiser keep Oobolo and his shockingly well-armed freighter distracted, and she'd do the rest.

The lifepod was sluggish, reluctant. Worse than a Podracer with a belly full of

sand. *Stang*. What she wouldn't give to be a Jedi! Swearing under her breath, Myri coaxed and cajoled and bullied the useless piece of junk into an intercept course, feeling her bones creak and her muscles shriek as she willed the kriffing 'pod to close the gap… close the gap…

The lifepods connected with a teeth-jarring thud.

As searing lines of laser-cannon fire criss-crossed the darkness of space, she bounced her lifepod dent by dent along the hull of her father's crippled craft, nudging and compensating until she was locked

towards them, their Alliance uniforms familiar and welcome.

A tech popped her lifepod hatch from the outside. "Hey in there. You all right?"

Myri nodded. "I'm fine. Thanks." as she clambered out. The tech was staring, his expression peculiar. She put it down to the garish crystals she wore, and turned in search of her father.

"Myri!" he said, approaching. The blood on his face had dried to a red mask, clashing horribly with the mauve skin. "Good job."

Two small words holding a galaxy's worth of pride. She smiled at him. "Thanks."

A crowd had gathered, and she noticed they were all staring with that same peculiar expression. Then someone started to clap. Within moments everyone was clapping, even her father.

Disconcerted, Myri blushed. "What? Cut it out, would you? Seriously, people. *Dad?*"

The crowd parted to reveal a familiar, rangy figure. Garik Loran. His lean face somber, he let the applause continue a few more heartbeats, then halted it with a raised hand.

"That was some stunt," he said, eyes hooded. "Guess we'll have to call it The Antilles Maneuver."

She could never tell if her father's old friend was joking, or not. All she knew for certain was that Garik Loran didn't care for show-offs. "Sorry, sir," she muttered. "But I couldn't leave General Antilles to be fried."

"I suppose not," Loran agreed. He regarded her quizzically. "You do know that what you did with those lifepods is technically impossible?"

Her father was grinning. "No such thing as impossible. Not for an Antilles."

As Loran rolled his eyes at her father, Myri felt her blush deepen. Okay. Enough. "Sir, the mission. Did you –"

Loran nodded. "Yes, we received your transmissions intact. Oobolo made a run for it just as you reached us, but don't worry. We tagged him in time. He and his friend and the intel will soon be in Alliance custody."

"That's good to know, sir."

"Indeed," said Loran, and stepped back. "Now if you two would come with me, there's some debriefing to be done." His eyebrows lifted. "And after that, Myri, there's another mission I'd like to discuss with you. Everyone else? Back to work."

"Ah well," said her father, as they walked side by side from the hangar. "You know what they say, kiddo. The reward for a job well done is another job."

That was very true. But she didn't mind. She smiled as her father's fingers clasped hers once, then let go.

"Bring it on, General," she said. And laughed. ☾

---

in behind him, and they were in line with the Alliance cruiser. Her lifepod's cramped interior strobed with white-hot lightning, making her blink. She couldn't believe Oobolo didn't turn tail and run. That intel the Besalisk had passed him had to be explosive if it was worth this kind of risk.

She glanced again through the viewport. Her father stared back at her from his lifepod, close enough to touch, his mauve face wet with blood. But he was grinning at her, waving. Holding up his comlink. She snatched up her own, thumbed it back to its default setting and clicked it on.

"*You're good?*" her father demanded, his static-crackled voice loud in the 'pod's near-silence.

"Yes. You?"

"*Good enough. But my controls are fried, kiddo, so it's up to you. Get us home.*"

His confidence killed her fear. Myri laughed. "Yes, sir!"

She aimed their lifepods at the Alliance cruiser's open hangar deck and wrung every last spark of power from her sputtering,

inadequate engine. Stared white-knuckled at their destination as the sweat poured down her face, feeling the skin between her shoulder-blades crawl. One lucky shot from the freighter, just one, and they'd be tiny bits of slagged metal, blood and bone, floating forever in the vast cold of space.

Time slowed. The lifepods swam through the void. Suspended between possibilities, Myri felt her scrapes and bruises complain. Felt her pilot instincts move her fingers on the controls, a tweak this way, a shimmy that, as the sublight engine labored and plasma fire etched threats of disaster into the night.

And then, between blinks it seemed, the sky was full of safety.

Dreamily, she watched the Alliance cruiser's shadow swallow them, felt the darkness fall over her face. Blinked again as the hangar lights banished darkness, bit her tongue bloody as her lifepod struck the hangar deck, hard. Through the viewport she saw her father's lifepod crunch to the deck in front of her, then tip onto its side like a stricken shaak. She saw people, running

WRITTEN BY **ARI MARMELL**
ART BY **TOM HODGES**

It wasn't even genuine rain pattering down around him, muting the hum of the speeders and skiffs high above. Real rain could never have wormed its way among the various obstacles to reach the city's lower levels. No, this was condensation, dripping from the undersides of bridges, roadways, and TaggeCo grav-cranes overhead. Oily, polluted, stinking and stinging, it was enough to drive almost anyone to seek the nearest shelter.

Almost anyone. Not the hunter.

Broad-brimmed hat and sturdy coat of nashtah hide shed the putrid water as efficiently as any forcefield, but even if they hadn't, the figure crouched beneath them would likely never have noticed the precipitation. From a flat and leathery face beneath that brim, the sinister crimson eyes of a Duros peered not at the multitude of towers above and ledges below, or the glimmering of a thousand lights, but into the years ahead.

War's coming.

Most people didn't like to think about it, didn't want to admit it. They pretended the Trade Federation's recent embargoes were flukes; ignored the growing whispers

field—independent from the building's internal security, and not nearly as easily bypassed—the Duros had placed on the roof below. Indeed, even as he rose for a better view, a glimmer of green luminescence shone, briefly but brightly, from a darkened hatch.

"Suppose it's about that time, then…" the hunter muttered, his voice a rasping, rolling growl. Spindly fingers ran across the custom blasters at his waist in a final check, and then he was off and running. Coat flowing behind him like wings, boots spraying a wake of filthy water, the bounty hunter hit the edge of the platform and leapt.

"Blast doors down! Blast doors down!"

Akris Ur'etu, lord of the youthful but rich and brutal Skar'kla

a holdout blaster in one paw, hidden behind his magnificent desk of blood-red greel wood.

"Is it him?" he demanded, his tone now slightly more under control. He ran his empty paw over his head, as though he could force his fur to relax. "Are we certain it's him?"

A bronze-scaled Trandoshan thug opened his maw to speak, but the answer quickly became moot. A pinprick of glowing heat blossomed through the blast door; molten durasteel trickled from the breach, disturbingly like seepage from a ruptured cyst. Swiftly, smoothly, that point became a line, tracing its way down the surface of the door. Ur'etu could

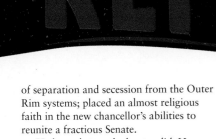

of separation and secession from the Outer Rim systems; placed an almost religious faith in the new chancellor's abilities to reunite a fractious Senate.

He knew better, the hunter did. He could smell it in the air, across the length and breadth of the Republic. Might be a few years, yet, but war it would be.

And there was money to be made in war. A lot of money; more wealth than even the greediest Corellian could imagine. But he needed the name, the reputation, to claim it, which was why he'd taken this fool's errand of a job in the first—

His eyes snapped back into focus with a single blink at the sudden vibration in the metallic band on his left wrist. Something had tripped the portable sensor

Consortium, cringed at the sound of his own voice, shrill enough to drown out the slamming of the heavy slabs. He knew it made him sound panicked, even cowardly, and couldn't do a bleeding thing about it. When the Bothan crime boss grew agitated, his shadow-gray fur stood on end and his voice screeched like the felines he so greatly resembled.

Still, whatever his people thought of his bravery—or lack thereof—they obeyed. Half a dozen guards, human and otherwise, crouched throughout the room or flattened themselves against the walls, blasters and slug-throwers trained on the nigh-impregnable door. Ur'etu himself clutched

practically envision the brown robed figure on the other side, lightsaber pressed tight to the portal.

"As he likes it, then," the Bothan sneered, his worry drowning in a growing tide of anger. "I don't know why this Jedi's been interfering with my operations—or what happened to the bounty hunter who's supposed to get him out of my fur!—but it ends here! The instant that door opens, I want that hallway filled with enough blaster fire to charbroil a Hutt!"

When the Bothan crime boss grew agitated, his fur stood on end and his voice screeched like the felines he resembled.

Guards grunted, fingers flexed on triggers and firing studs—and slowly, methodically, the sizzling outline in the blast door grew...

When the cut was finally complete, a chunk of durasteel simply slid away and toppled into the chamber. Clearly, the Jedi had canted the cut downward so gravity alone would do the job of moving the heavy slab; had any of Ur'etu's men been fool enough to stand too close, they'd have been pulped.

Blasters screamed and bolts flew even as the room shuddered at the impact, so many and so rapidly that the ambient air grew charged, but no target stood revealed for them to hit. After a few volleys that served no purpose other than to score the walls beyond, it finally dawned on the lot of them that they were firing into an empty corridor.

Empty... until, just as the Trandoshan began to edge forward, a tiny metallic sphere bounced into the room from off to the left of the gaping hole in the door.

"Detonator!"

Ur'etu dropped beneath his heavy desk with a horrified yowl; guards dove for cover or turned to run, as though there were any real way to escape.

The blast, when it came, was almost pure heat and flame without concussion. The Trandoshan and two other thugs were incinerated outright, the others singed to various degrees of pain. Smoke, far more than any traditional thermal detonator should have emitted, billowed upward to cloud not only the doorway but that entire half of the room.

"Eyes on the door!" the Bothan shrieked from beneath the desk. "He'll be—!"

He already was. From the very top of the smoke, carried through the fumes in a leap that no normal human could have duplicated, the dark-clad intruder rolled. A sizzling *snap-hiss*! and an emerald reflection in the cloud heralded his arrival. The lightsaber flashed, and the first of the surviving guards went down.

From well behind the Jedi—who, it turned out, was a black-haired and bearded human of average height, clad in a dark-hued

variant of the Order's traditional garb—the bounty hunter watched through narrowed crimson slits. One finger idly tapped at his chin, while the other kept the same rhythm on the butt of a holstered blaster.

These were no Jedi tactics he'd ever heard of! Slicing through the blast door, that was one thing, but the Duros had never seen a lightsaber like this one. The shaft alone was over a meter long, as though the weapon had been stuck on the end of a small pike, turning it into more of a spear than a sword. And he'd watched as the Jedi ducked aside, hunkering behind the segment of the door still standing until the inevitable barrage had passed, and then…

"Since when," he asked himself softly, "does the Jedi satchel of tricks include thermal detonators?"

Most curious of all, though, was the leap that carried the intruder into the chamber beyond the wall of smoke. For just a split second, as the Jedi crouched, the bounty hunter swore he spotted tiny flashes of light from the soles of the man's boots.

"Well, now. What exactly are we looking at here?"

Tugging the collar of his coat high and tight to filter the worst of the fumes (Breathing tubes! Best add breathing tubes to my own sack of tricks…), the bounty hunter crept toward the smoke.

When the boss of the Skar'kla Consortium had ducked beneath his desk, it wasn't only because he'd hoped the heavy greel wood might shield him from the blast. A hidden switch, a quick turn, and the floor beside the desk hissed open. By the time the last of the guards fell to the lightsaber, Ur'etu was already dashing along a metal-paneled corridor, swearing up a storm in Bothese between ragged gasps. He'd expected he might have to retreat, that the guards upstairs might not be enough—but he thought they'd at least have slowed the blasted Jedi down a little! With every step, he had to quash the urge to look over his shoulder, convinced he heard pounding footsteps or the sinister hum of the blade close behind him. A dozen times he started at sudden movement, and a dozen times it proved nothing more than his own reflection in the polished walls.

Finally, after what felt like a sprint of roughly a light year or so, he came to the end of the corridor, and a heavy door

These were no Jedi tactics he'd ever heard of! The Duros had never seen a lightsaber like this one.

not substantially thinner than the blast doors above. Somewhat frantically—for now he really did hear the rapid steps of the oncoming Jedi—he waved a paw over a sensor recessed into the durasteel. Instantly the portal slid up into the frame, revealing Ur'etu's security center.

From amidst a ring of standing monitors, the Bothan's Weequay security chief peered at him.

"Problem, boss?"

The clunk of the closing door masked another stream of Bothese obscenities. "What the mradhe muck kind of stupid question is that?!"

The Weequay shrugged, and if he felt at all contrite, it didn't show in the crags and wrinkles of his coarse face. "Thought you said you'd call me when you needed—"

"Wasn't time! That Jedi tore your men apart!"

"My—?"

"He's coming through that door any second," Ur'etu continued between wheezes.

"Good!" The security chief stepped away from his post, a stubby force pike clutched in his left fist. It began to crackle and spit, as though just as anxious as its wielder for the coming chaos. "Been wantin' to try my hand against a Jedi."

"You don't have to beat the son of a mynock! Just lock him up long enough for..." The Bothan hefted his blaster.

"Just don' hit me, boss."

"Oh, thank you so much for the—"

No lightsaber cuts this time; the door simply slid upward once more to reveal the cloaked and cowled figure beyond.

Instantly Ur'etu stepped back and to one side, raising the small but deadly weapon in hopes of a clean shot. The Weequay strode forward, force pike spinning idly at his side.

The Jedi's left hand rose, fingers pointing at the Bothan.

Ur'etu gasped as the blaster abruptly tore itself from his grip and sailed across the chamber to slap into a dark-gloved palm.

The Weequay had crossed roughly half the distance between them in a sudden lunge before the Jedi flipped the blaster around and shot him in the face.

"Now… now wait a minute…" the Bothan protested, backing away with both paws raised. "Look, I don't know what grudge you have against my organization, but I'm sure there's some arrangement that we can glrk…"

The Jedi stepped to one side, left hand pointing once more, and Ur'etu began to choke.

"Right. Think I've seen about enough, then."

Two faces, one hooded and one furred, twitched around as the bounty hunter stepped calmly into the security chamber. Ur'etu made a peculiar gurgling in his throat, gesturing madly toward the Jedi with one paw while the other continued to grab futilely at his own neck.

The Duros watched the Jedi's arm shift beneath his robes, saw the indecision on the man's face, and offered a broad, sharp-toothed grin.

"Don't mind me. I got no intention of interfering. By all means, finish up."

One wouldn't have thought the suffocating Bothan's eyes could bulge any wider. One would have been wrong. Ur'etu, boss of the Skar'kla Consortium, died staring in horrified rage at the blue-skinned bounty hunter.

"Now," the bounty hunter began as the body slumped to the floor, "let's you and me talk a minute."

"What about?" Even had the Jedi's words not swum in a soup of suspicion, the hand he rested on the hilt of his lightsaber would have been indicator enough.

"Mostly about how you faked all…" Long blue fingers waved idly at the room in general. "All this."

The hand on the lightsaber shaft tightened.

"I don't recommend it, son. Not even a Jedi'd be fast enough—and we both know you're no Jedi."

The man's answering hiss of astonished anger led into the louder hiss of plasma, the lightsaber blade once more snapping on to bathe him in a faint green glow…

And just as swiftly shut down as a blaster bolt tore through the shaft, sending metal shrapnel, burnt wiring, and crystalline shards tearing through cloth and, in a few painful instances, skin.

"You're lucky I made that shot, by the way. I don't typically practice shooting to wound."

"Stolen lightsaber, right?" the bounty hunter continued, as casually as if discussing the latest slingball match. "Extra haft makes it easier to wield without leaving a few of your own limbs behind, that one's obvious. What else you got?"

The "Jedi" leapt, clearing the control panels and half the chamber in a bound, heading toward the fallen Weequay and —presumably—his weapons.

"The boots, right. Impressive." A second blaster bolt flew, piercing miniature engine, leather, and flesh alike. Smoke, so thick it was almost a fluid, gushed from the human's right heel. Propelled only by the other, now, his leap veered off course, slamming him into the wall with a bone-bruising crunch. He slid to the floor, groaning. "Smallest personal jet I've seen was 30-kilo pack," the Duros told him, gesturing idly with the pistol. "You're lucky I made that shot, by the way. I don't typically practice shooting to wound."

Fingers shaking, the supposed Jedi raised a hand once more. The blaster quivered in the hunter's hand, then began to pull away.

"Mono-filament cable with a magnetic grapple?" The bounty hunter yanked, and the wounded man slid across the floor, dragged by his own wrist. "Probably looked just like the Force to that scared Bothan idiot when you snagged his blaster." The human fetched up against the hunter's feet with a pained gasp.

"And the suffocation. Let me see…" He bent low, studying the other's wrist gauntlets. "Gas emitter. Wouldn't recommend trying that, not with you and me so close. Might choke the both of us, hmm? Real clever scheme, I'll give you that." The Duros holstered his weapon, then again started to idly tap a finger against his chin. "Leave behind a few bodies killed with a lightsaber or choked without any bruising, make sure witnesses see you performing a few tricks, and everyone's thinking your target riled up the Jedi something fierce. So nobody—not the authorities, not Ur'etu's allies—are looking at any of his business rivals. Smart.

"So which Hutt are you working for?"

"What did—? I never said… How—?"

"Not hard to figure. Not like anyone but the Hutts have been trying to move on Skar'kla territory."

The "Jedi" nodded once, his teeth clenched.

"All right. Then here's the deal, son. I took Ur'etu's job—that's killing you, in case you still weren't sure—because I figured taking down a Jedi would garner some attention. But everyone would've figured it out, once I brought you in. So here's what I figure: The Hutt's bounty on the Bothan must be pretty sizable, so I'm going to collect it.

"And you… You're gonna convince me I made the right call letting you live by teaching me how to construct this kind of miniaturized equipment." Already the hunter's mind was reeling with the possibilities; energy fields, ship controls, hidden weapons, code breakers…

The false Jedi was clearly wise enough not to bother asking what would happen should he refuse. Instead, he nodded a second time, even more stiffly. "I didn't catch your name, bounty hunter."

"Bane. The name's Cad Bane."

"Never heard of you."

"No." Bane couldn't keep a broad and vicious smile from spreading across his face. War was looming—and the hunter with access to this kind of gear, and the right attitude to use it, would have more than enough of a reputation to cash in when the time came. "No, you wouldn't have.

"Not yet." ☻

ERUPTION

WRITTEN BY **JOHN OSTRANDER**
ART BY **JAN DUURSEMA**

Hawk Ryo drifted in and out of the shadows, a shadow himself. The moon world Zerist was located far from the sun, and most of the available light was reflected off the gas giant, Obri, around which the moon orbited. Kainnan was typically bustling with activity, but the workers' town was now deserted. Like all the surface towns on Zerist, Kainnan was located near an active volcano for its much needed warmth, despite the risk of occasional eruptions. The authorities usually predicted the eruptions in time and evacuated the threatened areas, just as they had recently done with Kainnan. No one was left in the town except Hawk.

In theory.

In reality, the Je'daii Ranger spotted two figures atop the flat-roofed building less than a kilometer away. Despite being only five stories high, it was still the tallest building in the area. They were Twi'leks, like himself. And they were armed. Hawk opened his comm channel and called his partner.

Her surroundings, Lanoree Brock decided, were very beautiful. Underground seas flowed through large caverns smoothed with high vaulted ceilings, and natural minerals gave off enough light to create a twilight effect. It was no wonder the rich of Zerist chose to live in the warm caverns rather than the cold surface of the moon. It was calm on this island, lending itself to meditation.

Peaceful.

The negotiations were not. The management of Dessain Mining and the manual laborers were now simply shouting at one another; ill will was building. Lanoree was finding it difficult to maintain balance between the light and the dark sides of the Force as she was taught.

Management consisted entirely of the extended Dessain family, which was headed by Eomin Dessain, the tall, pale, patrician head of the clan. The workers, both human and alien, were led by short, weather-beaten Arko Santis, and demanded a voice in how the company was run. They left Zerist to labor at the gas mining operations floating above Obri. The pay was steady, if not generous, but it was a hard life.

For their part, the Dessains were loath to cede control to anyone who was not family. The solution, it was decided, would be a marriage between Brom Santis, Arko's oldest son, and Oma Dessain, Eomin's youngest daughter. Brom would become part of the Dessain family and a voice for the workers. Lanoree had gotten stuck with the role of negotiator, and though it wasn't the solution she would have suggested, if it satisfied all parties concerned, then it satisfied her.

That was before Oma Dessain vanished.

Each side blamed the other for her disappearance. Work at Dessain Mining had ground to a halt. Tempers flared and open class warfare looked not only possible, but likely. Lanoree and Hawk had been sent by the Je'daii Council on Tython to prevent violence and find the girl.

Lanoree's comm buzzed. The Ranger swung her long legs out of the chair, turning away from all the shouting. "Please tell me you found the girl."

"I may have found her," Hawk replied. "I went to the spaceport to check who arrived or left around the time of the kidnapping. I discovered a Shikaakwan ship registered to Baron Volnos Ryo."

"Your brother."

"My brother the crime lord." Lanoree could picture Hawk's lips twisting in distaste. "He owns interests in the mining operations on Obri's two other moons, but he's never been able to get a foothold with the Dessains. One of the ways to increase the value of his own holdings is to decrease the value of his rival's holdings. Are you growling?"

"Maybe. Will Oma still be alive?"

"Her body hasn't been found, so it's likely. If they intend to kill her, it'll be when the two sides are at each others' throats."

"Which will be soon."

"You have to keep them from reaching the boiling point. I think I've spotted where Oma is being held, but you can't say anything until I know for sure. I'll let you know what I find. Keep the workers and management from killing each other."

"Right. You get the easy job."

"The Force be with you."

Lanoree turned back to the round wooden table and narrowed her gray eyes. Both sides were already at the breaking point. Violence was ready to erupt. But Lanoree had a theory: Sometimes the best way to cut off violence was to use it first. Her right hand dropped to the slugthrower at her hip. She didn't often carry one—

didn't need it most times—but something told her to wear one today. If there's one thing Lanoree learned through her experience, it was to listen to her instincts.

With one fluid move, she aimed the slugthrower straight up over her head, and fired three bursts into the ceiling. The arguing stopped dead and all eyes went to the auburn-haired Ranger. Je'daii were mysterious beings to most of the sentients of the Settled Worlds. They went where they willed and intervened where they chose or, they claimed, as the Force directed. They had strange powers and were both respected and feared. Right now, Lanoree was feared.

Good. That meant she had their attention.

The slugthrower still in her hand, the Je'daii Ranger sat back in her chair, placing the weapon on the table before her, the barrel pointed at the now silent delegation. She spoke quietly. "The last time I was a

balance. Right now he needed to use aggression, however, which meant channeling the dark side. He eased into it with a comfortable familiarity while he crouched and then leaped straight upward, letting the Force carry him. Hawk cleared the edge of the roof, right in front of the very surprised Twi'lek guard, and without hesitation slashed his sword across the guard's neck. He died silently.

The other guard sensed something amiss and started to turn. Hawk gestured with the Force and pulled him across the roof. The guard gasped

Holding his sword in his right hand, the ranger let the balance within him slip to the dark side.

negotiator was on Ska Gora. Before I was done, forests were ablaze and one of the parties was dead."

She leaned forward. "I was hoping these negotiations would go smoother."

In truth, the deaths and the burning forests on Ska Gora haunted Lanoree. The negotiators here on Zerist, however, didn't need to know that.

"Perhaps we should begin again," she suggested in a low murmur. They did, quietly, and with nervous glances in her direction.

Certain he hadn't been seen by anyone, Hawk reached the side of the five-story building and glanced upwards. One guard was directly above him and the other would be across the roof. It was vital that he silence both before they could give alarm—assuming the girl was alive.

The Ranger brought his sword out of its sheath without a whisper, holding it in his right hand as he let the balance within him slip into the dark side. Hawk knew the dark side well; he dwelled too deeply in it once and it got him sent to Bogan, a moon of Tython where those who drifted too far to the dark side were sent by the Je'daii Council for solitary reflection and meditation until they returned to the

for a moment before being impaled on the Ranger's sword. Their eyes met and Hawk recognized him. Deon Aarlaa—one of his brother's personal guards. Aarlaa's eyes registered recognition as well, and then life faded from them. Hawk felt his death in the Force and part of him, the part that fed on the dark side, felt a deep satisfaction.

The Ranger let the body slide off his sword and took a deep breath, centering himself again in the balance. It was tempting for Hawk to just stay in the dark side as had once before. It was seductive but dangerous.

Hawk found a stairway in the middle of the roof leading down into the building and descended cautiously. Two floors down were two large rooms on either side of the stairwell, the doors left wide open in the haste of the evacuation. At first blush, they appeared to have been used as dormitories for workers that were unmarried; cots were overthrown and debris littered the floor.

Hugging the stairway wall, Hawk glanced through the doorway and found Oma. The girl was bound and gagged on a cot next to the wall opposite the door. A large and surly-looking Twi'lek stood guard, a slug thrower at the ready, but he was looking at the far end of the room.

Focusing his senses through the Force, the Je'daii heard two more Twi'leks at

the other end of the dormitory. Neither sounded happy.

"...Thought this would be over by now!"

"You got other things to do?"

"Other than sit next to a sokar volcano? Yes!"

"The problem is that Je'daii sitting at the table. Not for long, though. Our contact will take care of her. Then we off

the girl, leave the corpse where it can be found, and get gone."

Hawk couldn't risk comming a warning to Lanoree. His best bet was to settle things here and hope that his fellow Ranger was still alive. However, the moment he made a move, the two guards at the end of the room would see him and the guard closest to Oma would certainly kill her. He needed a diversion.

The volcano provided a spectacular one. Ahead of schedule, the eruption started with a clap of thunder as plumes of pumice, flaming ash, and molten lava were belched into the air. Everyone was stunned for a moment, but then Hawk Ryo moved. His sword in his right hand and a long knife in his left, he swept into the room. Hurling the knife towards the guard standing next to Oma, he guided it with the Force into the Twi'lek's neck. The guard's finger tightened on the trigger of his slug thrower as he dropped; the shot went wild but was audible even over the roaring volcano.

Hawk pivoted towards the two other guards and sped towards them as they turned to the source of the slug fire and spotted him. A moment for their reaction. A few steps for Hawk. A moment as they brought their slug throwers around. Another few steps. They aimed their weapons. Hawk threw himself into a forward roll beneath their shots and pushed off of one leg as he came forward and up. Flipping in mid-air over the guards, the Je'daii shoved his boot down hard into the upturned face of the one to his right. Nose bone and cartilage cracked as the Twi'lek fell backwards. The Je'daii landed, spun, and thrust his sword into the fallen Twi'lek's chest—a quick and clean kill. His partner kept firing, but always where the Je'daii had been. Hawk landed in a crouch and, with a gesture of his hand, delivered a Force blow that sent his target backwards through the window. The Twi'lek's scream was covered by the volcano's roar.

Hawk preferred not to kill when he had the option, but there was no time and no other choice. Still, the dark part in him exulted and he struggled to bring himself back to the balance.

Hawk squatted next to Oma. "I'm Je'daii ranger Hawk Ryo and I've been sent here to rescue you. Try to be calm." Picking the teen up, Hawk threw her over one shoulder and raced back up to the roof. Superheated volcanic debris rained down on the town, the wooden buildings starting to catch fire. Hawk again tried to warn Lanoree, but the ash jammed the comm's signal.

It was hard to see through the ash and the Ranger tightened his grip on Oma. Calling on the Force once more, he leaped to the next nearest roof, ran across, and then jumped to the next roof after that. He could barely breathe and was jumping blind, but he hoped he could trust in the Force that he was taking them out of danger.

And that Lanoree was not dead.

R anger Brock eased back into her chair. The discussions were still going nowhere but at least everyone was civil. A servant brought her a goblet of wine, a Vaisamond red, something she had developed a taste for on Ska Gora. Lanoree raised the goblet to her lips—and paused. She knew the bouquet of the wine and something bitter underlay the aroma.

Lanoree turned her head to glance at the servant who had given it to her: a nervous little man, as old as Eomin Dessain. Fear came off him like a wave, a bitter aroma of its own. The servant turned to run. Lanoree caught him with the Force, lifted him up, and dropped him onto the round table. Thrusting the goblet in his face, Lanoree whispered, "I think this vintage is off. Please. Taste it."

The man's eyes went wide as he babbled incoherently. Lanoree growled, "Drink it, little man, or I will make you drink it." She didn't have that ability, but it was commonly believed that the mysterious Je'daii could seize your mind. That fear, that superstition, sometimes served the Je'daii almost as well as the Force did.

The servant certainly believed the stories. "No! It's poisoned!" he blurted.

Lanoree folded her arms, keeping her eyes on her would-be assassin. "Master Dessain, you have a traitor in your midst. The kidnappers would have needed someone on the inside to reach your daughter. That traitor is this man."

Eomin Dessain looked at his servant, appalled. "Betolo? All these years, you have been a trusted servant, almost a member of the family... why?"

"Because all these years I have only been a servant." Betolo said quietly. "Never a member of the family. I wanted to have something of my own before I died. A chance to leave this wretched rock."

Dessain's voice seethed with fury. "Where is my daughter?"

"With any luck... dead. My lord."

Lanoree's comm buzzed. "With any luck, my lord, she is not," she said as she activated the comm. "Hawk?"

"Lanoree, someone is going—!"

"Yes, I know. He tried and failed. Is Oma Dessain with you?"

"She is," Ryo said, "but we have another problem."

"W hat do you mean you refuse to marry Brom Santis?!" Eomin, while relieved to have his daughter back, was furious.

Oma Dessain stood alongside Hawk Ryo with the delegations on the island in the cavern. She, like him, was covered with ash, making her pale skin even whiter and powdering her dark hair the same hue. Free from her bonds, she stood glaring defiantly at her father.

Oma's chin jutted out. "I mean I won't marry him! No one asked me if I wanted to get married! I don't and I won't!"

"You have your duty to the family!"

"I also have a duty to myself! I don't know this Brom, I don't love him, and I won't marry him to settle some dispute!"

This set off another round of arguing between father and daughter with Santis pitching in.

"This is breaking down quickly," Hawk murmured.

"Actually, my sympathies are with the girl. She shouldn't be a clause in a treaty," Lanoree murmured back.

"If she doesn't relent, the negotiations will likely collapse and everything we've done will be for nothing."

"I think I may have another solution," Lanoree said. "First, I'll need to get their attention." She shot her slugthrower three times into the air. And again, with the same effect.

Very pleasantly, Lanoree spoke. "In other parts of the solar system, rival

Lanoree folded her arms, keeping her eyes on her would-be assassin.

interests have a developed a practice called fostering. I suggest you try it. Oma would become a foster child in the Santis household and Brom would be the same with the Dessains. Each would be treated as a full member of the family they are with. They would spend six months with one family and six months with the other. The workers would have a voice through Brom and Oma, would learn firsthand about the workers' lives."

"I think this is a very reasonable suggestion," Hawk added, equally pleasantly.

But the expressions on the two Je'daii firmly suggested that all sides accept the deal. Oma looked pleased; at least she wasn't getting married.

Details were worked out, Hawk cleaned up, and the two Je'daii met at the spaceport to take leave of Zerist and of each other.

"The Council has summoned me back to Tython for a special mission," Lanoree said. "It's been four years since I've been back; it's time."

"I'm heading out to Furies Gate," replied Hawk. It was the outermost planet in the system. Great Generation ships left from the small world, seeking a path through the maze that was the Core and looking for ways back to the rest of the galaxy. The Settled Worlds jointly maintained a station there. "I like to look out into the stars and quietly meditate," he said.

A small shadow passed over Lanoree's face. "My brother used to look out at the stars and wonder if there was a way back to the rest of the galaxy. He was never very happy on Tython," she said softly. She was quiet for a moment, then shook it off and said, "It was good working with you, Ranger Ryo. I look forward to the chance to do it again."

Hawk nodded. "I do, too, Ranger Brock. The Force be with you."

Lanoree smiled. "And you," she replied. The Je'daii then crossed to their waiting ships and took off into the star flecked skies. ☻

CURRENT FICTION

The following stories represent tales from current continuity, that ran from 2014 to 2017.

ONE THOUSAND LEVELS DOWN

WRITTEN BY **ALEXANDER FREED**
ART BY **JOE CORRONEY AND BRIAN MILLER**

Level 2142 was a bust. Anandra realized it as soon as she stepped up to the counter of "Hangra's Meat Shack," pressed her palms onto the greasy metal to quell the shaking in her arms, and asked the old man tending the grill about the "Centax 3 delivery." He looked at her with confused condescension, like she was lost and out of her depth—which, Anandra supposed, she probably was—and it made her want to drag him over the counter and swear in his face until he somehow made things right.

She didn't yell. She couldn't afford to make a scene. She forced herself to stay calm, to look pathetic and confused and earn the man's sympathy. By the time she returned to her brother—still in the alley where they'd slept the night before—she had her next lead. Her next hope of escaping the stormtroopers.

The alley was formed by metal train grates and Anandra settled beside Santigo against the wall, watching shadows cross his face as speeders flitted high above. She passed him the greasy packets of meat and cheese the old man had given her and waited for the questions to start.

"So are we leaving?" Santigo asked.

Anandra balled her hands into fists and didn't look at him.

"We missed our chance."

"We shouldn't have rested," Santigo said.

At eight years old, he was barely half Anandra's age, but his bitter determination reminded her of her father.

"The transport left two days ago," she snarled. "Four hours didn't make a difference."

She took a long breath and reached for one of the wrapped packages as Santigo began to eat. She felt hollow and nauseated at the thought of food. "Besides," she said, "we don't have to leave Coruscant. The guy said he knew someone on 1997 who might give us shelter."

"What level are we on now?" Santigo asked.

Anandra didn't answer. It wouldn't comfort him, and she didn't want to argue. Yes, one hundred forty-five levels was a long way on foot; yes, they were both tired; and yes, they had to do it.

They ate in silence until Santigo spat out a chip of bone and said, "I wish we had starblossom."

He'd spoken almost to himself, but Anandra pressed her thumb into Santigo's shoulder and wrenched him to face her.

"Well, we *don't*," she said. "We can't have fruit whenever we want and there *isn't* any more starblossom. There isn't *ever* going to be more."

Santigo was trembling. Anandra felt a rush of guilt and pulled away as she snapped, "It's gone. Just like Alderaan. Get used to it."

The riots hadn't started as riots. They'd begun as vigils, a way for the people of Level 3204 to grieve for the missing and dead in the wake of the Disaster. Hundreds of locals packed together in the streets, bringing holographic snapshots, handwritten letters, and children's toys to makeshift monuments in parks and community centers. As days passed, however, and official statements and pirate newsfeeds converged on a common truth, anguished wails became cries for justice and revolution.

The planet Alderaan was gone, destroyed by the Empire for crimes no one understood. The Alderaanian people—first- and second-generation immigrants who had shops and restaurants and houses on 3204, who celebrated Coronation Day and imported their favorite fruits from a planet they rarely visited—were alive and frightened and angry. The rest of Coruscant nervously stayed inside and watched the news because Alderaan wasn't, after all, *their* planet.

Anandra couldn't blame them. She'd never thought Alderaan was her planet, either, until the underworld police and the Imperial stormtroopers came.

When the troops marched into the street and shot her uncle's neighbor Reffe, cutting short his tirade against Imperial corruption, Anandra's mother promised it was over, that no one was going to fight and that the stormtroopers wouldn't make trouble.

"You and Santigo will be safe," she said with a faded smile over breakfast, as she absently bent a spoon in her hands.

She'd already promised that Anandra's father would be fine. That he'd be home on Coruscant as soon as his trade mission was over. Even Santigo hadn't believed that.

"You, I can take," the Pau'an said. The leathery gray skin around his mouth tightened as he grimaced. "You and the boy? This is more difficult."

Level 1997 smelled like soot and human waste. Sparks from industrial compactors drifted lazily to the streets, and lurid signs in pastel pink and blue invited passers-by to sample local "entertainments." Anandra had been to 1997 once before, on a dare with a schoolmate; they'd taken a lift down, snapped their image with a holocam, then returned skyward. Her parents hadn't found out.

Now she was back, staring down a man with a face like a corpse in a cramped corner of a painfully bright cantina. Santigo stood behind her chair, a hand on her shoulder.

"I'm not leaving my brother behind," Anandra said.

"I sympathize." The Pau'an tipped his own chair back and grinned at his monstrous partner—a hulking black-skinned alien with a mouth wider than Anandra's shoulders and oily quagmires for eyes. Anandra didn't recognize the species.

"Family is family. But I need people to run goods, make deliveries. You can do that, and I can protect you."

Anandra suspected she knew what sort of "deliveries" needed to be made on Level 1997. She could adjust, though. She might have to.

The Pau'an kept talking. "Yet the boy is so little, and can give me nothing. You see my dilemma?"

"I could work for you longer," Anandra said.

The Pau'an sighed and glanced at his companion again.

"I am not sure this is enough. You are both a risk, running from the underworld police..." He paused. "What *is* your crime again?"

Anandra winced as she heard Santigo's soft, defiant voice. "We aren't criminals."

"Then you have nothing to fear, eh?" the Pau'an said, the stains on his jagged teeth etched by the intense light. He pointed a finger toward the entrance.

Two newcomers had entered the cantina, both in full body armor. They might have been droids, Anandra thought, if it weren't for their swagger. One wore the blue-gray of the underworld police, amber lights gleaming from the sockets of his helmet. The other wore the white of an Imperial stormtrooper, stark and blinding in the cantina's illumination.

The day after the stormtroopers shot Reffe, security forces began arresting anyone in the streets. Anandra's mother sat on the orange couch in their apartment and cried while Anandra kept Santigo away from the windows. By that time, there was no HoloNet service either—no way to spread news apart from neighbor to neighbor.

The Pau'an tipped his own chair back and grinned at his monstrous partner.

The day after *that*, stormtroopers began going door to door. Rebel spies, they said, had been recruiting locals, and anyone born on Alderaan needed to be taken in for questioning. Rumor was that second-generation immigrants were being given "the benefit of the doubt" and relocated to temporary housing for their own safety.

The young woman who lived next door—the droid mechanic with a chipped front tooth and blond hair who'd babysat Anandra years before—had repeated that particular rumor with a cynical grin.

"That's how I got my first airspeeder," the woman said. "When they relocated the Mon Calamari after the Old Market Sector riots. Dad found this B-14 some poor family left behind."

"I don't remember it," Anandra said. "I was really young."

She shifted her weight from one leg to the other, awkwardly wiped her palms on her hips. "You think they should've run?" she asked. "The Mon Cals, I mean."

"Sometimes you can't know," the woman said. "You just have to wait and hope things get better." Then she hugged Anandra and slipped back inside her apartment, locking the door behind her.

The rest of that afternoon, Anandra and Santigo stayed close together. Anandra's mother shut herself in the bedroom, but Anandra couldn't hear crying anymore.

Level 1996 was a maze of pipes and catwalks between the compactors above and a humming abyss below. The plating and sluices that canopied the level breathed heat onto Anandra and Santigo as they hurried away from the lift.

The stormtrooper had seen them. He wouldn't be far behind.

Anandra knew she'd made a bad choice. She could've lived with herself, carrying packets of death sticks or spice to the Upau'an's clientele. Santigo was smart and resilient and he could've *learned* to live with it. But she'd bitten her lip when the Utpau'an had made his final offer, and instead of taking shelter with the gangs of Coruscant she'd pulled Santigo toward the cantina's back exit.

Now they were paying for her squeamishness. The catwalks turned and branched, but there were no walls aside from the curtains of pipework—nothing to hide them from a stormtrooper with heat displays and sensors and who knew what else. Her brilliant plan of "run to the next level and find shelter in the deepest, darkest hole around" was turning out to have flaws.

Anandra stopped on a long, narrow span between maintenance platforms. There was nothing on either side, nothing below except the weird lights and humming sounds of Level 1995.

"You need to run, okay?" Anandra said, turning Santigo to face her.

"What about you?" Santigo asked.

"Don't talk back," Anandra snapped.

She didn't expect her brother to obey, but he did. She looked away and breathed in relief as she heard his footsteps ring on metal into the distance. Then she put a hand on each guardrail and waited.

When the stormtrooper came out of the lift, his white armor shone like a spotlight. He came without the underworld police officer; that was good. His blaster was still holstered; that was better.

He spotted Anandra in seconds. She stayed put as he wove among the catwalks and arrived on the nearest platform.

"Walk slowly in my direction, please. Hands on your head," the stormtrooper said. She couldn't read his tone under the electronic hiss of the helmet.

"I didn't do anything," Anandra called.

"Facial ID confirms you're Anandra Milon, age sixteen, 3204 resident scheduled for relocation. Pre-convicted of juvenile

noncompliance. You'll receive a fair hearing taking into account age and psychological state."

"You going to stand there, or are you going to arrest me?" Anandra asked. To her surprise, she felt calm. Almost giddy.

The stormtrooper glanced behind him, then back to Anandra. "Come on, kid. You got a raw deal, but it's not the end of the world."

"It kind of was," Anandra laughed, and lowered her knees to the catwalk. The stormtrooper put a hand on his blaster and began to cautiously approach.

"I have to put you in stuncuffs," the stormtrooper said.

As he reached for his belt, Anandra sprang for the blaster in his holster.

She didn't try to retrieve the weapon. The trooper would have caught her, broken her wrists and pried the blaster back. She only needed to pull it out of its holster, maintain momentum and release. It went sailing, skidding across the catwalk and quivering at the metal's edge. For that moment, Anandra had the advantage.

Then the stormtrooper kneed her in the chest. She fell back, barely tried to break her fall. He can't shoot me, she thought. If he killed her now, at least she'd cost him his dignity.

Two solid kicks to her midsection, and her whole body seemed to fold. When he hesitated, she was up again, jumping forward, wrapping her arms around his neck and jabbing her thumbs under the rim of his helmet. His fingers dug into her sides as she tried to crack the helmet's seal. She slammed her head against the black eyeplate, saw red, hoped she'd bought herself a few moments.

Somehow, when her vision came back, she was on the ground and looking up at the stormtrooper's unhelmeted face—the face of a scarred, middle-aged man who vaguely reminded her of her uncle. Then the stormtrooper screamed as he rose into the air and plummeted over the railing.

Behind him stood the Pau'an's monstrous partner, nearly too big to fit on the catwalk, flicking stubby fingers as if the stormtrooper had left a residue.

"Level 1782," the creature said, its voice higher-pitched and breathier than Anandra had expected. "You may find shelter there." It stared for another moment before adding, "I had no part in this."

Anandra realized she had the stormtrooper's helmet in her hands. The white surface was stained with her blood. "Why are you doing this?" she asked.

Enormous muscles rolled under skin as the creature seemed to shrug. "You are of Alderaan, yes?" it asked.

"Yes," Anandra said.

"I know what your people suffer," the creature said, and turned away.

When the stormtroopers came to the door of Anandra's apartment, Anandra and Santigo were huddled in the empty fluid bucket of a cleaning droid floating outside their bedroom window. The droid normally washed the building once a week. It had already come two days before, and Anandra guessed she had her neighbor to thank for its change in schedule.

Anandra heard her mother open the door. She heard the static of a stormtrooper's voice. Then she felt the cleaning unit carry them away, and she put an arm around Santigo and tried to focus on her mother's instructions.

They were to go to Level 3108 and find an old friend of the family. Their mother would meet them, and they'd all leave Coruscant together.

Level 3108, of course, had been the first of many disappointments. The "family friend" had offered nothing but excuses and apologies, and finally a promise that a smuggler on 2142 would get them offworld. Santigo hadn't wanted to leave without their mother; Anandra and a close call with the underworld police convinced him otherwise.

They'd been running ever since.

Level 1782 was an endless junkyard walled by scrap metal and overlooked by swaying towers of debris. It was built of crashed airspeeders, decommissioned hovertrains, and broken billboards cast down from their homes in the sky; when a vehicle fell from the upper levels, 1782 was its final destination.

Anandra and Santigo walked together, Santigo clutching Anandra's right wrist. In her left hand she held the dead stormtrooper's blaster. She hadn't put it down since she'd retrieved it from the catwalk.

They'd been exploring the junkyard for nearly an hour, alone except the oversized rats, when a humanoid figure slunk out from behind a rusting tram car. He wore a workman's vest two sizes too large, and his bulging eyes were set at opposite sides of his teardrop head. Anandra knew his species—Mon Calamari—though she hadn't seen his kind for years.

He carried a steel hydrospanner, long and heavy, in one webbed hand. He was probably salvaging junk, Anandra thought, but she remembered the stormtrooper's boot in her chest and she wondered how fast and hard the Mon Calamari could swing.

Anandra pointed her blaster in his direction. "Don't come closer."

The Mon Calamari stopped. Santigo squeezed her wrist and said something, but Anandra wasn't listening. The blaster seemed to twitch in her fingers.

"We won't hurt you." Anandra said. "Just give us some food and credits and we'll head to the next level."

The Mon Calamari bobbed his head but otherwise didn't move.

"You said someone would be here to help us," Santigo whispered. Anandra ignored her brother. She was in control for once, and she didn't need another disappointment.

"Can you understand me?" Anandra asked, harsher. Her palms were sweating, and she tried to grip the blaster tighter without pulling the trigger.

The Mon Calamari spoke in a guttural voice in a foreign tongue. When Anandra

Anandra looked from the barrel of her blaster to the face of the Mon Calamari.

gestured with her blaster, he tried again: "Yes," he said, spitting and fumbling with the word.

"Don't hurt him," Santigo urged.

The Mon Calamari raised his free hand—the one with the hydrospanner stayed at his side—and pointed at Santigo.

"Alderaanian?" he asked.

Out of the corner of her eye, Anandra saw Santigo nod.

"Follow," the Mon Calamari said, and began to creep backward.

Anandra looked from the barrel of her blaster to the face of the Mon Calamari. She thought of all the ways this encounter could go wrong: he could be a slaver working with the Pau'an, or planning to sell her to the stormtroopers, or he could beat her and her brother to death for no reason at all.

Santigo was watching her. Slowly, she let her breath out and lowered her blaster.

They followed a twisting path through the wrecks and descended a hill of upholstered train seats and window frames toward a great steel cavern. As they came closer, Anandra realized the cavern was the hull of a starship; it must have crashed planetside during some long-forgotten conflict and since been gutted. What

remained was an open space glowing with blue and yellow light.

The hull was filled with makeshift camps, tiny stalls, tents strung with lanterns and batteries, portable stovetops sizzling with grease, buckets full of rainwater, and hundreds of life forms from a dozen species. Mon Calamari roasted mynocks on spits while tattooed near-human children tossed a ball nearby. Anandra spotted a hulking creature she thought, for an instant, was the Pau'an's partner —but its coloring was off.

"Stop," Anandra said, sharper than she expected. She tugged at Santigo, drawing him close. "What is all this?"

"Home," the Mon Calamari said. "Stay. You are expected."

Anandra shook her head in confusion. Men and women began to emerge from the hull, observing with cautious interest. The Mon Calamari didn't look away from Anandra.

"Mon Calamari," he said, tapping his chest. "Empire takes." Then he gestured behind him.

"Herglic, Empire takes." Another of the hulking creatures was trundling into view.

As the crowd grew, the Mon Calamari pointed to the strangers one by one, naming species and planets Anandra barely knew—names she'd only heard mentioned in muted asides. Then finally, he pointed to her.

"Alderaanian," he said. "Empire takes. But here, we all share."

And whether because of the Mon Calamari's words, or the sad, strained gazes of the people behind him, or the sheer extent of her exhaustion, Anandra dropped her gun and began to weep.

Santigo squeezed her arm again, and Anandra cried like her mother had cried during the riots; she cried without dignity or reason, cried until her nose streamed and strangers guided her into the warmth and safety of the hull. Santigo clung to her, and when she could speak and reason and act again, she helped her hosts prepare a meal, found a place for her brother to rest and eat.

She knew she would have questions tomorrow. She would need to learn how these people lived, what they hoped for. She would need to share news from the upper levels. She would need to decide whether to give up her blaster or use it against the Empire.

But that night, she could put those concerns aside. That night, she'd found home and family in the depths of Coruscant. ☮

ORIENTATION

WRITTEN BY **JOHN JACKSON MILLER**
ART BY **BRIAN ROOD**

Battle stations! Hostiles off the starboard bow!"

In the command well of the Imperial cruiser *Defiance*, 20 members of the skeleton crew hastily turned to their terminals, ready to defend against attack. Every mind was attuned to the situation—save the one belonging to the figure looming dark and large above them on the catwalk. Darth Vader looked on with utter disinterest.

There was nothing in this "battle" to engage the Dark Lord's attention. It wasn't real. There was no one to challenge the Empire. He and his Master Darth Sidious, who now ruled the galaxy as the Emperor, had brought the Clone Wars to a conclusion not long before; and while the two were on their way to Ryloth now to root out insurgency, the "hostiles" outside were pure fiction, part of a training exercise.

"Hard about, my cretins," shouted Commandant Baylo, passing Vader as he stalked along the catwalk. "While I've been waiting for your picnic to end, you've lost your forward shields!" He clapped his hands on the railing and leaned over to bellow. "We have an observer today. Are you trying to make me look bad?"

Vader thought he already did. Well past 70 and with a nose too long for his face, Pell Baylo walked with an exaggerated limp that caused the stumpy man to bob up and down like a flying thing. He nonetheless commanded the attention of the cadets in the pits on either side of the catwalk, all of whom were now scrambling to correct their errors.

Vader thought his own presence here was a mistake, too. But Sidious had brought him to *Defiance*'s bridge and left him. It was his duty to remain, even if he saw no other reason for being there.

Crossing the vast swath of cosmos between Coruscant and Ryloth, Darth Sidious had ordered a stop in the Denon system so he could consult with several chiefs of the navy, visiting there to discuss how the jumble of affiliated military schools that had existed under the Republic might be better integrated into the Imperial Academy. His livelihood under review, Baylo had suggested a timesaving solution:

> Crossing the vast swath of cosmos between Coruscant and Ryloth, Darth Sidious had ordered a stop in the Denon system so he could consult with several chiefs of the navy.

the meeting could take place aboard *Defiance*, the cruiser he'd operated as a flight training school for nearly 50 years. The commandant could show his students in action while they conveyed his Imperial Highness on one leg of his trip.

The Emperor had praised Baylo for his suggestion. Vader saw through the offer. *A futile effort to save his school.* The Clone Wars had brought the *Defiance* Flight Training Institute—known to most spacers as "the Baylo School"—directly under the umbrella of the Republic Navy, with Baylo receiving a rank as a line officer. Yet the commandant treated the institute as

his personal property, ignoring schedules and asserting he knew best when recruits were ready for service. Even now, with the Empire in charge, naval leaders were loath to rein Baylo in; he'd trained many of them aboard *Defiance*, after all. Vader expected that resistance would wilt, now that the Emperor was on the scene. Baylo was just another fossil, married to archaic practices.

But his Master had spent half a minute on the bridge before departing for his meetings with the naval chiefs who were Baylo's superiors—leaving Vader behind to observe Baylo's silly pantomime show.

Vader had objected, as strenuously as he dared: "I would serve you better elsewhere, Master." The Emperor had not been amused. "I decide where you are needed. You will remain and be my eyes."

That was hours ago, and Vader hadn't seen anything worth his attention. Baylo had run his cadets through their paces, dressing down one after another and spewing aphorisms. The first mock attack concluded, he unleashed another one.

"—it's all about attitude, in more ways than one," Baylo was saying to someone, mid-rant. "Think about your direction, your facing. Don't you know where you're going, cadet? Because if *you* don't, your ship certainly won't…"

The trainees—humans in their early twenties, some on their first orientation flights—seemed almost happy to absorb the platitudes and abuse. Vader knew Baylo had a mythic status in naval circles, and not just for his exploits. *Defiance* had fought pirates when it was in patrol

service, yes—but Baylo's spine had been injured, and now his daily battle was with near-constant pain. Twice since he had been aboard, Vader had heard cadets whispering of Baylo's bravery in working despite the agony.

Ridiculous. Baylo knew nothing of pain.

A voice came from behind. "Shuttle arriving from Denon, Commandant. Vice Admiral Tallatz aboard."

Baylo stood back from the railing. "That'll be the last of Palpatine's—of the *Emperor's* guests for his meeting." He checked the time. "Navigator, plot our hyperspace route to—"

"I already have it, sir," called out a female voice from the pit.

"I'll be the judge of that." Forcing one atrophied foot in front of the other, Baylo fought his way down the steps into the command well. A woman with deep brown skin, dressed in sharp cadet grays, slid her chair from her terminal, allowing the old man to approach. She wore the trace of a knowing smile as Baylo read the monitor.

"I'm impressed, cadet," he said. "You'll go far—and so will this ship. Or did you *not* intend to plot a course into Wild Space?"

The cadet's grin vanished. The young woman looked past him at her calculations, suddenly puzzled. "It is a course to Christophsis, sir, where the *Perilous* will meet us."

"You've failed to account for a singularity along our route which will reshape our hyperspace passage in a most startling way. We now know who our next admiral will be," he added with a snort. The young woman stepped away in humiliation as Baylo began to work the console. After a moment's effort, he stepped back. "There. Small repair, major difference." He looked around and about. "Details matter, everyone. A navy isn't built on captains—but on crews that watch their work."

"Aye, Commandant," came the response from the cadets.

Aware of Vader's gaze, Baylo looked up at the Dark Lord. "They don't learn right away, but they do learn. I get results. You can tell your Emperor that."

"He is your Emperor, as well." They were the first words Vader had spoken before the trainees, and several shifted in their seats on hearing his powerful voice.

But if Baylo was shaken, he didn't show it. "I'm sorry. I forget—what are you to the Emperor, again?"

"You would do well never to learn."

That time, Vader got a reaction. Baylo straightened—a strenuous feat for him—

and he slapped the back of the chair of the woman he had corrected. "Well, I can still teach my people a few things. Extra courier detail for you, Sloane, once you're done here. You can think about navigation while you're finding your way around ship."

"Aye, Commandant." The cadet returned to her station and stared blankly at the screen before her, trying to understand her mistake.

Baylo hobbled back toward the staircase. "You have the settings. Take us to hyperspace as soon as the admiral's docking is complete. I need to prepare in case they need me." He struggled up the steps and made his way past Vader. "Carry on, cadets."

Vader watched the aged commandant exit—and then thought about the exchange. The man Vader had been would have bristled at such treatment. His Jedi teachers all thought they knew better than he did. And they were so smug, always pretending they knew some secret

> Vader's Jedi teachers all thought they knew better than he did. And they were so smug, always pretending they knew some secret about the universe he was unworthy to learn.

about the universe he was unworthy to learn. It was all a lie, a false front to hide their weaknesses. Darth Sidious, now the Emperor, had the secrets, not them. It had been a delight to prove them all wrong.

But Sidious was now in that same role as teacher, and he was doing many of the same things: acting as though he knew better, and doling out information only as he chose. Vader had traded all the masters on the Jedi council for one. A better one, he knew: the secrets of power Sidious shared were real. And yet, as different as their master-apprentice relationship was, he had served Sidious long enough to get that familiar feeling. The Emperor had something else to do—and he had given Vader busy work.

No. That concept fundamentally clashed with something Vader had long known about himself. *Every job I do is important—because I am the one doing it.*

His cape trailing behind him, Vader descended the stairs into the command well. There, at the end, sat the chastened cadet from earlier.

"Tallatz has debarked," called out her neighbor. "His shuttle's clear."

Sloane looked at the numbers before her again and sighed. "Commandant's coordinates locked in the navicomputer. Stand by for hyperspace jump on my mark."

"*Hold.*"

Vader's voice startled her, and she turned her chair. Brown eyes widened as she looked up at him. "Yes, my lord?"

"What do you see?"

"N-nothing."

"You fear to contradict your master."

She shuffled in her seat. "My lord, I don't wish to say the admiral is wrong about—"

"No. That is *exactly* what you wish to do." The woman had hidden her emotions from her companions, but could not fool Vader. He had felt her anger at being embarrassed—and it had bubbled up since, finally breaking through his own preoccupied thoughts. "Speak, cadet—?"

"Sloane." She swallowed hard. "Rae Sloane, of Ganthel." She gestured to the panel behind her. "I've studied our orientation and done the math, with the computer and without. Something isn't right..."

Baylo was waiting in the anteroom as Vader stepped onto the administrative deck. Wearing an antique greatcoat, dress attire for the era during which he trained, Baylo leaned near a large viewport looking out upon the streaming stars of hyperspace. He was using the window frame for support, Vader saw. He looked old, even for Baylo.

He straightened as he saw Vader. "Told you we'd get underway on time."

Vader said nothing.

"Hmph." Baylo looked back at the closed door. "Not used to waiting outside my own office."

"It is not your office."

Baylo looked at Vader—and chuckled lightly. "Whatever you say," he said. Before the old man could return his gaze outside, the door to the office opened. Three women and one man emerged, admirals all: chiefs of various branches of the Imperial Navy. Each glanced briefly at Baylo and silently headed for the elevator.

That evoked a frown from the commandant, but only for a moment. "The Emperor will see us now," Vader said.

"Who told you that?"

Vader simply pointed to the door. Shrugging, Baylo took a breath and started for it, shadowed by the Dark Lord.

The master of *Defiance* stood in his own office, hands clasped and eyes directly forward. The room was windowless save for a single viewport—and the walls were covered with plaques and pictures depicting the names and faces of cadet classes from the past. Vader thought the room somber, a pathetic shrine to a soon-to-be-forgotten past. An appropriate setting, too: seated at Baylo's desk, the black-robed Emperor began to describe his just-settled plans for the Imperial Academy. They included several modifications to streamline operations, making the body more responsive to him. And one other change: "*Defiance* is approaching obsolescence—and we will employ no one who is unresponsive to command. The 'Baylo School', as you call it, will be folded into the existing training center at Corellia. And you will take a chair at the navigation institute planetside."

"No."

The Emperor was more surprised by Baylo's response than Vader was. "Repeat yourself," his Master said, in a voice nearing a hiss.

"No, I will not transfer this vessel to your new command." Still standing as erect as his gnarled frame would allow, Baylo

nodded toward the great seal on the wall to the right of his desk. "*Defiance* was commissioned by the Galactic Republic— and detached to me so those who trained here might serve that Republic. I do not recognize your order as legitimate."

The Emperor frowned. "Don't play games, Commandant. Whether you've had time to redecorate or not, the Republic is no more. The Senate decided—"

"—to dissolve its pact with the people," Baylo said, voice rising in volume. "What I owed allegiance to no longer exists. I consider the Galactic Empire a hostile power—and I can't fulfill these orders." He reached inside his waistcoat, an act that drew Vader's immediate attention. But before he reached through the Force to summon his lightsaber, Vader saw

Baylo produce a datapad. "This is my resignation." He offered it to the Emperor.

The Emperor simply stared. Then he chuckled. "A republican, Baylo? I was told you were more intelligent."

Finding no takers, Baylo returned the datapad to his pocket. "I am, of course, willing to report to the brig until we reach our destination. I understand the need to keep an orderly ship." He fixed his eyes on the Emperor. "But order's place is in the military. Not in civilian life." Baylo looked back toward Vader. Seeing no response, the commandant shrugged. He looked up to the viewport, and the stars streaking by. "Enjoy the rest of your journey. I figure I'm dismissed."

Vader took a step toward Baylo. He, too, had been watching the stars flying

> Vader took a step toward Baylo. He, too, had been watching the stars flying past outside while listening to the man's little speech—and waiting to see how the Emperor would react.

past outside while listening to the man's little speech—and waiting to see how the Emperor reacted. Baylo turned to discover Vader barring his way. "This guy again." Baylo spoke through clenched teeth, trying not to betray any fear. "I don't care if you kill me."

"No," Vader said. *That much is true.* "Because you think you are already dead."

The Emperor looked keenly at Vader. "His ailments?"

"No. He plotted a course that will cause *Defiance* to emerge from hyperspace at Christophsis—and plunge into the sun."

The Emperor's eyes widened a little.

"I countermanded the orders."

Now they narrowed. His Master asked, "And?"

And as if in answer, *Defiance* returned to realspace at that moment—with millions of safe kilometers between it and the aforementioned star. Vader could see it shining outside the viewport, along with something else: *Perilous* was there, waiting as instructed.

Seeing them, Baylo mouthed an obscenity. The Emperor saw them, too. "Very good, my old friend." He looked kindly on Vader. "This is part of what I expect from you—to manage the petty problems so that I can focus on larger matters."

Vader felt a surge of pride. He had

suspected it was a test the Emperor had placed in his path; instead, he'd caught something his Master had missed. Even so, the word "petty" didn't sit well with Vader, and he could feel it bothered Baylo more. "You have something to say?" Vader asked.

"You bet," Baylo said, throwing caution away. He'd sagged on learning of his plot's failure, but in focusing his pain and anger on the Emperor he seemed to gain strength. "I've watched you and your cronies, Palpatine. Corrupting the navy, bit by bit during the Clone Wars. Turning something noble, something meant as a shield, into a weapon. Something *oppressive*. A service it's taken generations to build, that students of mine have given their lives to!" He thrust his finger to the images on the far wall. "I'm older than you, 'Emperor'—no matter what you look like now. I remember when this was an honorable calling!"

Vader had been waiting for his Master's angry reprisal ever since Baylo opened his disrespectful mouth, but instead the Emperor seemed amused. "You would have killed several of your own colleagues."

"Traitors, trying to save their posts."

"And a crew of your cadets, for vengeance?"

"A better fate than turning them into droids. Because that's what you want, isn't it? Mindless slaves, just robots in your—"

The words caught in Baylo's throat—as

did his breath. Vader clutched the fingers of his right hand together, summoning the dark side of the Force to snap the commandant's windpipe. He fell to the deck like a Toydarian whose wings had been clipped; a not unpleasant comparison, Vader thought.

But the Emperor's smile vanished. "Lord Vader!" he said, rising from his seat. "I did not instruct you to kill him."

Vader looked at the Emperor and said nothing. Alone again, they were master and apprentice, Sidious and Vader: and the elder Sith Lord spoke freely and angrily. "I would have kept the wretch alive, to take pleasure from his pain as I transformed his Navy—while I broke down his precious ship into cafeteria trays." He mused as he looked on the corpse. "And a teacher who could so easily kill his students might be molded into something I could use."

"He was a threat," Vader said. "He is finished."

Sidious scowled. "Still, I did not command it."

"He is a petty thing, one of those you expect *me* to deal with. My way is faster," Vader said, before catching himself, and adding: "—Master."

Sidious looked at him. But before more words could pass between them, a chime came from the door. "Enter," the Emperor said.

The door slid open, and Sloane stepped forward. "Captain Luitt of *Perilous* has hailed," she said. Reluctant to look directly at the Emperor and his ominous servant, she sought for something else to focus on. "He's ready to resume your journey to Ryloth as soon as you..." The proper cadet trailed off as her eyes discovered the body on the floor. She gasped.

"Commandant Baylo succumbed to his injuries at last," the Emperor said, indifferent.

Sloane looked startled. Baylo had been all right the last time she'd seen him. But she could not be unhappy, Vader thought: Baylo had belittled her in public. Sloane would probably realize that later, once she remembered where her priorities lay. She was smart, and smart people could figure that out.

But now the Emperor claimed her attention as he stepped past the fallen commandant en route to the exit. "I have an additional instruction for you to convey to your superiors at the Academy."

"Y-yes, my lord?"

"This training vessel's name is to be changed," the Emperor said, looking back purposefully at Vader. "From *Defiance*— to *Obedience*."

"Of—of course." She bowed and prepared to follow.

And Vader did, as well. ☙

BLADE SQUADRON

WRITTEN BY **DAVID J. WILLIAMS AND MARK S. WILLIAMS**
ART BY **CHRIS TREVAS**

Gina Moonsong popped her cockpit hatch and slid down the ladder onto the flight deck. She yanked off her flight helmet to reveal the red buzz-cut she'd had ever since Dantooine, and wiped the sweat from her olive skin. Before she could hand off the flight log to the crew chief, the booming baritone of the deputy wing leader's voice echoed through the hangar.

"Front and center, cadet!"

Moonsong froze and saluted, the ghost of a smile hovering just short of insubordination as Lieutenant Braylen Stramm pushed his dark brown face right up to hers. He looked about as annoyed as any officer would who had just watched a vital training exercise go bust—all the more so when the order to advance on the Imperial Fleet might come down any day.

"What in the three suns did you think you were doing out there, Cadet?"

Moonsong hesitated as pilots exited the ships all around her. The expressions on their faces ranged from annoyance—the outsider was causing trouble *again*?—to professional interest: how was their by-the-book commander going to handle the latest infraction by the squadron's problem child? She met Stramm's eyes, and grinned.

"Completing the mission, successfully sir."

"Successfully? The computers say different. You were *destroyed*. Along with half the squadron."

"Sir, we scored three hits on the Star Destroyer. Sir."

"Except that wasn't a Star Destroyer. That was a bunch of drones in space simulating the *position* of a Star Destroyer. And you broke formation to score those hits. After which you got annihilated."

"With due respect, sir, the calculations the wing leader sent in were off."

"And after less than fifty hours you're an expert at flying a B-wing? This isn't the same as smuggling off Coruscant, Cadet. When we go into battle it won't be against some local security cruiser. We'll be facing the Imperial Navy."

"Well, you'd know all about that, wouldn't you?"

A moment of astonished silence. Then Stramm drew in a deep breath to cite Moonsong for an inevitable disciplinary infraction. But before he could speak:

"That's enough."

Wing Commander Adon Fox strode over to them both. Rotund and red-faced, he made up for his lack of warrior physique with reflexes and mental agility. He was known across the fleet as a first-rate leader of pilots. Yet right now it was all he could do to keep them from killing each other.

"I'm going to pretend the last five seconds never happened," he said. "Because the cadet's right. My numbers were off." Moonsong started to reply, but Fox cut her

off: "But instead of hot dogging in there, you should have told us what you were doing first."

"Sir, I didn't have time—"

"Then make time."

He said it with such steel that Moonsong knew better than to question him.

"The whole point of a B-wing squadron attack is that the combined ships act as a force multiplier. If we integrate our attack vectors, we have a far better chance of finishing the mission successfully—*and* alive. Understood?"

"Yessir."

"I don't think she understands at all," Stramm muttered.

"She did get the job done, Lieutenant; nobody ever said this war was going to be easy." Fox turned back to a chastened Moonsong. His black eyes reminded her of her old mentor, Barthow Quince. They had that same look of disappointment that set a lump in her throat.

"This is not your personal war, cadet. If I thought it would do any good I'd revoke your flight status right here and now, but frankly we don't have enough pilots as it is."

He pitched his voice a little higher, letting it ring out across the hangar floor.

"As it stands, I've just received our orders from Admiral Ackbar. Tomorrow's the big show. The fleet moves on Endor. But we won't be participating in the main assault. We'll be safeguarding the fleet's

lines of communications and guarding the rear—"

"*Rearguard*?!?" Moonsong couldn't hide her disappointment. "I didn't come all this way just to—"

"Enough, cadet. We have our orders. Dismissed."

Fox turned on his heels, and strode off the flight deck. He had mixed emotions that the squadron wouldn't be going into the kill-zone. On the one hand, he longed to strike a blow at the Empire. But (much as he hated to admit it) the squadron just wasn't ready. And as for Stramm—he meant well, but frankly he was trying way too hard. Which was to be expected; Stramm was a former Imperial Naval officer who was used to strict discipline and the chain of command. What he needed to realize was that the Alliance did not have the same resources to train its pilots. Most of them had never flown a snubfighter before in their lives. Hell, most of the new flight cadets were from backwater worlds with little to no military experience.

Case in point, one Gina Moonsong. Like so many others who flocked to the Rebellion, she had no formal training and had learned to fly on smuggling routes off Coruscant. Moonsong might have a standing aversion to rules and regulations, but there was no denying she was an amazing pilot. Certainly better than himself, maybe almost as good as the legendary Wedge Antilles.

Fox couldn't help but smile as he considered the true reason for the friction between the two pilots. They thought they had been so careful, but Fox was nothing if but perceptive, and had seen chemistry flare between them from the moment they first laid eyes on each other. Whether or not they had taken things any further than that—well, it was none of his business. Relationships with subordinates were unheard of in the Imperial Navy, but matters were a little more lenient in the midst of the Rebellion, where there were no such restrictions beyond what wing commanders were willing to put up with. And not only did Fox have bigger things to worry about, he wasn't about to invoke a double standard. Everybody on the squadron grapevine knew how generals were cavorting around with princesses, and if anything the Rebellion was the stronger for it. Illicit relationships in his squadron weren't Fox's problem; training was. His people were still scared.

He'd been the same, not too long ago. When the Battle of Hoth began, he'd had less than one hundred hours of flight time and yet they expected him to fly his single X-wing as an escort to an escape

transport. At first it looked like a suicide mission, but he'd somehow soldiered on, and survived. What he hadn't counted on was his wife's transport being destroyed by the Star Destroyer blockade as it took off. But after that, Fox wasn't afraid anymore. He didn't feel much of anything these days, truth be told. And he was fine with that. He lay down on his bunk, knowing that there was no way he'd get any sleep before the operation tomorrow. He knew exactly where his dreams were liable to venture, and figured no dreams at all was better than dealing with ghosts of the past.

Stramm wasn't sleeping either.

He'd brewed himself some coffee, and settled down with schematics of B-wings, X-wings, TIE fighters and Star Destroyers. Not to mention the original Death Star. He'd gone over all the accounts of the Battle of Yavin—focusing in particular on the ship logs of Antilles and Skywalker. They'd accomplished the impossible, but even they hadn't had to contend with capital ships guarding the station. Stramm knew that this time around the Imperial Navy wouldn't be as lax, especially since the station was far from operational.

He knew the imperial logic, of course—knew it first hand. They'd have at least a few Star Destroyers on hand, and would probably employ a lot of TIE fighters as long-range pickets. Admiral Ackbar's plan of popping out of hyperspace as close to the Death Star as possible seemed like the only possible course of action but the thought of doing so twisted Stramm's stomach into knots.

It wasn't death he feared, though. It was failure. His faith in the Rebellion wasn't exactly boundless; he hadn't joined up because he thought they would win. It was just that he was tired of fighting for an oppressive force—of putting his boot on the throat of provincials whose only crime wasn't kowtowing quickly enough. It had been only a year since he deserted from his post in the Imperial garrison on Naboo and made his way into the Outer Rim to join the Alliance. He'd finally snapped, figuring it was better to die fighting tyranny than continuing to be its willing servant.

And right now it looked like he was finally going to get his wish.

The door chime broke his concentration. Stramm was more than a little surprised when he opened it to find Moonsong standing there. Her emerald eyes seemed to almost glitter in the darkness. He took her by the arm, pulled her into his quarters.

"Did anybody see you coming?" he asked.

"Frankly, people have more important things to worry about." Moonsong gestured at the schematics. "Doing a bit of last-minute studying, Lieutenant?"

"What do you want, Cadet?"

For a moment they stared at each other. Then—

"I want to apologize," she said.

"That's a first."

"For what I said in the hangar. I didn't mean to question your loyalty. I was mad and I was out of line."

Stramm shrugged. "You were just stating a fact."

"You know what I mean."

"Sure. I came on a little heated too... it's only because—"

Moonsong stepped forward and put her hand softly against his chest. "I know why."

Stramm placed his hand over hers. "We're going to make it out of here."

"Don't say things you don't mean."

"What do you want me to say?"

> ## Montferrat believed in dealing with failures swiftly and definitively. So an opportunity to demonstrate the penalty for transgressions was always welcome.

"The truth."

"The truth is none of us know what's going to happen tomorrow."

That made her laugh out loud. "What's so funny?" he demanded.

"'None of us know what's going to happen'—that's precisely why we have a chance."

He grinned at that, and drew her to him.

A dmiral Jhared Montferrat was getting annoyed at all the screaming.

It wasn't a noise one usually heard aboard the *Devastator*. His crew was the best there was, and they took a justified pride in their ship's unique legacy. And right now, that pride couldn't be greater: after months of raiding Rebel commerce, the ship was rejoining Vader and his fleet at Endor. The final battle of the war might be in the offing, and that meant that there really wasn't time for distractions. So when the *Devastator* captured some suspected smugglers on the way into the system, Montferrat's orders were as simple as they were harsh.

Which meant there was a lot of screaming.

Montferrat regarded the four shackled men with his single gray eye. He'd heard enough of their desperate protests about how they weren't rebel spies. Certainly there was the faint possibility that they might be telling the truth about being traders, but ultimately it made no difference. Montferrat had found over his many years of command that it was best to keep a crew focused on their mission. That was one of the many lessons he had learned back in the days when the *Devastator* served as Darth Vader's personal flagship. A focused crew was a crew less likely to make mistakes, and Montferrat believed in dealing with failures swiftly and definitively. So an opportunity to demonstrate the penalty for transgressions was always welcome.

He gave the stormtroopers a curt nod; they slammed the airlock door, cutting off the screams. One of the smugglers began banging on the window, but Montferrat didn't bother to look. He hoped if his day ever came, he'd meet it with more dignity than the men he was dispatching. The stormtroopers cycled the airlock and the banging stopped. The sergeant stepped forward.

"What should we do with their ship, Admiral?"

"Set it adrift and let the gun crews use it for target practice. Score the drill and let me know if any gun crew fails to achieve one hundred percent."

Without waiting for a response, Montferrat turned on his heels and headed back toward the command deck. He took the long way there, of course. He always walked the decks before a big operation; he liked to let the officers and crew know that he was watching their every move. That was one more thing Lord Vader had taught him. Truth to tell, he didn't expect much in the way of action in the upcoming operation; there was no way the surprised rebels would be able to withstand the awesome display of power the Emperor had amassed to put an end to their seditious nonsense once and for all. Even so, his analytical mind had gone over the mission details time and time again, and he intended to carry them out to the letter.

Montferrat arrived on the bridge to find Commander Gradd wearing his immaculate flight suit. There was no question that Gradd was one of the best TIE fighter pilots in the whole fleet, but Monferrat found his ostentatious nature to be a continual source of annoyance. He cleared his throat.

"Commander, I want to take your interceptors out and take up position aft of the ship."

Gradd cocked an eyebrow and ran a finger over his pencil-thin mustache. "I thought we were going to support the Battle Station's operations, Admiral."

"You are, only now you will be doing it closer to this vessel when we move to engage the rebel fleet."

"Sir, may I suggest—"

"You may not. Considering that even the smallest of their attack craft have hyperdrives, I don't want to be taken by surprise by any snubfighter attacks, and I want to be free to maneuver against their capital ships as soon as we have the go ahead."

Gradd bowed slightly and gave Montferrat a crooked smile. "A sensible alteration to plan, sir. Allow me to compliment—"

"Spare me, commander. After the battle is won I am sure there will be time enough for appropriate congratulations. Dismissed."

The fighter ace headed toward the bridge exit. Somehow his ego wasn't too large for him to get through the door, but in his wake Montferrat was quietly seething. No one would have dared question Vader's orders when *he* was running this ship. Montferrrat could testify personally to that, having seen Vader Force choke more than one hapless Imperial officer in front of his own eyes. Montferrat had lived in daily fear of that deadly grip when he was subordinate to Vader on board the *Devastator*—and had (though he would never have admitted it to himself) been more than a little relieved when Vader transferred his flag to the *Executor*.

Not that Vader needed to be on the same ship to exact punishment. And anyway, the *Executor* was visible on the screens right now—an impossibly vast vessel, the Star Destroyers arrayed it like minnows to a shark. Looking at the new flagship, Montferrat half-wished that Vader had taken him as an officer to serve on the *Executor's* bridge. But he knew such thoughts were foolish. Montferrat was caretaker of a vital legacy—a sacred trust. The *Devastator* had witnessed historic battles—it had served on the blockade at Hoth, and it had even once captured Princess Leia Organa. Who knows, maybe it would have another chance against her in the coming battle. The ship had been refitted dozens of times with the latest systems and weapons, keeping her more than competitive with the newer capital ships now operational. The *Devastator* thus remained one of the most prestigious commands in the fleet. Montferrat would have been the first to say that he was lucky to be where he was, but it was well known to all who served under him that the admiral firmly believed there was no such animal as luck. He looked up from his reverie to see an excited bridge officer gesturing at a tactical display.

"Admiral: the rebel fleet just emerged from hyperspace."

Shock was far too mild a word for what the Rebel fleet experienced as it realized the partially completed Death Star's shields were up. But even more alarming was the fact that they were effectively cut off by the largest flotilla of Star Destroyers ever assembled—a mass of ships stretching across the sky. They were trapped. Fox let out a low curse as his A-wing's com filled with the urgent voices of the other wing commanders asking for instructions. He took in the situation; the main rebel strike force led by General Lando Calrissian in the *Millennium Falcon* had broken off its attack on the battlestation and was slugging it out with swarms of TIE fighters dispatched from the Imperial fleet. Behind them, Star Destroyers were moving in for the kill. Fox's tactical display looked like a multi-layered spider web of electromagnetic interference. He wasn't surprised at all when he got orders cancelling the rearguard mission and reassigning his wing pronto.

"About time," said Moonsong.

"Stow that talk, Blade Three," snapped Stamm. Moonsong shut up as Fox spat out the new orders. There was no time to tell them the why of the situation. It wasn't their job to think—in fact, the less thinking they did at this point, the better. But on the off-chance that the rebel commandos who had landed on the moon somehow brought the shield down, the fleet was going to need to pivot quickly and vector onto the Death Star. They were going to have to make every second count. And they weren't going to have time to fight their way through still more Star Destroyers. One in particular was deploying just in front of the shield...

Fox recognized it as the *Devastator*. The ship that Vader had once commanded. The ship that had killed his family. He gritted his teeth and keyed his mike.

"Blade Leader to Blade Squadron. Follow me in on heading one-seven-zero-delta."

Blade Squadron broke apart, then reformed like a flock of birds streaking towards the huge ship in an arrowhead formation. But any hope Fox had for a quick strike against the massive ship disappeared as two dozen TIE Interceptors swept in from the ship's aft and came at them head to head. Fox watched them

rush in on the screens with a sinking feeling. He knew in his heart of hearts that most of his pilots had just barely grasped the techniques needed to make attack runs on a capital ship. And now they were going to have to dogfight for their lives with seasoned TIE fighters. Yet the situation here was the same as everywhere else in the fleet. They were surrounded. It was over. But it wasn't.

Fox cracked a smile. They might not be able to win, but at the least they would be able to give the Imperials a fight they would never forget.

"Blade Squadron... Start your attack run!"

It had all been leading up to this moment. Gina Moonsong could see that now; could see how all the paths and permutations of her life had led, inexorably, to this place: somewhere in space near Endor, an absolutely insignificant moon, which was now—thanks to the Empire's decision to build its battle station there—the most important place in the galaxy. All her time as a smuggler back on Coruscant, all her resolution to stay one step ahead of the law and never to get involved... well, it hadn't worked. She'd gotten involved and then some.

And now there was no turning back. Moonsong had seen her share of security and police cruisers—had either flown in, or run from, virtually every type of ship out there—but she'd never seen an actual Star Destroyer before. Sure, she'd watched a million holos, participated in endless training runs, studied schematics till her eyes glazed over.... but this was different. This was a monstrous slab of metal covered with guns and armor, crewed by enough men to fill a city... the kind of ship other craft never went near if they wanted to live to see another landfall. Every instinct in Moonsong was screaming at her to turn her B-wing around and flee—but somehow she controlled her nerves and held her course, accelerating in toward the *Devastator*. For the first time since she had joined the Rebellion she realized the true magnitude of her situation; the fun and games were over.

All that was left was to die bravely.

She pulled into formation behind Blade Leader, rotated her ship's wing thirty degrees around the gyro-stabilized cockpit in which she sat; Moonsong's wingman Blade Four executed the same maneuver as he brought up the rear. She didn't need to check her scanners to know Lieutenant Braylen Stramm and his wing man were matching her course and speed. All the fumbled training missions and mishaps were forgotten; the real thing was underway, and the squadron was rising to the moment, finally working together as a single seamless unit. The ships resembled some great avian flock as they fell into attack formation. On Moonsong's tactical display the *Devastator* was a huge spinning ball of electronic countermeasures punctuated by an outgoing hail of laser cannon fire. As the ships accelerated towards the behemoth, Moonsong could feel her craft's S-foils buckling as she struggled to keep on course while hits from the *Devastator*'s laser cannons drained her

deflector shield power and rocked the ship. Unfortunately there were few real options for getting close to a Star Destroyer, except to go straight at it. But at the moment, incoming fire was the least of Moonsong's worries; they were approaching far too fast for the ships' gunners to lock onto, and even then it would take several direct hits to knock out one of the B-wings. She was just starting to think they might make it all the way to the Star Destroyer itself when...

"Stay in formation people! Interceptors incoming!"

Wing Commander Fox's voice echoed through her headset as a squadron of TIE interceptors poured around the Star Destroyer and rushed in toward her. They must have been in a holding pattern immediately aft of the ship, but now they were deploying in earnest against the B-wing menace. On paper, the mismatch was considerable: B-wings were assault fighters that maneuvered like freighters, stuffed as they were with avionics packages usually reserved for the smaller capital ships. Pilots relied on the complex nav systems to enable them to score hits—but in a ship-to-ship dogfight, the B-wing was

"Every instinct in Moonsong was screaming at her to turn her B-wing around and flee."

at a considerable disadvantage even with the A-wings that were flying escort. All they could do was accelerate toward the target, hoping that at least some of them would get close enough to deliver their payloads. Moonsong watched as the TIE fighters broke formation and swept past them, executing seamless loops that put them on the squadron's tail, opening up a withering blast of fire all around the B-wings.

Admiral Montferrat could not believe the audacity of these rebel scum. Didn't they realize they were facing the Devastator? Vader's onetime flagship, the pride of Death Squadron... Montferrat prided himself on having the best trained crew in the entire Imperial Navy. Ever since he had taken command of her at the battle of Hoth, Montferrat had personally and ruthlessly combed the ranks, recruiting and promoting only those officers and ratings who had met his meticulous and exacting standards. And even though he found TIE fighter commander Gradd personally distasteful, there was no doubt that his skills as a fighter ace were almost on a

par with Darth Vader himself. Montferrat watched the engagement unfold on the *Devastator*'s giant tactical display. Several rebel ships had been destroyed already; the remainder were taking heavy fire from the TIE interceptors. At this point most sane pilots would have broken off their attack to deal with their pursuers, but the rebels waited until they were deep within the Devastator's flak envelope before executing their own high speed turns, insuring the ensuing dogfight would occur in uncomfortably close proximity to the monolithic ship. And the irrational human factor didn't stop there: Montferrat watched as a single B-wing fighter spiraled back, directly into the heart of Gradd's squadron. The pilot knew full well what he was doing: buying time for his comrades. One surprised TIE pilot died in a hail of laser fire from the B-wing's quad cannons before he even knew what had hit him. The rebel pilot then abruptly cut his speed, allowing two TIE interceptors to pass, which he then lacerated with pinpoint shots from his craft's ion cannons. He might have been able to score a fourth kill had Gradd not threaded the needle of fire and blown the B-wing to pieces. Montferrat rounded in fury on one of his gunnery officers who had continued to shoot into the dogfight, hitting one of the B-wings but just missing two of the TIE interceptors:

"Cease fire you fool, you'll hit our own pilots!"

The blood drained from the gunnery officer's face—he stopped firing as Montferrat turned back to the tactical display, absorbing the fleet positions of the larger battle raging all around.

"Helm, change course by seven degrees, keep us between the rebel attack force and the Death Star. We'll make sure none of their ships reach the station."

Commander Gradd couldn't help but grin as he zeroed in on another B-wing. Panicked, the rebel pilot attempted erratic evasive maneuvers. Gradd's smile intensified as he fell in behind him and blew out the starfighter's quad engine system with a single shot. He didn't even bother looking at the snub fighter disintegrate as he sped past. There was no question in Gradd's mind that rebel pilots were mostly inferior, if not just outright incompetent. He'd heard a lot of talk about the B-wing before this battle—how they posed an unprecedented danger to Star Destroyers if they could get enough maneuvering room to deploy their

weaponry. But Gradd had no intention of giving them that room. Not that it would matter anyway; regardless of B-wing specifics, Gradd had always placed far more faith in the man than the machine. Though he would have been the first to admit that maxim was double-edged; it chafed him to no end that the most famous pilot in the galaxy was a twenty something farmboy who had somehow managed to blow up the first Death Star. But sometimes luck was a fickle mistress. Unfortunately, Gradd's secret hopes of cutting Skywalker's legend down to size in

a glorious ship-to-ship encounter had been dashed when he heard that the Emperor himself had sent Darth Vader to bring the boy to him alive. Gradd would just have to make up for the lost opportunity by killing as many rebel pilots as he could. He could tell that whoever was running the rebel wing of pilots had some combat experience. That was going to make the kill all the more satisfying. He checked his scanner, searching for the fighter receiving the most com traffic; it was an old trick he used to find the enemy wing leader. The tactic didn't fail him: one of the escort

A-wings lit up and Gradd locked him into his targeting computer.

"Break, break, break!" Fox yelled into his comlink. Blade Squadron broke formation several thousand meters above the *Devastator*'s topside and went ship to ship, an angry swarm of TIE interceptors, A-wings and B-wings buzzing around the gigantic vessel. It only took a few seconds for things to go from bad to worse; Fox's long range scanners picked up a huge electromagnetic buildup around the new Death Star. Before he could even ponder

Before Fox could even ponder what the station was doing, a bright beam of green light leapt from its radial cannon and incinerated an entire rebel cruiser.

Fox's speed, staying on him despite Fox's weaving flight pattern. Fox gritted his teeth and leaned forward.

"Okay fella, you wanna play," he muttered. "Let's see how good you really are"—and promptly swerved hard, taking the ship through a dizzying set of maneuvers. But the interceptor matched them, moving ever closer, filling Fox's display with the ominous gray shadow of his foe. His sensors showed its forward lasers charging for the killing shot.

Gradd smiled as his targeting computer locked onto the A-wing. The board lit up green as Gradd unleashed a barrage of fire from the interceptor's laser cannons—at first cascading off the A-wing's heavy shielding, but quickly punching through. Parts of the rebel ship began to burn. Gradd was astonished at the amount of damage his quarry was taking while still remaining operational—and even now it took all of Gradd's concentration to keep up with the rebel pilot's evasive maneuvering. Back in the early days of the Rebellion, Gradd had once been impressed by these intuitive upstart fighter pilots, making up for skill with sheer audacity and will. Now he'd killed far too many of them to give any credit to their unorthodox piloting.

Which is why what happened next took him so completely by surprise.

At the last possible second Fox flipped his A-wing over, yanking back on the stick and executing a high G-force barrel roll under the attacking interceptor. The Imperial pilot gave up the advantage of pursuit so he could take a final shot, scoring a direct hit on the A-wing's drive systems, which much to the TIE interceptor's surprise, did

what the station was doing, a bright beam of green light leapt from its radial cannon and incinerated an entire rebel cruiser.

The station was operational.

Admiral Ackbar and General Calrissian's voices echoed over the fleetwide com, ordering the rebel fleet to engage the Imperial Star Destroyers. But Fox had more immediate problems at hand, with no less than three interceptors on his tail and two more coming for him over the bubble's horizon. They had identified him as the leader and were going to try to shut him down hard. Fox

dialed back his speed, spoiling the shots of the interceptors on his tail. One veered past him at high speed, forcing the ships on that vector to swerve off to avoid a collision. As the starfighter overshot, Fox's wingman Blade One managed to get off a bracket of fire, knocking one of the delta-shaped wings clean off, causing it to spin out of control and smash into another interceptor. But Blade One's triumph was short-lived as two of the interceptors caught him in a cross-fire, opening up so quickly that he probably never even knew what hit him. The remaining interceptor matched

not result in a killing shot. He most likely died wondering why that was as Fox came out of the roll behind him and blew him to pieces. But Fox had no time to savor his triumph; his vision flared red from all the emergency lights in his cockpit, and he became aware that he was choking back blood. He opened up the comm channel.

"Blade Leader to group; if you make it past the fighter screen, execute your primary mission. Over and out."

Stramm saw Blade Leader's ship spiral off from the attack, obviously fighting to maintain control—so much for Fox, he thought. There wasn't time to think about whether their leader would survive. It was just one more factor in the chaos of the battle as he attempted to mobilize an attack run amidst the dogfight. But the hysterical yelling in his headset wasn't helping.

"Too many TIE fighters! We've got to get out of here!"

"That's a negative Blade Four," said Stamm. "Keep the comms clear of chatter!" His attack computer told him Blade Three and Four were with him inside the Destroyer's defense envelope—and he knew the ships would be syncing their fire control systems, coordinating laser fire and proton munitions.

"I know you've got the attack data ready, right Blade Three?"

"I'm working as fast as I can!" said Moonsong. She was facing considerable distraction. Despite the death of their wing commander, the TIE interceptors were redoubling the fury of their attack; she could see their glittering lights as they maneuvered to get behind the rebel fighters. Then Stramm broke off from the attack formation and swung his craft around to face the fighters on their tail.

"Get that attack data; I'll hold them off."

Moonsong bit her lip. She couldn't worry about Stramm. He knew what he was doing, she hoped.

The system-wide tactical display was a web of blinking multicolored lights and indicators that stretched from Endor's high orbit all the way out to the titanic battle that raged between the two fleets and the new Death Star.

It was a fitting place for the Rebellion to end.

And yet—despite his satisfaction—Montferrat felt shame that his own part in this had been so less than perfect. He could only marvel at the level of incompetence Gradd had displayed. Not only had his arrogance gotten him killed, it had actually increased the previously miniscule threat the rebel fighters posed for the *Devastator*. But he wasn't worried—not yet, anyway.

"Fighter control, report."

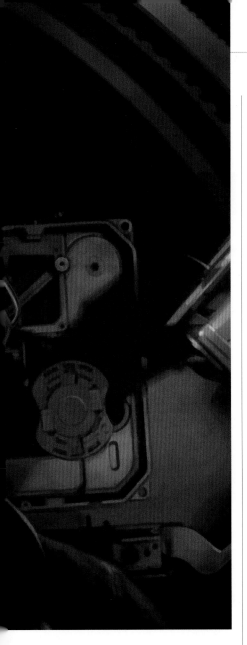

An ashen faced junior officer stepped forward. "The rebels are down to less than half a dozen ships, sir."

"And our fighter screen?"

"We've sustained major damage to our flight deck and can't launch or recover any more interceptors. Should I signal to another ship for fighter support?"

Montferrat gave the officer an icy stare. "Everyone else is a little busy. Set all weapon batteries for point blank range and fire at will."

Moonsong had a plan. It wasn't much of one, but it was the best her ship's computer could do given the timing. Her nav-systems lined up the angles, finding the pathway through the Devastator's electronic defense grid. She rapidly typed in the new attack vector and hit the transmit while simultaneously lining up the crosshairs projected onto her helmet's heads-up display. Her board went green, indicating that Blade Two and Four had received the data—but then it suddenly flashed back to yellow. Blade Four's targeting system must have been damaged and wouldn't lock on.

"Reset your targeting computer, Fanty!" Moonsong barked into her comm.

"No can do, the whole system's crashed. You go in without me." Moonsong's scanner's showed a TIE interceptor vectoring in to target Blade Four as he peeled out of formation. Moonsong cursed under her breath; there was nothing she could do—the pair of TIE interceptors on her tail would have their firing solutions in a matter of seconds. Moonsong fully expected the next shots to end her short career as a rebel pilot— but instead both interceptors blew up as Blade Two swept in behind them and took them out with clean precise shots that only an expert could have pulled off. The blasts they'd just unleashed ripped past Moonsong, missing her and striking the Star Destroyer, impacting harmlessly against its armor. Moonsong knew better than to waste time thanking Stramm; instead she locked flight paths with him. They both pulled back on their throttles, rotating their wings through a one-eighty and bringing their ion cannons to bear, unleashing their proton torpedoes and scoring direct hits on the weak points in the Devastator's navigational shielding. The ship's hyperdrive detonated, causing a chain reaction of explosions which blew back into the Star Destroyer's primary generators.

Montferrat pulled out his pistol and shot the panicking officer. So much for insubordination. As klaxons blared and warning lights flashed all around him, Montferrat made his way across the burning bridge to an engineering station and shoved the dead officer who had manned it out of the way so he could see why the drive section had stopped responding to his frantic queries for more power. The answer was as simple as it was definitive: an ion overload had destroyed the cooling manifolds and ruptured the hyperdrive's magnetic containment bubble, which meant that everybody down in the power plant was either dead or dying, and the ship was undergoing systematic demolition.

"Sir!" screamed a badly burned officer. "The Death Star's shield is down!"

Montferrat looked around at the dying screens. The whole moment seemed like a dream. How was this possible? How had the mightiest space force ever assembled been bested by a bunch of misfits, rejects, and malcontents? He took a last look around the bridge as he slowly pulled off his black gloves and laid them down on the shattered console. He could feel the floor plates shudder and for a moment he seemed to rise into the air as the craft's artificial gravity flickered out. He felt light as a feather, and for some unknown reason the sensation seemed right and proper.

As Moonsong and Stramm's B-wings accelerated to maximum speed, the Devastator burnt in their wake. Stramm opened up the comm-channel.

"Blade Two to Admiral Ackbar—the course is clear. Tell General Calrissian he's got nothing but empty space all the way to the Death Star."

"Acknowledged, Blade Two. Good work."

Stramm switched frequencies back to the squadron. "Blade Two to all surviving units, form up on me. This fight isn't over yet."

But all Moonsong could hear was the echo of static—static that had never made her feel more hollow.

"Blade Four here." Fanty's battered ship pulled into formation. "I think we're the only survivors."

"Not quite," said a voice.

Moonsong and Stamm looked up to see Fox's A-wing angling toward them. Even as they took that in, the Devastator started to explode behind it, lighting up the ships, a tiny daytime star in the skies over Endor. But Moonsong's elation quickly faded as her sensors told her Fox's ship was experiencing multiple critical systems failures.

"Eject Blade Leader," she said. "We'll recover your pod. Get out of there now."

But Fox's voice was resigned to the inevitable. "I already tried. The main interlocks are fused. They won't let me disengage."

"Hold course; I'll intercept and—"

"That's a negative Moonsong. Regroup and form up to assist the fleet. Nobody's called off the war on my account."

Moonsong hesitated. "You heard the man," said Stramm. Was his voice breaking? Moonsong couldn't tell. She steeled herself, locked course with Stramm and Fanty; the three B-wings veered off toward the rest of the rebel fleet. The fight was now raging all around the Death Star. The shield was down and rebel fighter wings were calling for help as they barreled in to attack the unfinished station. There were still a number of Star Destroyers trying to stem the seemingly endless tide of rebel interceptors. Moonsong watched as Fox's ship faded on her rear screens.

Ahead lay the Death Star. ☻

BLADE SQUADRON
ZERO HOUR

WRITTEN BY **DAVID J. WILLIAMS AND MARK S. WILLIAMS**
ART BY **CHRIS TREVAS**

The planet's vast wall of huge, swirling storm clouds looked like infinity itself: It filled the view, broken only by the patches of orange-gray terrain visible here and there beneath the roiling weather. Gina Moonsong accelerated her B-wing to attack speed as the rest of her squadron fell into formation behind her. She gritted her teeth and opened her comlink.

"All units, on my mark... three... two... one... mark."

The battle-computers of the B-wings synced; the next moment, over a dozen ion cannon beams converged at precisely the same coordinates on the planetary shield that protected Malastare. For a moment a portion of that shield flickered into the visible spectrum—and then splintered, disrupting just long enough for the squadron to pass through. Moonsong felt the chop as her ship passed through the compromised shield. All around, her pilots were struggling to maintain an ever-more precise heading as they vectored through the shield's weakest portion—a struggle that grew increasingly desperate as the atmosphere built and the gravity intensified. For one ship it was too much: Moonsong watched on her screens as the electromagnetic surge of the flickering shield caught the tail of Blade 7, whipping the ship back up against the deadly wall, fireballing the craft before Karls even knew

what hit him. Moonsong cursed under her breath even as she checked that Fanty was still in position on her wing, that Stramm and the rest of the Squadron were right behind. They had penetrated the planet's first line of defense but were continuing to struggle against the overwhelming force of the maelstrom.

And it was about to get a lot worse.

"Blade Five to Blade Three; I count at least a dozen TIE fighters inbound." The coolness in Cutter Poole's voice belied his complete lack of experience in battle.

"There sure are a lot of them..." Blade Six chimed in.

"Charge deflectors to full," said Moonsong. "Let's do what you were trained for."

Yet even as the deflectors went up, and her reflexes took over, she felt her mind going back to events after the destruction of the second Death Star. It was so recent and yet it seemed like such an eternity ago...

The ceremony on the flight deck was short and to the point. Some admiral (whom Moonsong had never heard of) droned on about duty, sacrifice and heroism before proceeding to award the B-wing pilots who had survived the Battle of Endor their Medals of Bravery. Moonsong couldn't help but think they should have given them to the pilots who didn't make

it. It made her promotion to lieutenant feel more than a little hollow. The only happiness Moonsong took in any of it was that Braylen Stramm had been promoted to wing commander. As the ceremony participants headed back to their duty stations, Moonsong made her way over to him. She gave him a lopsided smile and a jaunty salute, both of which he returned with less than the usual enthusiasm. In that moment, she knew everything—almost like they were playing out roles that had already been rehearsed.

"The medal looks good on you, Commander," he said.

She wasn't going to let him duck out of this. She looked around to see that nobody was in earshot—then moved closer.

"What's on your mind?" she asked.

"Nothing," he replied.

"We both know that's not true."

Stramm looked past her at the confetti dangling from the rafters.

"I'm not sure how to say it."

"I'll say it for you. You think your promotion means that we have to stop seeing each other."

"It does," he replied.

"That's a ton of bunk," she said evenly. "You're scared of how serious we've become."

"Of course I'm scared," he shot back. "Scared of having to choose between you and the rest of the squad."

"Sounds like you already have."

"Gina, I may have to order you to do something that might... well, if that day comes I don't want to doubt whether I'd give the order or if you would even follow it."

"I'd follow it. You know I would."

"That's my point," he said—and when she didn't reply: "I— look, we can figure things out between us when the war is over."

"The war *is* over," she said.

"It's not." He sat down on the edge of the stage, let his feet dangle—for just a moment, he looked like a helpless child. "I shouldn't be telling you this, but... the Imperials aren't beaten. What looked like just a rearguard action is turning out to be something more serious. All leave is getting canceled and Blade Squadron is getting a fresh batch of recruits. And I need you to train them. Okay?"

She smiled with a calmness that she knew he could see right through. "Okay," she said.

Stramm and his B-wings peeled off, deploying their ECM packages while Moonsong led the rest of the squadron straight down on the incoming TIE fighters. Blade Squadron's penetration of the planetary shield had woken everybody up planetside, but hopefully they were going to be focused on her and not Stramm. Fanty's voice echoed through the squadron's headsets.

"Stand by for Ground-Hogs...." Moonsong smiled grimly. Ground-Hogs was the nickname for the Imperial pilots who flew planetary atmospheric missions. Steering a TIE fighter through the mess of a planet's atmosphere was tougher than it looked, and the Ground-hogs made it look easy. Even with all the terrible weather, the B-wing's battle computers showed them in a tight formation and closing fast. Over the years the 'Hogs had developed skills and tactics that made them as dangerous as any type of combat pilot you could think of. And right now Moonsong wasn't thinking of anything else; she pushed the stick forward, diving down to intercept the incoming TIEs in what was arguably the most gut-wrenching part of Stramm's plan. Her battle computer indicated that Stramm's ships were vectoring straight in toward the target, unnoticed by the TIEs or the ground defense batteries. She and her pilots had the Imperials' undivided attention.

"Initiate maneuver orenth," she barked— and her B-wings initiated a steep loop that took them away from the TIE fighters, giving the impression that they were in full retreat. Sensing an easy victory, the TIE fighters closed in after them, following the B-wings all the way up to the edge of atmosphere beneath the shield.

Which was exactly what she wanted.

Moonsong knew it was too late— the TIE fighter was already dropping into Poole's blindspot, peppering him with laserfire.

"My name is Lieutenant Gina Moonsong."

She gazed at the new faces. Above them, up in the hangar's observation deck, she caught a glimpse of Stramm watching over the railing. Each of her cadets was untested. And she wouldn't have time to teach them much.

"The three of you have been assigned to my section." She glanced down at the datapad containing the personnel files. "So welcome to Blade Squadron." She paused.

What else was she supposed to say?

"Well, don't be shy," she said. "Sound off."

The tallest of them spoke up first. "Pilot Cadet Yori Dahn reporting."

Moonsong gazed at her appraisingly. "It says here you used to be first officer on a tramp freighter."

"Yes, Lieutenant."

"And what led you to join up?"

"The Imperials executed my crew."

"So you're here for revenge," said Moonsong.

lieutenant. If any of you joined up thinking you'll take a quick rumble through the war and be home before the next Founder's Day, I have some sad news for you. This thing isn't over by a long shot. I hope you're reading me."

"Yes, Lieutenant," they replied in unison.

"Welcome to Blade Squadron then. Now... this is my wingman, Fanty. He's going to get you all squared away. We start training exercises tomorrow at oh-six-hundred sharp." Moonsong motioned to Fanty, who stepped up and carried on.

"Okay you heard the El-Tee; let's go."

Moonsong looked back up at the observation deck, but Stramm was no longer there.

As the atmosphere frayed, so did the Ground-Hogs' advantage. Moonsong fired her afterthrusters; the B-wings broke formation, spun around and rocketed headfirst back towards their pursuers, causing them to scatter in surprise. Moonsong and Fanty dropped in behind a pair of TIE fighters, and unceremoniously shot them out of the sky. Suddenly B-wing pilots who had never engaged a foe before found themselves winning their very first fight. Poole and Dahn whooped as they engaged a disoriented TIE, making short work out of him. Poole's excited voice crackled over Moonsong's speakers.

"Just like shooting mouse droids in a barrel!"

"Blades Five and Six, look out!!" Even as she snarled the warning, Moonsong knew it was too late—a TIE fighter was already dropping into Poole's blindspot, peppering him with laser fire. The B-wing's cockpit belched a plume of smoke before turning away and plummeting down through the clouds. Moonsong veered sharply leftward, riddling the TIE fighter that had brought down Poole, sending it spinning down after him. But the payback brought no solace.

"Come in," said Stramm. She stepped inside his wardroom, but didn't close the door behind her.

"Here's the operation," he said without preamble. This routine was new to both of them, and they were making it up as they went along. He keyed up a map of a star sector and pointed at an insignificant cluster at the edge of it. "Commander Antilles scouted out the target: an Imperial communications hub on Malastare. I'm working up the program."

She studied the map. "Looks like the planet's shielded."

"I suppose so, Lieutenant."

"That's a terrible reason to fight."

"Is it? I thought that—"

"It's likely to get you killed. Find a better reason."

"Yes, Lieutenant."

Moonsong had already turned to the next cadet. "And who are you supposed to be?"

"Pilot Cadet Jordan Karls." He was a stout Togruta who wore a pelt-sash made from what Moonsong suspected was a particularly nasty predator. Karls looked like he had killed it himself with his bare hands.

"Your file says you saw action near Bespin. What makes you think you'll be a good B-wing pilot?"

"I'm highly adaptable, Lieutenant."

"What's that supposed to mean?"

"I've flown everything but X-wings."

"B-wings are a lot more temperamental than X-wings," said Moonsong. "Your file says you did okay in training. We'll see how that works in practice." She turned to the last cadet, but he spoke first:

"Pilot Cadet Cutter Poole, ma'am." Poole was young, square jawed, dark-haired and blue-eyed. He looked like an action hero right out of the latest holoplay.

"What are you smiling at?" she asked him.

"I'm just glad the war didn't end before I got here, sir. I mean, ma'am."

"Oh I see. A glory boy. We've got all kinds of uses for you. Just so you all know: I don't like being addressed as ma'am, skipper, sir, or boss. You all get to call me

"Thankfully the shield generator is right next to the primary target. We can hit both at the same time."

"How do we get in?"

"Well." Stramm looked uncomfortable. "Ackbar's techies think if we aggregate our ion cannons, we can create a temporary aperture."

"That sounds crazy."

"Do I look like I'm arguing?"

"And even if we..." She caught sight of a locale planetside, tapped it. "What's this?"

"That's Moff Pandion's vacation palace."

"Pandion... Didn't he used be the head of some slaver cartel?"

"Still is. He supplies a lot of the Empire's work camps. "

"And we're not planning on hitting him?" Moonsong struggled to keep her voice level.

"Let's stay focused, Lieutenant. If we hit the station and knock out the defenses we'll be able to get boots on the ground and secure the planet." He gave Moonsong a hard look. "That's what counts. We need to be disciplined and make sure we bring everyone back in one piece. Right?"

She shook her head. "Playing it safe isn't going to win us the war, sir. If Moff Pandion is there, we need to consider hitting the target."

"Well, that's part of the problem. We don't *know* if he is there or not, and I don't want to risk anybody's life going after him."

"We've risked our lives for a whole lot less."

"Gina—"

"And who do you think is doing the actual communicating? Hitting the hub might hurt Pandion—but killing him in his palace will put an end to any orders he might want to send out. Not to mention making it that much more likely that his troops will take *our* orders to surrender."

"Lieutenant, you have *your* orders. Are we clear?"

She hesitated for the tiniest of moments. For anyone who wasn't a fighter pilot, it wouldn't have even been discernible. For someone who was, it was unmistakable.

"Yessir," she said.

The communication array and the shield generator disappeared in a massive explosion that kicked thousands of kilograms

of orange-gray dust up into the air. Stramm's bombs had found their marks. The ground forces would have a much easier task now.

"Blade Leader to Blade Squadron; we have knocked out the targets and are heading to the rendezvous point." Moonsong watched on the screen as Stramm vectored skyward as she dispatched the last TIE fighter. She keyed the mic:

"Fanty. Get Yori to the rendezvous."

"I'm not leaving you, Lieutenant. What are we doing?"

Moonsong hesitated. *What the hell*, she thought. "Drop to one-zero-zero meters and target that power signature at oh-seven-five northwest."

"That's the Moff's palace."

"Exactly. We're going to hit it."

"We just got the order to bug out, Lieutenant. Besides, we—"

"Won't have enough fuel to make orbit? I just did the calculations. We can make it, but it's going to be close."

"Let's do it," said Yori, speaking up for the first time. "I'm having a blast."

Fanty laughed mirthlessly. "This is not a good idea."

"You don't have to come with me," replied Moonsong.

"That's where I disagree."

The three ships plunged in toward the ground, the few remaining TIE fighters left far in their wake. Most of the ground fire was still focused on the fleeing Stramm; it took the turbolasers a while to pick up on Moonsong, but when they did they started to make up for lost time with a vengeance. Moonsong watched as orange-gray spread out on all sides and streaks of fire rose toward her.

"Picking up some pretty hairy flak, boss," said Fanty.

"We'll go down to the deck and use proton torpedoes. When we get inside the perimeter, pull up and run like hell."

"Blade Three, what are you doing?" Stramm's voice echoed in her headset. "Get back in formation!!"

"Can't read you," said Moonsong. "Picking up a lot of static—"

"Dammit you can hear me just fine! I told you to stay on—" His voice cut out as Moonsong cut the communication channel. Stramm would have to wait until they rejoined the squadron to yell at her. The three B-wings swooped down until they were less than fifty or so meters above the ground. Moonsong's battle computer sounded a variety of alarms as they drifted into a sea of anti-aircraft fire. All she could do was hope against hope that the B-wing's powerful ECM bubble and high speed approach would prove too much for the Imperial targeting computers on the ground to handle.

"Stay in formation," she said. "We're only going to get one pass." The B-wings roared into the grass-covered valley that contained the sprawling estate. The barrage of torpedoes turned the various buildings into pillars of flame, which then collapsed in on themselves. In moments, the whole valley was a roaring inferno. Moonsong didn't know if the Moff was there or not, but she knew that if nothing else, he wouldn't be hosting any more lavish dinner parties. It might not have been much, but for now it was enough. She pulled back on the stick and led what was left of her squadron up, racing into thick clouds. The ship shook so hard it felt like it was about to come apart. The clouds got thicker and thicker. Her instruments went dark. She kept on accelerating upward. If she made it back, she could only imagine what kind of reception she was going to get from Stramm.

Truth was, she couldn't wait. ☙

BLADE SQUADRON
KUAT

WRITTEN BY **DAVID J. WILLIAMS AND MARK S. WILLIAMS**
ART BY **CHRIS TREVAS**

reen lights flashed up from Lieutenant Gina Moonsong's battle computer as she watched the Kuat Drive Yards' defenses go on alert. The yards consisted of a massive ring of steel that encircled the planet Kuat like a giant metal serpent. The dry docks, warehouse, machine shops, and immense orbital habitats made the station the premier facility for producing some of the Empire's most fearsome weapons, among them the *Imperial*-class Star Destroyer, the AT-AT, and new tech-monstrosities rumored to be in the prototype phase. The New Republic had decided it was time to deal with the Empire's main supplier of arms, and had committed itself to an assault that rivaled the attack at Endor. Hundreds of laser batteries lit up as the yard's defenses opened fire on the approaching New Republic fleet.

Moonsong eased back on the B-wing's throttle and checked the squadron formation. To her rear, Mon Cala cruisers and other capital ships stood ready with their massive torpedo batteries, while the X-wings in the vanguard locked their S-foils in attack position. To her right and left, dozens of other snub fighter squadrons were taking up their positions as well. Ahead, a fleet of Star Destroyers and their complement of TIE fighters moved out of the planet's high orbit behind the ring and accelerated to engage. Three assaults so far and the Imperials were still using the same tactics. The problem was they were

effective. The sheer number of forces they had committed to the yards represented a major investment. The Imperials wanted to keep this facility at nearly any cost and had dispatched more of their deep space assets than the New Republic had anticipated. They were only a few days into the campaign and it was clear to everybody that this battle would be neither short nor easy.

"Look who's come out to play."

"I see them, Fanty. Lieutenant Li, we're going for the SD's in Quadrant Four. Close up formation and wait for the word."

"Copy, Blade Leader." Lieutenant Sandara Li commanded the new X-wing escort section that had been added to Blade Squadron. So far Moonsong's relationship with Li had been less than warm. Moonsong figured Li would have preferred to fly with Stramm—but Stramm was back on the carrier *Amalthea* helping the commodore coordinate the overall fleet action.

Explosions off to the right drew Moonsong's attention as the New Republic's first wave clashed with Imperial forces. Dozens of New Republic and Imperial fighter squadrons spun about in the solar winds, lighting up the darkness while capital ships launched wave after wave of proton torpedoes at each other. Yori Dahn's taut voice crackled through Moonsong's headset:

"I got one on my tail! I can't shake him."

Moonsong rolled her B-wing and dove at full speed on an intercept course. Just as the TIE fighter lined up for the kill, Moonsong's lasers cut it in two.

"Thanks boss," said Dahn.

"Don't thank me too quick," shot back Moonsong—even as flames streaked up and down a nearby Star Destroyer; the next moment it exploded, flinging debris in all directions. A piece of wayward metal smashed a B-wing in half just as its X-wing escort disintegrated from enemy fire. As Moonsong tried to issue a course correction to her people, a message from the commodore rang through every pilot's comm-set:

"Central command to all fighter squadrons: this is a recall order. I repeat, all squadrons return."

"What the hell's going on?" Li blurted out over the comm.

"You heard the order, Lieutenant. I'm sure command has a good reason for it. Now let's get back to the barn." Moonsong swung her ship around as she wondered just what that reason could be.

raylen Stramm stood next to Captain Tane by the holoprojector. Moonsong couldn't help but think Stramm looked odd in the khaki and powder-blue uniform instead of his flight suit. Odd, but handsome nonetheless. Even more odd was that Moonsong was the new acting squadron leader. When command temporarily transferred Stramm to Combat Operations Planning, she figured they would have tapped one of the other squadron commanders to take over.

So now Moonsong, Fanty, Li, and Li's wingmate—Johan Volk —sat with the other

squadron leaders from the Mon Cala cruiser *Amalthea*'s fighter group. Stramm stepped forward and let his baritone fill the room.

"All right, people, we've been analyzing the enemy, and it's become clear that we need to change our tactics. We simply do not have the firepower to overwhelm the target's defense fleet with a single strike. Therefore we have decided to focus on strategic bombing of key parts of the yard's infrastructure. Fuel dumps, supply monorails, and sensor arrays will be the primary targets, going forward. This means our timetable will change, but all our simulations validate the new strategy." Li raised her hand, and Stramm acknowledged her with a nod of his head; Li stood up to her full height and tossed her long black hair out of her eyes. Moonsong couldn't help but notice that every eye in the room locked on Li's imposing figure. Heck, the lady looked like one of those tough heroines from a Coruscant holodrama.

"Commander, does this mean that the X-wing elements will now be equipped with proton torpedoes so we can participate in the bombing?"

"That's a negative. So far the addition of X-wing elements to the B-wing bomber group has been successful in the escort capacity, but our B-wings will still rely on you X-wing pilots to keep the TIE fighters off their backs."

Li's wingmate Volk stood up next. He was a huge bald man with a tremendous beard and a bigger smile. Scuttlebutt was that he and his wife Vira were legendary guerilla fighters on the backwater world they came from.

"Excuse me, sir, but who is going to keep those Star Destroyers off us?" Captain Tane waved at the holo display of the yards, and zeroed in on a cluster of Star Destroyers.

"Elements of the fleet will engage the enemy, here, here, and here... forcing them to commit the bulk of their destroyers and support ships against us, thus allowing you pilots to make your strikes. We'll take some damage...that's for sure—but if you pilots are able to cripple their supply depots and command centers it will be worth it." Then, as if sensing the general tension in the air: "Look, we know we've asked a lot of you; and frankly we'll be asking for more. This fight is critical—if we lose, the stability of the New Republic will be threatened." Tane stepped back and allowed Stramm to wrap things up.

"Squadron leaders will receive their new mission packages and will be responsible for making that data available to their pilots. If there are no more questions... Ok, then. Good luck out there and good hunting. Dismissed!"

Moonsong tried to focus past the chaos around her as the squadron rocketed towards the supply monorail. In theory, if they destroyed enough of the yard's capability to move supplies and ammunition, certain areas would become far more vulnerable. A shrill scream filled her headset as Blade Nine's ship indicator disappeared from Moonsong's heads-up display.

"They got—"

"I know, Fanty!" Yori Dahn's B-wing pulled up next to her. Her voice broke as it came over the channel.

"Lieutenant, are you seeing what I'm seeing?"

On top of the ring in front of the monorail stood a cluster of AT-ATs and AT-ACTs, an older Clone Wars–era AT-TE or two... along with several unfinished AT-ATs that looked like giant skeletal troop transports with just the heads and powerful cannons functioning. The Imperial walkers spat searing plasma up at them. Li's voice rang out.

"X-wings, we're attacking those walkers!"

"Stay in formation," said Moonsong. "We need you to deal with those TIE fighters."

"This will only take a minute and there's no way you'll get to the target if we don't clear them! Save your bombs for the target. Let's go!"

"I'm with you, boss," Volk said with no hesitation.

"*Hold your formation*," snapped Moonsong. But it was too late; the X-wings were already peeling off and diving for the goliaths. For a moment Moonsong actually thought they might pull it off… until several cargo freight elevators rose up, carrying more partially completed AT-ATs and armored Star Destroyer laser turrets. Moonsong saw two X-wings take fire. One blossomed into a radiant fireball, while the other spun out of control and impacted against the side of the shipyard. Even more alarming was the fact that the X-wing lasers weren't powerful enough to penetrate the walkers' heavy armor in a single shot. Moonsong knew that if they didn't concentrate their fire on the makeshift gun emplacements, the chance of any of her group getting out alive would be exactly zero—and the only way to knock off those walkers was with the torpedoes earmarked for the monorail.

And that meant the monorail would just have to wait.

"Blade Squadron, follow me, and concentrate ion cannon fire on those emplacements." The group of snubfighters wove an impressive pattern as they changed their trajectories, increased their speeds, and zeroed in on the enemy. "Use your torpedoes on those walkers!"

"But what about the primary target?" Dahn asked.

"This *is* the primary target now, so open up!" The B-wings leveled out in front of the walkers and unleashed a rain of deadly fire on the behemoths below. Moonsong's B-wing swooped in over the main ring of the yard as the AT-ATs loomed ahead. While the armored beasts' weapons could punch though most snubfighters, they were not as effective at tracking them at high speeds. Moonsong lined up her shot and let loose a pair of torpedoes that annihilated an AT-AT crew compartment and sent the walker toppling over onto a half-built scout model. Unfortunately the pilot behind her was hit by an attacking TIE, and clipped the walking tank as he went down—sending his own craft spiraling out of control and crashing into another walker's legs. The explosion knocked the massive vehicle right off the ring and down towards the planet below. Everywhere the armored giants were getting turned into piles of spare parts. Pieces of shattered walkers floated away into space. The ring itself cracked in multiple places from the barrage of torpedoes the B-wings fired as they shot past. Moonsong cursed under her breath—what a waste. What a diversion.

"OK, people, let's get out of here. The target isn't going anywhere."

Li climbed down out of her battered X-wing and found herself face to face with a furious Moonsong. The mechanics and hangar crew gave them a wide berth while the other pilots remained at a respectable distance… but close enough to be within earshot of the fireworks.

"What in the blazes did you think you were doing out there?"

"I was doing my job," Li responded evenly.

"Your job was to protect us from TIE fighters, not engage the bombing targets. I lost a good pilot. The only reason you aren't dead too is because I scrubbed the main mission to pull your fat out of the fire. That was reckless—"

"Oh, that's rich coming from you, Gina. You think I haven't heard about you?"

"Heard about me?"

"Word travels. You think I don't know the only reason you got named acting squadron leader was because your boyfriend handed you the command?"

"You're out of line, Lieutenant." Li

Moonsong fought fatigue as her targeting computer screamed out the coordinates for the command hub.

snapped to attention and clicked her heels together. Moonsong stepped back, rubbed her eyes, and let out a long sigh.

"You know what your problem is, Lieutenant? "

"No, ma'am, I do not. Perhaps the acting squadron leader will enlighten me."

Moonsong cracked a smile and lowered her voice. "First of all I got this command in spite of Stramm's recommendations. Truth be told he wasn't sure I was up to it, but they needed him planning ops and somebody had to step up. I stepped up. But the *real* issue here is the fact that you're just like me, only a few months back. See, it took me too long to realize that the only way any of us make it out of this war alive is if we work together. You're a damn fine pilot, Li, maybe even as good as me, and with a little discipline you could be one of the best. And I'm not just saying that. You spotted those emplacements; you just lacked the experience to know that your armament wouldn't scratch them. So yeah, you just might be that good, and yeah, maybe I feel a little threatened by you, but

I'll tell you what: if anybody can find a way to smash these imp pigs out of the sky, it's you and me. What do you say?"

Moonsong pulled off her flight glove and stuck out her hand. Li looked down at it in amazement. And then she shook it.

The chaos and intensity of the campaign blurred days into weeks until the New Republic fleet and its pilots were stretched beyond thin. Moonsong fought fatigue as her targeting computer screamed out the coordinates for the command hub. Moonsong had to hand it to Stramm; he and his little band of rear-echelon planners had discovered the hub by studying the combat footage brought back by a dozen fighter squadrons. At this very moment the fleet was engaged in a spectacular battle against the Imperial's main defense force and had baited them into a close-quartered slugfest over the planet's northern pole. The maneuver should have allowed a trio of B-wing squadrons to strike the command hub virtually unnoticed. Unfortunately, the Imperials managed to scramble a makeshift group of TIEs that outnumbered the B-wings three to one.

"Have your ships hold their positions and cover us."

Moonsong balked at that. "That's too dangerous, I can't—"

"Hey, it's not like we haven't had people shooting at us from the front and back before. At least this way we can follow your shots in and confuse their sensors. If you've got a better plan, I'd love to hear it."

"You want a better plan?" asked Moonsong. "Okay. All B-wings cut power and hold positions. Set laser cannons to rapid fire and target your Ion cannons past the target. We'll wait for you to start our bombing run, Lieutenant Li."

"That sounds worth a shot…"

As the B-wings let loose their devastating barrage against the TIEs, Li threaded her X-wings through the friendly fire and into the heart of the enemy formation. Moonsong couldn't help but smile as she watched a pathway clear on her targeting computer. Her smile grew wider as she spotted an even better way to nail the command hub.

"OK, boys and girls; follow me in on the following trajectory. Let's go." The B-wings formed up on Moonsong and sped toward the ring, where they all saw the huge hangar open, its energy blast shields still down. The B-wings entered the hangar; as they flew under the command hub section, they targeted their laser-guided bombs and torpedoes deep into its heart.

Moonsong's craft glided above the flight deck, firing on enemy craft that had not been quick enough to launch. As the squadron exited the hangar on the other side of the ring Moonsong heard Fanty and Dahn scream in triumph as the hub erupted behind them. She grinned and keyed her comlink.

"Way to go people! Now that's how you do it!"

Moonsong checked her watch; she had less than an hour before the squadron launched on another strike mission. She'd lost track of how many mission hours she'd flown. For Blade Squadron, it seemed like every time they kicked over a rock, more Imperials would scurry out from under it. Her people, like everybody else, were tired and stretched thin. As she made her way through the hangar she passed Volk's badly mauled X-wing. Volk had managed to pilot the ship back, and he was now in the infirmary, though his bird would never fly again. But it was the ship next to his that contained the real surprise.

"Braylen—I mean Commander Stramm; what are you—" She trailed off as Stramm climbed down from the X-wing cockpit and faced Gina with an awkward smile.

"We're short on X-wing pilots and we need every fighter out there for the strike," he said simply.

"I didn't know you could fly an X-wing."

As Stramm's smile broadened, it seemed to lose its awkwardness. "I may not be as good a pilot as you, but there's not a snubfighter built that I can't fly. Besides, things were getting a bit boring up on the bridge."

I've missed you, she wanted to say. But when she opened her mouth, all she heard herself saying was just:

"Well... Your squadron is ready."

"You mean *your* squadron," he replied without missing a beat. "You're still the boss. Technically I'm still with planning ops. Since Volk is in the infirmary, I'll be slotted in as Lieutenant Li's wingman."

"Seriously?" she said.

There was a long pause.

"So let me get this straight," she said. "You broke up with me because you didn't want to have to order me into battle, or put me at risk. And now you're asking me to do the same to you?"

"Do we have to have this conversation now?"

"Yes."

"Okay." Stramm hesitated. "It's really pretty simple. I trust your judgement more than I trust mine."

"This is our last mission together," she said.

"You sure about that?"

"I'm not sure about anything," she said. "Not anymore." She turned and walked away.

"Hey Gina," he called after her. "Good luck out there."

"Luck's the least of my problems," she replied.

"Bandits coming in, lieutenant." Stramm's voice was strained, and with good reason. It seemed like he and Moonsong had spent the last day or so in constant combat. Her torpedo launchers were empty, and her B-wing's maneuver drive redlined every time she engaged the thrusters.

The X-wings and their pilots were just as battered and just as exhausted. But somehow the squadron was holding it together.

"We've got them," Moonsong answered. "Lock your S-foils in attack position and hold your fire until they get close." Common sense told her she should turn her bird around, re-arm, maybe even grab twenty winks on the flight deck…but this wasn't a time for common sense. It was time to push all the way to the end.

The two battered opposing fleets dispensed with fancy maneuvering and barreled straight at one another. Both commanders knew that all the tricks and clever stratagems were over. Both sides had lost too many ships and pilots, and all that was left to decide was how many of the shipyards would be intact after the final clash of arms. A cloud of TIE fighters, TIE bombers, TIE interceptors, and heavily armed shuttles spread out from the Drive Yards in a last ditch attempt to break the New Republic's cruiser flotilla. The formation was met in kind with every fighter the New Republic fleet could throw back at them.

Li and Stramm's X-wings shot out in front of the formation and engaged in a deadly dance with TIE fighter after TIE fighter. Gina had to admit that they were a very effective team.

"Stick close Fanty; let's earn our pay."

"Roger that, boss."

Moonsong led her pilots through a hail of laser fire towards a damaged Imperial light carrier. She relayed an attack pattern to the rest of her pilots; and like a well-oiled machine, they slotted past the TIE fighters and unleashed their devastating payload into the carrier's open hangar. The carrier exploded, debris and flame shot in all directions.

"Good work people! Let's regroup, and let's find a new target."

Even as she spoke those words, Moonsong was scanning: she saw that the New Republic fleet was taking quite a beating. Her carrier, the *Amalthea*, was limping away trailing drive plasma. That did not look good at all. If they were caught out here beyond carrier-range, they were either going to get picked off by Imps or run out of fuel… or both.

But then the situation abruptly changed.

As one, the Imperial forces broke off and scattered in numerous directions. Those vessels too damaged to flee transmitted code designating the signal for their surrender.

"My god… They're surrendering…"

"We did it!" Gina leaned back in her acceleration chair and closed her eyes. Pure relief flooded her body as the whoops and yells of her pilots filled her comm-set. Finally the commodore's voice came over the fleet-wide channel:

"All New Republic forces, I have just accepted the surrender of the Kuat Drive Yards from Moff Maksim. I repeat: we have accepted their surrender." Gina gazed out the cockpit window at the splintered yet still-mighty ring. Fires raged across it, surrounded by the debris of hundreds of fighters and starships. Against the lights of the fires and explosions, that debris looked like a gigantic asteroid field. It was so beautiful that it was easy to forget it was nothing but tombs for fighters on both sides. Moonsong took a deep breath.

"Okay… Let's go home."

She turned, and her squadron swung into formation behind her. ☻

BLADE SQUADRON
JAKKU

WRITTEN BY **DAVID J. WILLIAMS AND MARK S. WILLIAMS**
ART BY **CHRIS TREVAS**

*A*s the battle rages over the backwater desert world of Jakku, the vaunted Blade Squadron flies its B-wing starfighters against a decimated Imperial war machine. Having played a crucial role in the Battle of Endor by destroying the Imperial I-class Star Destroyer Devastator, the fearless pilots engage in another heated confrontation in the ongoing Galactic Civil War....

*A*ll available ships, concentrate your fire on the engines of the *Ravager*. Repeat, concentrate on the engines—"

Admiral Ackbar's words were still ringing in Gina Moonsong's ears as she keyed her comm.

"OK Blade Squadron, you heard the man." Moonsong tightened up her squadron's formation as the B-wings swooped in to attack the Super Star Destroyer *Ravager*, flanked on either side by their X-wing escort. She found herself keeping a particularly close eye on the X-wing piloted by Braylen Stramm. Given how much Kuat had depleted their pilots, he'd remained with the squadron; they needed every able-bodied pilot on deck. Officially, their relationship was strictly professional. In reality, though, it was more complicated than ever.

Fanty's voice cut through her reverie: "Fifteen seconds out."

"No TIE fighters, just capital ships." Lieutenant Sandara Li's contralto echoed

over the squadron's frequency; she and her wingman Johan Volk rolled in to cover Moonsong's approach. Gina smiled grimly as the *Ravager*'s aft filled her cockpit window. To her surprise, there was almost no return fire—the vast ship was beset from too many directions to worry about a small squadron. And there seemed to be some kind of issue with its drive-system... the craft was shifting course at an unpredictable angle. But that wasn't Moonsong's problem.

Her problem was finding a way to make it even worse.

"Stand by to fire ion cannons. Transmitting targets in three... two... one. Weapons free! I repeat, weapons free!" The B-wings of Blade Squadron unleashed a withering barrage of fire, scoring multiple hits on the drive systems. Moonsong hung back, allowing her pilots to take their shots and peel away. It wasn't until after Stramm and her wingman Fanty cleared the area that Moonsong started her own attack run. There was an undeniable pleasure in delivering the coup de grâce, and as the squadron commander Gina reveled in it. Moonsong reduced her speed, lined up the engines and let loose with everything her B-wing had. She was rewarded with orange blossoms of fire and molten debris as the Super Star Destroyer pitched and heaved. Gina's readouts were going haywire; there was massive EMP interference, and what little she could decipher made no sense: had someone unleashed a *tractor beam* on the enormous ship? What was going on?

She swerved away but there was nowhere to swerve; all of a sudden, the *Ravager* was losing traction and plunging toward the planet Jakku below. Leaving Gina right between the two.

She heard Ackbar's voice echoing on override across all channels:

"Soldiers and pilots of the New Republic! The dreadnought Ravager is down—it falls to Jakku! Beware debris and take cover!"

—and then the admiral's voice was cut off by a sudden explosion that sounded like it was right next to Moonsong's head. She wasn't sure if she had taken a direct hit from a laser, or if a piece of debris had smashed into her B-wing—but whatever clobbered her had collapsed her shields, and knocked out her maneuver drive. She was drifting dead-stick right into the debris field of the crashing Super Star Destroyer. She managed to bring up the auxiliary power, but the readouts told her she was past the point of being able to punch out. She was already in the grip of Jakku's gravity; all she could do was try to redirect her B-wing to bring the craft in line behind the dying *Ravager* in a desperate attempt to use the giant craft as a heat shield for re-entry. All her sensors were now in the red; alarms were warbling right next to her head, and she smelled acrid smoke. But through those alarms she heard a voice:

"Gina! Gina can you hear me?"

She could, but as the comm died, it became clear Stramm couldn't hear her. She wanted to tell him she was sorry, that

they should have ditched this whole war and made for some world where no one had ever drawn weapons... but now it was too late. The G-forces were hauling her down toward blackout; the prospect loomed before her almost inviting, like some kind of ultimate solace. But she fought for consciousness—and then stopped fighting gravity; instead, she vectored down and past the *Ravager*. They were well beneath the heat of re-entry now; all she had to worry about was surviving the crash—not to mention crashing in a place that didn't promptly get smashed by millions of tons of falling metal. She made some guesses on the fly, used the little power her ship had left to accelerate well past its safety limits, the craft shaking like a leaf in the winds of atmosphere. A vast ceiling of falling metal loomed above. Desert stretched below. With her last breath of consciousness, she engaged the auto-landing sequence...

I t was a steady sound; like a drumbeat, or somebody tapping the inside of her skull. As her eyes opened, Moonsong realized that there was some strange looking bird pecking at the glass of her cockpit. She unstrapped herself and activated the emergency explosive that blew the canopy clear. The bird took off just in time and flew away with an annoyed squawk. Moonsong unstrapped herself, pulled herself free of the wreckage and stepped out into a wilderness of sand. She didn't know much about Jakku, nor had she ever planned on finding out. The place looked like a wasteland. It was a hell of a place to make a last stand. Especially since half the sky was on fire. Miles away, the huge wreck of the *Ravager* sat like a volcano, spitting plasma-charged steel and smoke into

Moonsong didn't know much about Jakku, nor had she ever planned to find out... it was a hell of a place to make a last stand.

the air, while the sand all around had been blackened by its impact. Looking back at her wrecked B-wing, Moonsong realized it was a miracle she was alive, but she seriously doubted that was going to remain the case for long. She pulled off her helmet and thermal gloves before disconnecting the controls for the suit's systems. She felt more than a little conspicuous in her red flight suit. She quickly discovered that the B-wing's survival kit was destroyed and if you didn't count the signal flares she carried—which she didn't—then she had absolutely no weapons.

Of course, things could always get worse: the distinctive whine of TIE fighter engines high above brought her to her feet and running. She ran up the side of a dune and dived for cover behind a cluster of rocks as the TIE fighters swooped in, firing wildly and quickly turning what was left of her B-wing into a molten heap of burning scrap. So much for honor among pilots; it seemed that neither the New Republic nor the Empire would be taking prisoners this time. She watched her beloved ship burn and took a deep

breath. No comm, water, survival supplies, homing beacon. But heading in the opposite direction of the gigantic funeral pyre of the downed Super Star Destroyer seemed like a good start. She folded her lucky flight gloves into her suit and started walking...

M oonsong was burning with thirst. She estimated she had trudged a good ten kilometers or so from the crash but still had no point of reference to tell her where she was. Darkness was falling fast and she was more than a little concerned about sleeping out in the open. She scurried up the side of a particularly high sand dune and peered down into the valley below—to find herself looking down at the shattered remnants of an Imperial stormtrooper camp.

this though..." Temmin dug deep into a flight suit pocket and pulled out a pair of nutritional supplements. Each bar could sustain a human for up to three days. The downside was the terrible taste. Though at this point Moonsong wasn't complaining.

"Well, at least we won't starve. We've got to link up with the ground forces if we're ever going to get off this rock."

"Yes si—I mean yes, ma'am—"

"Call me Gina. It's easier."

Moonsong took the first watch while the kid slept. Though that was really just a way to make sure he got some rest, because as soon as he woke, Moonsong skipped her watch and got them on the move instead. She figured they could make some real distance before the sun came back up. The kid seemed sullen and stayed quiet. Moonsong figured a little talking might ease the time and lower the panic factor. Too bad she was terrible at making small talk.

"So, um... what happened to the rest of your squadron, kid?"

"They're still up there fighting. But... some of them are dead now. They were my friends."

"I've lost good friends too," she said. She touched his hand gently. That was when she got a glimpse of his face in the starlight. "But they're not the only ones on your own mind..." It wasn't a question, just a statement. But still he hesitated...

"No... I mean, yes. I mean, I hope my mom's okay. She's a pilot too."

"No kidding," Gina paused. "Are you Norra Wexley's kid?"

"She was at the Battle of Endor," said Temmin with something close to awe.

"So was I, actually."

"Yeah, but did you fly a Y-wing into the Death Star and out the other side?"

"That'd be a negative."

"Well, she did!"

"That means she's a survivor," said Gina with a confidence she didn't feel. "Which means you'll see her again. I've got friends I want to see again too..." Moonsong's voice faltered as she thought about Stramm. She decided there and then that if she ever saw his face again she would tell him everything and see where the cards fell.

"Do you hear that?" Temmin asked.

"Hear wh—" But before either of them could react half a dozen figures popped out from behind a rock with weapons drawn. One of them called out the challenge.

"Thunder!" Moonsong let out a sigh of relief—they were friendly.

"Lightning!" Weapons lowered as the New Republic soldiers closed around them. One of them noted Moonsong's rank and gave a perfunctory salute.

Moonsong ran down to the scene of carnage, and carefully sifted through the remains of the dead troopers. Whatever had done this had made fast and terrible work of the squad. But Moonsong was intent on turning their bad luck into her good fortune and went to work scavenging through what was left of their equipment. She found a canteen of water—she didn't care it had belonged to a dead guy, he wouldn't be needing it. As she drank, she unclipped an E-11 blaster and a utility harness, then strapped on the utility belt, and unfolded the weapon's stock for maximum stability. She flipped the select fire switch with a degree of satisfaction. Maybe things were looking up.

And then she heard something behind her.

Moonsong spun around to find herself face to face with a boy in a torn flight suit.

"Don't shoot!" he said. And then, the challenge code: "Thunder!" He looked scared as hell. Moonsong slowly lowered the weapon but kept her finger on the trigger.

"Lightning. Who are you, kid?"

He gave her a crisp salute. "Temmin... Temmin Wexley, Phantom Squadron." He didn't look old enough to shave, let alone fly an X-wing, Moonsong allowed herself the ghost of a smile.

"Well, Temmin Wexley: I'm Lieutenant Gina Moonsong, Blade Squadron. Is your comlink still working?"

"Uh... no."

"Got a blaster?"

"Sure." Temmin pulled his DH-17 and checked the charge. "I've only got one spare power pack though."

"What about provisions?"

"Most of my kit was destroyed. I got

"Lieutenant, I'm Sergeant Agarne, Third Recon Group."

"You're a sight for sore eyes."

"We don't have much time. Group command is over there. He'll explain everything."

"Roger that. Lead the way." The group double-timed it over a few dunes to a rocky area where a squad of soldiers were digging in.

"Downed pilots to see the group commander," said the sergeant.

"Thank you, Sarge," said a voice from down in the trench. "Do me a favor and double check our lines of fire again." Agarne gave a curt nod and headed off to check the other soldiers. The group commander climbed out of the trench and faced the two newcomers. Blue eyes shone from within a scarred face.

"I'm Major Ranz," he said.

Moonsong saluted. "Lieutenant Gina Moonsong, commander Blade Squadron. This is pilot Temmin Wexley. If you don't mind us using one of your comlinks we'll get out of your hair and leave you to do your job, Major."

But Ranz shook his head. "Sorry Lieutenant, we're under orders to maintain radio silence until we make contact with our target—and even if I could give you a comm there's so much EMP interference, you'd need a full blown command-and-control sat-uplink to get through all the chaff."

Moonsong shrugged, burying her disappointment. This was war, nothing went as planned. "What is your target?"

Ranz gestured at the scrublands up ahead. "In about 30 minutes, an Imperial supply convoy is going to roll right through that pass. If they're able to reinforce Golga Station, they might be able to mount a counterattack that could make this battle drag on regardless of what happens upstairs."

"A supply convoy." Wexley looked around at the rebel troops. Some of them were wounded. All looked tired. "That sounds like it would be well protected."

"It will be. I expect at least one re-enforced company of stormtroopers to be traveling with it."

"Where are the rest of your men?"

"You're looking at them. Yesterday we had a full company."

"You don't honestly think you're going to be able to take out a heavily armored Imperial supply convoy with a dozen men do you? That's suicide."

Ranz laughed mirthlessly. "Didn't they say that about taking down the Death Star? Look, we have our orders. You're

welcome to some supplies if you want to make a run for it, but we're about a hundred kilometers behind enemy lines with nothing but thousands of angry stormtroopers between here and Base Alpha. It's up to you, Lieutenant."

It wasn't really much of a choice. "Count us in," she said. She glanced at Wexley. "I hope you know how to use that blaster, kid."

Then she turned back to Ranz. "I'd like to suggest a plan," she said.

The six Imperial Troop Transports skirted across the sands at 20 kilometers per hour. They were unbuttoned, with a single trooper sticking out of the top hatch manning the craft's main gun. Ranz waited until the very last second and gave the signal.

"Now!" The scouts detonated a jury-rigged cluster of power packs buried in the sand as the second transport passed over it. The ITT rose into the air on a pillar of sand and fire, then flipped over onto its back and split open, spilling supplies and troopers in all directions. The ITT behind it desperately turned, skidding to a halt as

"In about 30 minutes, an Imperial supply convoy is going to roll right through that pass."

it impacted with the wreckage. The lead transport stopped and spun its dorsal turret, spitting cover fire in all directions as the stormtroopers poured out, ready to meet their enemies. The remaining transports pulled into a triangle formation and stopped. On cue, Major Ranz and his New Republic troopers leapt from their spider holes and opened fire on the rear ITTs. Half a dozen rockets turned the rear transports into flaming coffins for the stormtroopers that had yet to disembark—but it didn't take long for the remaining Imperials to form a skirmish line and return fire. They even managed to deploy a heavy weapons team which struggled to set up a tripod-mounted blaster cannon. The surviving troopers from the front of the column raced to reinforce the rear and face their attackers... just as Ranz had anticipated.

"Now!" he shouted.

Moonsong, Wexley, Sergeant Agarne and three of the squad popped out of their hiding place at the head of the column and tossed the few remaining anti-personnel grenades they had before running down firing at the few troopers outside the command ITT. Moonsong felt the heated air of near-misses, did her best to forget just how naked and exposed she was to the

enemy's fire as she reached the ITT first and yanked a dead stormtrooper out of the smoking cockpit. She smiled as she saw the intact communication gear on the vehicle's dashboard. But that smile quickly disappeared as she realized the long range comm-dish was damaged.

"Temmin! We're going to have to align the dish manually!"

"I'm on it!" Wexley climbed atop the vehicle and pulled out his multi-tool to quickly unscrew the fitting that held the dish in place. An explosion went off nearby and Wexley fell from the ITT like he'd been hit by shrapnel; Moonsong somehow managed to focus anyway, keying up the coded channel to Fighter Command that piped her voice in directly to Admiral Ackbar's command ship *Home One*. Third Recon Group had no such access, but Moonsong did—and she had managed to persuade Ranz that even if the letter of his orders stipulated that they couldn't break radio silence until contact with the enemy had been made, well... that still meant that once contact had occurred, any and all signaling was just fine. It was a technicality, maybe, but it was one that might yet save all their lives. Sergeant Agarne poked his head in as blaster fire strafed their position.

"Pick up the pace, Lieutenant! They're on to us and we can't hold them off for much longer!" Moonsong climbed out of the cab firing wildly as she made her way to the wounded Wexley.

"Ok trooper, up and at them!" she shouted at Wexley. "I haven't given you permission to kick off!" She was relieved to see that he hadn't been hit—the blast had merely stunned him. He groaned as Moonsong pulled him to his feet and helped him limp off towards the nearest dune for cover. The stormtroopers had finished setting up their tripod-cannon, and proceeded to pour fire on the New Republic positions behind them while the bulk of the Imperials started to perform a flanking maneuver. That was when Moonsong heard a massive boom, followed by an enormous plume of smoke rising from where the major's position used to be. She realized he must have detonated the remaining explosives in an effort to stop the stormtroopers from overrunning his position. A few remaining New Republic troopers who had assisted with the assault on the lead ITT fell back and rallied around Moonsong's position. Sergeant Agarne fell in next to her and slapped a fresh pack into his blaster rifle.

"All right, you lot: set your blasters

on single shot and watch your aim. The only way we're getting out of this is if we conserve our ammo."

"You really think we're getting out of this?" someone muttered. That was when the unmistakable sound of fighter engines overhead drew Moonsong's attention. Diving out of the sun were the familiar shapes of TIE fighters streaking towards them. On their first pass, their deadly laser fire raked the area, killing most of the remaining troopers in Ranz's regiment as well as a few stormtroopers too close to what was left of his position. "It's over!" shouted one of the rebels. "They've got us... we've got to surrender!"

"I seriously doubt these guys take prisoners," said Moonsong. She stood up and raised her rifle to her shoulder; if this was it, she figured she would go down fighting. "Okay, you want some of this? Come and get—" but even as she said the words, the TIE fighter suddenly exploded, followed by the next one in formation, and then the next one... until finally the only fighter craft in the sky were B-wings diving down and strafing the ITTs. Snub fighter laser fire kicked up huge plumes of smoke and sand; the stormtroopers broke formation and scattered in all directions. The second pass of the B-wings finished most of them off. The rest ran into the desert. Moonsong waved to the sky as Blade Squadron sped past, waggling their wings and rolling in salute to the survivors on the ground. She wasn't surprised to see Stramm's marking emblazoned on the lead fighter. She stepped over to where Wexley was kneeling.

"What's happening?" he said looking up at her.

"We're going home," she said. "Your mother will be proud."

She knelt beside him—with a hand on his shoulder while the fighters that made up Blade Squadron landed all around them. Stramm stepped out and walked over to them.

"I see you've got a new friend," he said.

"This is Temmin," said Moonsong. "Temmin, this is Braylen."

"Good to meet you," said Stramm. He took Gina's hand. "You gave me quite a scare," he said. "Don't do it again, okay?"

"Hey, I thought you weren't going to try to give me any more orders."

They looked at each other for a moment, and then both started laughing. "I wouldn't dream of it," he said. Just before things turned awkward, she pulled him in and kissed him. She felt more than a little dazed—it seemed surreal that the sands of Jakku hadn't claimed her. As to what came next—well, she would just have to see. ☸

STAR WARS LIBRARY

STAR WARS: THE EMPIRE STRIKES BACK: THE OFFICIAL COLLECTOR'S EDITION

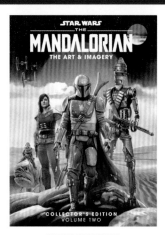

THE MANDALORIAN THE ART AND IMAGERY VOLUME 2

STAR WARS: THE RISE OF SKYWALKER: THE OFFICIAL COLLECTOR'S EDITION

STAR WARS: THE SKYWALKER SAGA THE OFFICIAL MOVIE COMPANION

MARVEL LIBRARY

THE X-MEN AND THE AVENGERS GAMMA QUEST OMNIBUS

MARVEL STUDIOS' THE COMPLETE AVENGERS

MARVEL STUDIOS' BLACK WIDOW

MARVEL: THE FIRST 80 YEARS

AVAILABLE AT ALL GOOD BOOKSTORES AND ONLINE

TITAN-COMICS.COM | TITANBOOKS.COM